KNICK̶̶̶̶̶̶̶̶̶̶̶ ̶̶̶̶̶̶̶̶̶̶ ̶̶̶̶̶̶̶̶

She had stayed perfectly still as June was beaten, bent
down with her head hung and her bottom well up. I came
behind her, to stroke her silky smooth skin and run a
teasing finger up the wet cleft of her cheeks.

'So, Miss Knickers, do you need a warm-up?'

'Whatever you see fit, Mistress.'

'That's better. You should learn from your little friend,
Boots.'

'That's what Master said.'

'I bet he did. Now, let's see about warming this sweet
little bum.'

Why not visit Penny's website at
www.pennybirch.com

KNICKERS AND BOOTS

Penny Birch

This book is a work of fiction.
In real life, make sure you practise safe, sane and
consensual sex.

First published in 2004 by
Nexus
Thames Wharf Studios
Rainville Road
London W6 9HA

www.nexus-books.co.uk

Typeset by TW Typesetting, Plymouth, Devon

Printed and bound by
Clays Ltd, St Ives PLC

ISBN 0 352 33853 9

You'll notice that we have introduced a set of symbols onto our book jackets, so that you can tell at a glance what fetishes each of our brand new novels contains. Here's the key – enjoy!

cp (traditional)

cp (modern)

spanking

restraint/bondage

rope bondage/hojojutsu

latex/rubber/leather/enclosure

fem dom

willing captivity

medical

period setting

uniforms

sex rituals

One

Gabrielle looked back at me as she bent to retrieve her knickers. She was pouting, and the sulky expression stayed on her face as she stepped into them, eased them up her legs and covered her neat little bum.

A tissue to wipe my pussy cream from her upper lip, a few more adjustments to her clothes, her hair twisted up into a neat bun, her glasses on and she had transformed herself from a spanked brat to a smart young lady. I couldn't help but giggle as she stepped to the door, so straight, so aloof; cold and untouchable. A few minutes before she'd been across my lap, nude from the waist down, bright red bum stuck up in the air, thumping the carpet with her fists and howling her head off as I punished her.

I'd had to do it. She'd been in one of her bossy moods, being Little Miss Efficient because she had a new client. I'd wanted my pussy licked and she'd said there wasn't time to play. That always warrants a spanking, and I do like to get her bum bare. Once her bottom was hot she'd licked willingly enough, and rubbed herself while she did it. That didn't stop her pouting.

'Very quiet, please, Poppy,' she said as she pulled the door to, just as bossy as ever. 'Sit and read or something, but don't be noisy, and do get dressed!'

'Cheek! Do you want another dose, Miss Gabby?'

'Sh!'

The door latch clicked to as she shut it, and I realised I'd been locked in.

'Gabrielle!'

'Sh!'

It was my turn to pout, but I really did have to be quiet while she was working. After all, if somebody is going to pay her extortionate fees to open their heart to her in therapy, the last thing they need is me banging about in the background. Besides, I wanted to listen to this one – Mr Stephen Stanbrook.

Most of Gabrielle's clients are young, professional types, and as dull as ditchwater. Half of them only use therapy to air petty, self-obsessed grievances about boyfriends, bosses, colleagues and how dreadfully hard it is to be on sixty grand a year in the capital of one of the world's richest countries. The other half just go because it's fashionable, also because they can afford it and want everyone to know they can.

Stanbrook was different. He'd heard about Gabrielle through Fat Jeff Bellbird, who's as big a pervert as ever pinched a girl's knickers, or in his case as ever dressed her up as a clown and spunked in her face. Stanbrook worked for the same company, some IT outfit, as head of sales. He knew Gabby was tolerant of kinky behaviour, and I was sure that was what he wanted to see her about.

The buzzer went while I was still trying to get dressed. All Gabrielle's clothes were in their proper place, ironed and folded. Most of mine were in the wash basket, on the floor or in the playroom. I couldn't pinch Gabby's either, as she's so long and skinny even her knickers don't fit around my bum comfortably. As for her bras, no chance. All I could

2

find was a pair of pink frilly knickers that should have been in the playroom, but I hurried into them, and had just shut the drawer when I heard his voice.

It was deep, very confident, masterful really, and even as I pressed my ear to the keyhole I was sure we had a spanker, or some other form of dominant and kinky male. I badly wanted to know what he'd done; why he needed to seek Gabrielle's help; and I was praying it wouldn't prove to be something boring after all.

She went through the formalities – couch, coffee and comfort. His response was polite, yet firm, his voice never wavering. In my mind I could just hear him telling a girl her knickers were coming down for a spanking. Once settled he got straight to the point.

'I understand from Jeff Bellbird that you are both discreet and broad-minded?'

'You can rely on my professional discretion, yes. I am not here to pass judgement, Mr Stanbrook.'

'Call me Stephen, please. I wish I could say the same, about passing judgement that is, on myself.'

'Yes?'

'Yes. I've always been very certain, very sure of what I want. Now I find myself split, on the one hand driven to do something, on the other guilty for doing it.'

He stopped and I carefully adjusted my position, making myself comfortable against the wall. Gabby spoke next, emotionless, her slight Strasbourg accent making her seem so cool, so clinical, very different from the real Gabrielle.

'Do go on, Stephen.'

'I'd better explain from the start. As you know, I'm head of the sales team at the company Jeff works for. It's a good job, varied, respectable salary, good perks. My wife Kate and I have been together since we met at university. She's a senior executive with GIC Yamoto, which brings her in roughly twice what I make. She also travels a lot, sometimes spending a month at a time in the Far East.'

I stifled a groan at the prospect of just one more man feeling inferior because he was earning less than his wife, but I kept my ear close to the keyhole as he went on.

'Now that our children have both left home, that leaves me with a lot of spare time. I've been going on the net, a lot.'

That was a bit better. He was going to be worried about how much porn he was viewing or worried about getting off on something he couldn't handle; fat girls, transsexuals, even farm animals . . .

'Communities mainly, message boards, chatrooms, you know.'

'Of any particular sort?'

'BDSM, that's bondage, domination, sadism and masochism. From a male dominant perspective, you appreciate.'

'I see, and is this a long-term part of your sexuality?'

'Yes . . . no. I always liked the idea of being in charge, or having a woman follow my orders. I suppose all men do.'

'Not invariably, but this is by no means unusual. Is your wife aware of this?'

'Good heavens, no! She believes in sex as an act of love and procreation. She's completely normal, as she's always quick to point out.'

'And you feel that you are not normal?'

'Yes . . . no . . . I don't know. I was never the New Man type, even when it was expected, and I've always regarded my dominant feelings as part of my masculinity, nothing more. Now I'm not so sure.'

He paused again and I heard the chink of a coffee cup against its saucer. So he was a male dom, just as I'd suspected – clever little Poppy. Gabby let him take his time, and the next voice was his again.

'The thing about this chatroom business is that I'm good at it, bloody good. When I started it was just a joke. All the guys in the different communities called themselves things like Slavemaster and Enforcer. I could hardly use my own name, so I started to put myself on the forms as The Master. The next thing I knew girls were calling me that and, believe me, I have never, ever experienced such a buzz. They wanted me to be dominant, controlling, something I've never been able to express with Kate. I went for it, and I challenge any red-blooded male not to do the same.'

'A very normal reaction.'

'Is it? I thought so, at first anyway. They appreciated it, so I didn't see there was any harm. I didn't even feel bad when it started to get a bit more serious. I began to whisper a lot . . . I don't know if you do chat at all?'

'I have a basic understanding. To whisper is to hold a private conversation off the main board, is it not?'

'Yes. As I was saying, I began to whisper a lot, particularly to this one girl, Nicola. Knickers she calls herself on line. She's very into calling me Master, and was soon asking very intimate questions, such as what I would like to do to punish her. We ended up having virtual sex.'

'Simply sex?'

'Hardly. I pretended to beat her, and make her give me oral sex.'

'I see, and you masturbated as you did this?'

'Yes.'

He was cool, admitting to tossing himself with a girl online and his voice not so much as wavering. Gabby went on.

'And who instigated this sex?'

'Neither really, it was a mutual thing.'

'So your concern is not that you are pressuring her into a sexual act?'

'No, not really, not then. I'm not too bothered about Kate either, or I wasn't. After all, I'd never met the girl, let alone actually touched her.'

'The situation has developed?'

'Yes. Nicola and I built up quite a thing, along with a friend of hers she'd met online, another submissive woman, June. Boots, she calls herself, because she likes to wear knee-high boots and nothing else. She was the one who suggested that we meet up.'

'And you agreed?'

'Not at first. I didn't feel right about it and, to be honest, I didn't want to ruin the fantasy image I'd built up of them. I suppose I was prejudiced, but I assumed that, because they were getting their kicks online, they wouldn't be up to much.'

'This was not the case?'

'Far from it. When I didn't immediately respond to their request to meet up, they sent me a picture, by email, of them together. Nicola's small, not much over five foot I don't suppose, very petite, and athletic too. She does some of this Oriental stuff, you know, twisting yourself into knots and standing on one leg for hours. June is taller, and bigger in general. She's not fat, by any means, but she looks quite fleshy next to Nicola. Very firm though.'

'They were naked in this picture?'

'As good as. It was taken in a bedroom, one of theirs, I suppose. They're both in just their panties, and June has her trademark boots on.'

'And having seen this, you found their request hard to turn down?'

'Did I!? Not only are they both so cute, but in the picture they're cuddled up together on the bed. That, and the way they behave online, has more than a hint of lesbianism. I'm sorry, but that turns me on like a switch.'

'There is no need to apologise. This is perhaps the commonest of all male fantasies. So you met?'

'Yes, on neutral ground the first time, at a munch, which is a pub meeting so that people who've only met online can get together in a safe and non-threatening atmosphere.'

'The three of you were not alone?'

'There were over twenty people there, but Nicola and June and I spent the whole time talking together. When it was time to go, they asked permission to take me behind the pub and give me oral sex. Asked permission! Two beautiful young girls, half my age, and they asked permission to suck me! The man who could say no has yet to be born.'

'So you did this?'

'Yes. June did it while Nicola held her pants down to show me her bottom. I was singing all the way home in the car. I have never felt so high, so elated. It was like being a teenager again, after having sex for the first time. Later I felt a bit guilty, for Kate, but also puzzled as to why Nicola and June would behave that way. I suppose it's just the way I was brought up, but I've always believed women see sex as a commodity, at least, more than men do. So the less attractive a woman is the more likely she is to be sexually adventurous.'

'This is a common misconception among your generation. May I ask how old you are?'

'Forty-eight.'

'Thank you. Do go on.'

'I meant to leave it like that, just one great experience not to be repeated. That wasn't so easy, because the girls were more eager than ever to play online, and wanted to meet up again. Kate was away, in South Korea, negotiating some deal or other. It was going to be over a month until I saw her again, and I had two attractive young women literally begging me to have sex with them.'

'Have you told Nicola and June that you are married?'

'No. I'd built up my personality online you see, and a lot of it was exaggeration, lies really. I said I was single, and a lot better off than I really am. Initially I was just creating a persona, an ideal me, I suppose you could call it. I never intended to meet anybody, and now I can't go back without breaking the trust we've built up.'

'So you allowed the relationship to build up?'

'Yes, Kate isn't really the issue. It is an issue, yes, but I realise that is something I am going to have to face. The reason I've come to you is rather different. There's another Group, more serious than UK Masters and Slaves, which is where I met the girls. I go on that, but I only really lurk ... that's reading messages and so forth without actually participating. In more than one discussion submissive women admit that their feelings derive from low self-esteem. It seems to be universal, the main cause, really. That is the source of my misgivings.'

'So you feel that, as low self-esteem has been a component in the evolution of their sexuality, it is wrong for you to interact with them?'

'Yes. I feel like I'm abusing them, and it's the last thing I want. I know this is not easy to understand. Even I think it's contradictory sometimes, but I want them to need me to control them, to dominate them, to look up to me, to see me as a protector, a provider, as a father figure I suppose. But I want them to feel good about it.'

'You wish them to be obedient to you, to be controlled by you, yet not to see your actions as abuse?'

'Yes. I want them to enjoy it. I've always hated the idea of any woman not being a fully willing participant in any sexual encounter, let alone one where I'm taking physical charge of her, even punishing her.'

'Yet you have said that this is what they want?'

'It is, but I still don't feel right.'

'You believe that their low self-esteem detracts from their responsibility, from their ability to give their consent?'

'Exactly!'

'And you are sure that this low self-esteem is an element of their sexualities? You have asked them?'

'No! I couldn't do that! You don't understand. We've created an idealised relationship, a wonderful relationship. To ask that sort of question would be to risk destroying it, if only because it reveals that I myself have insecurities and uncertainties.'

'So for all you know they might not feel that way at all?'

'No. I'm sure of it. It's a point women in the Groups make again and again.'

'Perhaps, but I can assure you that not all women with submissive sexualities suffer from low self-esteem. Indeed, in some cases the very highest self-esteem is necessary in order for a woman to have the confidence to express herself in such a way.'

'Hmm, that's interesting, certainly a very different way of looking at it.'

'Nicola and June are, from what you say, under no coercion to behave as they do.'

'None, but that makes no difference.'

'The expression of human sexuality is a complicated matter, Stephen, and far from fully understood. Nicola and June have chosen to give you an element of power over themselves, for their own complex and no doubt individual reasons. To put this down purely to low self-esteem is perhaps simplistic and may even be incorrect.'

'Sure. I mean, they certainly get their kicks . . .'

He trailed off, now with some doubt in his voice for the first time. That was typical Gabby. Her clients turn up with some nice clear problem and go away so confused they no longer understand what the problem is, or if it's a problem at all.

If I'd been in his shoes, I wouldn't have had a problem with the girls at all. I'd have had a problem with the high-energy wife finding out. It had been fun to listen to anyway, and I hoped Gabby would probe him on what went on with the girls. She didn't, and when he spoke again it was a simple question, the crucial one that never gets answered.

'So what would you advise?'

'It is not really my position to give advice, Stephen, but rather to listen and help you to resolve the situation in your own mind. The essence of my technique is that the individual should experience mental wellbeing on their own terms, rather than me attempting to guide you in any particular direction.'

'So you don't think I'm a bad person, mentally ill, anything like that?'

'By no means.'

'Well, that's a relief. The first person I went to talked about curing me of my sexual illness, and wanted me to refer the girls to him as well.'

'An outdated attitude.'

'That's what I thought. Well, thank you. You've

raised more questions in my mind than you've solved, but I do see it's not a simple matter of me taking advantage of their weakness. Next time I meet them online, it will be with a clearer conscience.'

'Not altogether clear?'

'No. There's Kate, of course, and I know full well that the next time I see some programme or article about sexual predators I'll end up feeling like I'm some sort of slavering sex fiend. I always do, but it goes away. Just my conscience, I suppose.'

'Possibly you would like to discuss the origins of your need for sexual dominance?'

He did, but I wasn't really up for hearing about testosterone levels and adolescent male hierarchy in the context of modern society, which was where the conversation was going. I wanted to hear about Nicola and June, and whatever delicious perversions they were into. My bum was also beginning to go numb and my left ear felt like a cauliflower.

I had to investigate UK Masters and Slaves. I'd tried joining Internet Groups before, as a pony-girl, but most of the time it had just been people bitching at others over tiny things, and some of them hadn't even been prepared to admit it was sexual. This sounded more fun.

Once I'd signed up, my first impression was that it was all a bit stiff. It was purely for submissive girls and dominant men, and the girls were expected to address the men as 'Sir' or 'Master' all the time. I like to switch, and I far prefer to be dominated by other women. The other drawback was that a lot of it was just technical, with a load of self-styled experts preaching about how SM relationships should work, or discussions on the best place to buy a suspension harness. I'd been there, done it and bought the T-shirt, almost without exception.

Had it not been for The Master, Nicola and June, I wouldn't have bothered, but I wanted to know, and the situation appealed to my sense of mischief. Gabby had assured me he had the look too, in so far as a man ever can. I hadn't seen him, my position at the keyhole providing only a view of a bit of couch and Gabby looking earnest and thoughtful. She'd described him, after smacking my bottom for listening. He was over six feet tall, slim, very straight, with short cropped grey hair and a neat beard, which sounded like a wonderfully stern look.

Nicola and June obviously thought so. Looking back through the old messages in the Group, I could trace their history. That fascinated Gabby too, both from a professional and personal viewpoint. At first there was no particular intimacy between the three of them, with each posting but few references to one another. Nicola was the busiest, and before long had begun to relate to him, and to June. Only later did his interaction with June become more frequent. Whoever got down on their knees, it was clear that Nicola was the one with the real drive.

There was a thread announcing the munch they'd been to, and after that the girls began to address him as their Master. He might have felt some doubt, but he didn't show it, taking a firm tone with both of them. In the last message he ordered them to attend the Thursday night chat session, and that both were to be bare between waist and socks.

He was a big contributor to the discussions on dress, and that seemed to be his thing, bare bums and pussies with the rest of the girl's clothing immaculate. When he did think knickers were appropriate, it was only so that they could be pulled down. He was also big on 'accidental' exhibitionism, such as making a girl walk down the street with her skirt up to show

12

the seat of her knickers, as if she'd tucked them up by mistake. That appealed to my own sense of exhibitionism. I love to feel the embarrassment of being made to show off, or of having no choice.

I had to join in the chat, despite Gabby's objections. So on Thursday we had an early supper and installed ourselves in front of the computer, me on the keyboard and Gabby sitting behind looking ever so slightly disapproving. She was in her work clothes, a smartly cut suit of fine, pale-yellow wool, with neat black heels, hold-ups and plain white knickers and bra. I'd wanted to play, and I was sure that someone would want to know what I was wearing.

It would have been easy to lie, as there was no camera facility, or even sound. I didn't want to, not about that anyway, and I'd put on a baby-doll, with big, blue, frilly knickers and a top with a fluffy trim, all see-through. It felt naughty, as always, and put me in the mood for mischief, which went a long way to bring Gabby out of her professional sulk.

Everyone else had nicknames, some SM-related, some rude, some silly, some incomprehensible. I'd chosen Poppet, as it was close enough to my real name and nicely submissive, pretty too. So I signed on, with just a touch of that lovely butterfly feeling in my tummy.

June was there, as Boots, along with another dozen or so, but not the other two. I typed in 'Hi', and Gabby leaned closer as it came up on the screen.

Poppet: 'Hi.'

Most of them responded in kind, one in detail.

Black Knight: 'Hi, Poppet. Do you know the club rules?'

Slightly taken aback, I typed my answer.

Poppet: 'I think so.'

Black Knight: 'Then you should know to address me as "Sir" or "Master", always.'

A thrill went through me, excitement mixed with resentment, leaving me wanting to pout but with a sudden sense of readiness in my pussy. Beside me, Gabby gave an amused chuckle as I typed my answer.

Poppet: 'Yes, Sir. Sorry, Sir.'

Black Knight: 'That's better. Good girl.'

A second jolt of submissive pleasure, blended with indignation, hit me. He was being so smug, so superior. In any other context I'd have turned my back on him or given him a lecture on respect. Not now, now it was time to play.

Poppet: 'Should I be punished, Sir?'

Black Knight: 'Perhaps. Do you have a Master?'

Poppet: 'No, Sir.'

Black Knight: 'Then who will punish you, and how?'

The other people had been discussing Japanese rope bondage, which was the official topic, but began to take notice. One man suggested I spank myself, another that I should be given a virtual caning, a third that I come to his house to learn my lesson properly. A flashing blue tab appeared at the bottom of the screen, making me jump slightly. I clicked on it and another window opened on the screen. A message appeared.

The Keeper: 'Pay close attention.'

I didn't, still trying to cope with the flow of suggestions for what should be done to me on the main screen. After a moment a new sentence appeared in the small box.

The Keeper: 'Attention, bitch! I am going to beat you, and fuck you in the cunt and arse. First, I must see if you meet my standards, which are high.'

'Close the window,' Gabby advised.

'Hang on . . .'

I was panicking, trying to think up a suitable response to The Keeper, who was being too pushy by far, and keep an eye on the main conversation, half of which was hidden by the small box. I was about to offer to take a virtual spanking, and had typed half the sentence in when a new message appeared in the small box.

The Keeper: 'You will follow these instructions, exactly. Tomorrow, at precisely 11 a.m., you will be in the Café Marseilles at the junction of Gray's Inn Road and Bedford Street. You will wear no underwear, only a red summer dress. You will wear your hair loose. I will be there, but I will not approach you if I am dissatisfied. You will not leave until 11.30.'

'Say you'll go,' Gabby suggested, 'and then don't.'

'Nah,' I answered, and typed a better response in.

Poppet: 'Go stick your manky little willy up your bum.'

It appeared, and an instant later the box closed. I turned back to the main screen, grinning, only to find that there were now so many messages my last one had gone off the top of the screen. Most of them were directed at me. Now completely out of my depth, I made a frantic entry.

Poppet: 'Sorry, can't cope!'

The response came almost immediately.

Boots: 'Lay off her, boys ... I mean, oh-so-high, infallible Masters. Are you OK, Poppet?'

I laughed, but there was gratitude too. I typed back.

Poppet: 'I'm fine, thanks, Boots. What I meant was that I couldn't keep up with the messages!'

Boots: 'Oh ... cool. They can get a bit rough sometimes.'

Black Knight: 'No bratting, Boots.'

Boots: 'Sorry, Master.'

A line of pale text appeared, announcing that The Keeper had left the room, then another, announcing that The Master had joined it.

'Here's Stephen, Gabby!'

'Poppy, you must not do anything to breach my profess–'

'Oh lighten up, Gabby! Or I'll post some photos to them of you in a nappy – a full one.'

'Poppy!'

She knew I wouldn't, but she went quiet anyway. On the screen the conversation had continued, but neither Boots nor The Master were contributing. I guessed they were having a private conversation. I moved to click on Boots' name, but hesitated, not wanting to push the way The Keeper had. Someone else asked me a question, but my heart wasn't really in it and I gave a non-committal answer.

'Is that enough for you?' Gabby asked.

'Not really, no. I want to know what they're talking about, June and Stephen.'

'It would be more sensible –'

She stopped. A new box had opened, this time from June. The rush was instant, my tummy fluttering as I bent to the keyboard.

Boots: 'Hi, Poppet.'

Poppet: 'Hi, Boots. Cute name.'

Boots: 'Thanks. It's 'cause I like wearing high boots.'

Poppet: 'And nothing else?'

Boots: 'How did you guess?'

'Poppy,' Gabrielle warned.

'Relax!'

Poppet: 'I know what bad girls are like. I am one.'

Boots: 'So I see! Do you mind me asking, are you really up for a virtual punishment?'

Poppet: 'From you? Sure!'

Boots: 'No, from my Master.'

Poppet: 'Who's that?'

Boots: 'He's The Master. He's good.'

Poppet: 'What would he want me to do?'

Boots: 'What are you into?'

Poppet: 'All sorts.'

Boots: 'Spanking?'

Poppet: 'Yes. I can do myself for him, if he likes, and I will be hard. But I have something better. I'd like to be made to wet my knickers.'

I felt the blood rush to my face as I sent the message. I hadn't seen any mention of watersports in the Group, only corporal punishment, bondage and a little pony-play. Yet if she and I were to play, even online, I didn't want to hold back my favourite thing. Her answer came back.

Boots: 'Dirty girl!'

It was followed by a big yellow smiley. I put my hand to my bladder in immediate reaction as the fluttering in my tummy grew abruptly stronger. I typed back.

Poppet: 'I know. Would he like that?'

Boots: 'I'll see.'

She was typing to him, I knew, asking if he wanted to make me wet my knickers. Just the thought was almost enough to make me do it, then and there. We'd shared a bottle of wine over dinner, and my bladder was already quite full, while being ever so slightly drunk was going to make it easier, and more fun.

My offer had pushed Gabby's button too. She should have been telling me off, but she stayed quiet, her eyes fixed on the screen, only to break off and share a tense glance.

I waited. There were plenty of messages coming up on the main screen, but I was barely aware of them, more of the muscles of my pussy and lower belly twitching and the curious way my frillies suddenly felt tight. I was praying he wanted to play, but the shame

17

of having asked, if he didn't, was growing quickly stronger as the computer clock showed one minute had passed . . . then a second.

A new box flicked into existence on my screen, The Master, Stephen Stanbrook.

The Master: 'I understand that you deserve to be punished?'

Poppet: 'Yes, Master.'

The Master: 'I will punish you. First, a few questions. How tall are you?'

Poppet: 'Five feet one inch, Master.'

The Master: 'Describe your figure.'

Poppet: 'Fairly petite, Master.'

The Master: 'In more detail.'

Poppet: '36D-24-34, Master.'

The Master: 'Busty then, and a full bottom.'

Poppet: 'Yes. I'm always told I have a cheeky bottom. Someone once said it was an "English Pear".'

The Master: 'Good. You're being honest with me. A liar will always pretend to be fashionably slim. That's important. Don't forget to address me properly.'

Poppet: 'Sorry, Master.'

The Master: 'That's better. Now, your face?'

Poppet: 'I have curly black hair, quite short, a round face, big brown eyes and a nose like a pig, Master.'

The Master: 'A nose like a pig?'

Poppet: 'A snub nose, Master.'

The Master: 'That's better, Poppet. You must learn never to put yourself down.'

Poppet: 'Yes, Master.'

The Master: 'You are to be punished now. As you have such a delightful bottom, it's a shame I can't be there to spank it. I could make you do it, of course, but I have something better in mind. What are you wearing?'

Poppet: 'A baby-doll, Master, blue.'

The Master: 'A shame. No doubt you look very sweet, but I would have preferred something more everyday because, Poppet, as your punishment you are going to pee in your clothes.'

Poppet: 'Pee, Master? Sitting in front of the computer, as I am?'

The Master: 'Yes.'

I knew we were playing, so did he. That didn't stop the now frantic fluttering in my tummy. I was going to wet myself, because he told me to, in my knickers and all over the chair.

'Gabby, get a splash mat from the playroom, please.'

'You are going to do it?'

'Yes.'

'You could pretend.'

'I don't want to.'

She gave an understanding nod and pushed her chair back, to nip smartly into the playroom and emerge a moment later with the biggest of our plastic sheets. I stood up, allowing her to spread the sheet and wheel the chair on to it. As I sat down I was typing again.

Poppet: 'I'm ready, Master.'

The Master: 'Good. Do it when you feel the need, and tell me how it feels.'

It felt wonderful. I closed my eyes, concentrating on the gentle pressure in my bladder. I held it, savouring that awful moment when it's about to happen, when you know you can stop it, stop being so dirty, so messy, so . . .

I let go. Pee spurted into my frillies, hot and wet as it soaked in over the bulge of my pussy and down between my bum-cheeks. My mouth came open in a long, satisfied sigh, and then I had leaned forwards and was typing frantically as my pee bubbled out underneath me, now flowing freely.

By the time I'd finished I was soaking. My bum felt squashy and wet in my sodden frillies and it was dripping off the sides of the chair. As I sent the message I wiggled in it, rubbing my bum in my own pee to really bring home the feelings of what I'd done. Then it was on the screen, and I was reading my own words, my own confession.

Poppet: 'I'm wetting my knickers now, Master. I can feel the pee coming out, and it's too late to stop. I'm wet, really wet. I've wet myself, Master, because you told me to, to punish me. Now I'm sitting in a pair of soggy knickers, and it's still coming, more and more. Thank you, Master, thank you for making me wet my knickers.'

I was reading it over and over as the last of my pee trickled out into the sodden gusset of my frillies. I'd done it, and it felt so good, too good not to finish myself off. He answered.

The Master: 'Now, stand up, pull your wet panties well up your bottom and stay that way, at attention, until I say otherwise.'

I was busy stroking my pussy through the wet gusset of my frillies and didn't answer. He could think I had obeyed or not. I had better things to do.

My legs came up, spread wide to the computer screen. I began to rub, delving between my pussy-lips to push the wet material on to my clitty. Gabby came behind me, her arms encircling my body. Her lips found mine as I twisted my head around, and we were kissing, just as she began to inch my baby-doll up. My boobs came out into her hands. She began to mould them, stroking gently to tease my already stiff nipples to full erection.

I closed my eyes, enjoying her attention and the feel of the wet, clinging material around my bum and pussy. It felt so good, so naughty, to be frigging myself in pee-soaked panties, with my bum in it and my own puddle underneath me on the splash mat. I was going to come, at any moment, and began to flick gently at my clitty, keeping myself high as I sought out the perfect fantasy.

He'd made me do it, a man, a confident, assertive man, punishing me by making me pee in my knickers. Only it wasn't a punishment, not to me. I didn't feel punished, nor ashamed, nor put down, just gloriously, wonderfully naughty. I need spanking, or the cane, to hurt me. That would have been punishment. This was nice, rude and wet, and even as I lay there masturbating I knew Stephen would be telling the two girls all about it. Maybe he would even paste them the filthy little note I'd written as my pee gushed out into my frillies. They'd see; they'd know I'd done it, but I wished they'd been watching.

That was perfect. They should have been watching, as Gabby had been. She was cool; she'd seen me wet myself a hundred times, and worse. They would have been shocked, shocked but delighted, giggling together as the yellow fluid bubbled out of the front of my knickers and soaked into my crotch. I'd have frigged off in front of them too, just as I was now, rubbing my wet pussy, my soiled knickers pulled tight over my bottom, completely see-through. Every detail of my pussy was on show, I knew, and my bumhole as I rolled my legs high. They'd stare, gaping as I started to come . . .

I was pressing my mouth hard to Gabrielle's as my muscles went into spasm. My whole body began to jerk, my bottom splashing in the pee puddle, my pussy and bumhole contracting, my back arched tight. My breasts felt huge in Gabrielle's hands, my bottom big and round in my tight, wet frillies, my pussy a furnace of damp heat, my whole body open, in one, long, beautiful high that broke only when I could bear the sensitivity of my clit no more.

Two

Stephen Stanbrook rang Gabrielle on Monday to book another appointment. It did seem funny, when he'd handled me with such confidence in the chatroom, but his dominant pose clearly hid a great deal of uncertainty. I had to listen, and persuaded Gabrielle to let me by refusing to put any clothes on until she was forced to lock me in the bedroom again. It was sure to mean she was going to turn dom on me afterwards, but being spanked by her isn't much different from having someone play pat-a-cake on my bum. This time I put a big cushion by the door to sit on.

He arrived on time; there was the normal preamble and, as before, he got down to business without hesitation.

'I've been trying to take in what you said last week, Miss Salinger, but I do actually believe you're wrong.'

'Yes?'

'Yes. Listen to this, and then tell me that these submissive women are in control, that they even understand what they're doing.'

'Go on.'

'I visited the UK Master and Slaves chatroom last week, as I do regularly. June was there before me, and when I logged on she told me, privately, that I'd just missed a new girl being teased over taking a punishment for breaking the Group rules. That's a common event, and sometimes it ends in a virtual punishment, sometimes it doesn't. This time it hadn't. So I ordered June to ask the girl, who was calling herself Poppet, if she'd take a virtual punishment from me. It's always better to get another woman to do these things, as new girls are much more inclined to be trusting to those men who've already established a good relationship with the other women.'

'An understandable reaction.'

'Poppet accepted anyway, and not just that. She told June that what she'd consider the most appropriate punishment would be to be made to wet her panties. That was new to me, but as a Master one doesn't show naivety, so I went along with it. Poppet did it, in her chair in front of the computer, or, at least, she said she had, and she did genuinely seem to be enjoying the experience. Then she went quiet, just as it got really intense. She didn't log off, but just stopped posting. We sent several messages, but they were ignored. I really think there's only one possible conclusion.'

'Which is?'

'That I freaked her out, of course! I mean, from what the guy I was with before told me, this need to wet herself will derive from some awful trauma, which she needs to re-enact in order to cope with her feelings.'

'That is by no means always the case.'

Gabby was good, so smooth, so cool, with never a hint of what she really knew. I wasn't; I was clutching my mouth and tummy in a desperate effort not to laugh, and close to peeing myself again. If I had, it would have trickled out under the door, which would have been completely surreal, and probably tipped him over the edge.

I held on, stifling my giggles by doing sums in my head, which generally works. Despite my reaction I did feel a bit sorry for him, but it was just so funny. There he'd been, after helping take me to ecstasy, getting in a flap over something that was entirely in his own mind. I hadn't logged off because as soon as I'd come I'd taken Gabby into the playroom to thank her for her unselfish attention to my boobs. Then, while he and June had been sending me concerned messages, I'd been applying cream and powder to my girlfriend's bum before putting her in a nappy.

She couldn't very well tell him, but her assurances were falling on deaf ears.

'It has to be that way,' he insisted. 'You weren't there. One last message, then nothing. Her name was still on the chatroom list three hours later when I had to log off because my son came home. He's just back from university this week.'

'Possibly she was preoccupied?'

I had been – playing nursemaid to his oh-so-cool therapist. After three hours, if I remembered rightly, Gabby would have come as she suckled on me, given me a second orgasm with me sat on her face and gone to sleep in my arms, the computer forgotten. That was not what he'd been imagining.

'No,' he answered, after a nervous pause. 'I'm sure of it. It's not just that either. When I asked her to describe herself she was putting herself down, saying she had a fat bottom and looked like a pig.'

'Self-deprecating humour is more often a sign of confidence than otherwise. Those who suffer from low self-esteem tend to be very sensitive about their appearance.'

'No, it wasn't like that, I'm sure. I feel I've exploited her dreadfully.'

'You simply responded to her request.'

'Yes, but a request she lacks the responsibility to make!'

'You don't know that.'

'Oh come on!'

'Stephen, it occurs to me that these feelings are more a product of your own mind. Last time you told me that you had been brought up to believe that women see sex as a commodity, rather than being driven by their libido. Surely this is the root cause of your concerns?'

She was right. She usually is. He wasn't so sure.

'Maybe, but that doesn't alter the facts!'

'The facts, no, but much of what you have said is supposition.'

He didn't answer, but I could imagine him shaking his head in doubt. Now I really did feel sorry for him, and promised myself to go into the chatroom again on Thursday and explain myself. After all, he was being a lot more considerate than many doms, male or female, and he didn't deserve his misgivings. As he went on I realised that they were pretty strong.

'So you say, but I wish I could be sure. We even tried to email this girl, Poppet, but her address is withheld to the Group. That also suggests to me that she's not comfortable with herself.'

I had withheld my email. It was *poppy@wholebeing therapy.com*, which would have been a dead give-away. I'd also knocked a few years off my age, something else he'd noticed.

'She's only twenty, as well.'

'You mentioned that your other contact, June, is nineteen?'

'Yes. June's more confident but, even then, I can't help but think it's just a front, a barrier she puts up to hide her pain.'

'Again, I feel this relates more to your own concerns than hers.'

Once more he didn't answer. My ear was beginning to hurt, and I pulled away from the door, grinning, but determined to set him right.

I could hardly wait for Thursday, because what had happened the week before had added a new thrill to my sex life. Gabby and I had been together a year and a half and, while I was as much in love with her as ever, the sex had settled down into a cosy routine. A pretty strange one, maybe, by any normal standards, but cosy for us.

Wednesday night looked as if it would be typical. With her working in the morning we would be sleeping in the normal bedroom, not the playroom. There would be wine for dinner, which would leave me pleasantly sleepy and pleasantly horny. In bed, we would probably go head to toe for a lick, and maybe liven it up with a bit of spanking, perhaps have some fun with each other's bum. Then it would be a quick shower, a cuddle and sleep.

We'd got as far as the wine, both slobbed out on the couch with our tummies full as we drank and chatted, when the bell went. Gabby sighed as she got to her feet.

'Let that be a friend and not a client.'

'I'll peep out of the window if you like, to check.'

'No, I have to answer anyway.'

She had reached the intercom, and spoke briefly into it. A voice answered, male, but I couldn't pick out the words. Gabrielle hesitated, bit her lip, then pressed the buzzer to let him up and spoke as she turned back to me.

'Jeff Bellbird.'

I made a face. Fat Jeff hadn't come all the way from Lewisham for a coffee and a chat. He knew us all too well, and sometimes he liked to take advantage. Sometimes we let him, but there was always a bit of a hurdle to get over before getting down to it. We both far prefer women for one thing. He was the size of a house too, at least twenty stone, with little piggy eyes peering out from the jungle of his facial hair, and always following our bums and boobs as we moved. He was also nuts, and seriously kinky, but those were his good points.

Gabby opened the door for him and he came waddling in, grinning through his beard like a cat who's had the cream, or maybe a sasquatch who's had a camper. It was a warm evening, and he was in outsize combat trousers and a string vest, tight over his vast gut and showing off even more hair than usual. It looked obscene, but he was oblivious, or simply didn't care. His eyes went straight to my boobs, as always.

'Hi, Pops.'

'Hi, Jeff. How are you?'

'Never better. So old Soapy Stanbrook's been coming to see you, eh, Gabs?'

He gave Gabby a resounding slap on her bottom as she passed, making her jump, then threw himself down in a chair, cocking one massive leg over the arm.

'That was hard, Jeff,' Gabby protested, rubbing her bottom. 'Yes, Mr Stanbrook has been to see me.'

'So what's his problem? Something good and dirty, yeah?'

'Jeff, you know I cannot possibly –'

'Hey, you can tell Uncle Jeff! I used to change your nappies, remember, even if it was only last month.'

He laughed, a curiously high-pitched noise for such a big man, then spoke again as Gabby sat down beside me.

'Come on, Gabs, tell. It's got to be something kinky. What's he into – ladyboys, Danish?'

'You know I cannot say, Jeff,' she answered. 'Also, I would be grateful if you did not discuss my sexual preferences with your colleagues.'

'I didn't,' he answered. 'He was going on about this crap shrink he'd had and I said I knew you. I suppose he reckoned, if you could handle me, you could handle him. He knows I'm a pervo; I never try to deny it.'

'We noticed,' I answered. 'How about you getting some therapy, Mr Clown Freak?'

'I don't need it. I'm into clowns. The bloke ones I shoot, the girl ones I fuck. What's to go to therapy for?'

'Lucky everyone's not like you, or Gabby would be out of work. What a pervert!'

'Yeah, and you love it. Fuck that anyway, I've got something you are going to love.'

He bent to the supermarket carrier bag he'd brought in to pull out a book. It was large, bigger than A4, and tall, with ragged-edged cardboard covers printed with a now faded design of green and gold. Gabby and I craned forwards as he laid it on the coffee table.

'What is it?'

'You'll see. I picked it up in Frankfurt, at the big tech conference last month. Fifteen Euros from some old bugger with a market stall.'

He opened the book, very carefully, and I immediately felt my mouth go dry. There was no text, just a drawing, ink line and watercolour, very delicate, very beautiful and very, very rude. It showed a woman on an iron-framed bed, her smart, twenties-style clothes in disarray. Her legs had been lifted and tied off to one of those things they lift broken legs up with in hospitals. Her big knickers had been pulled up her legs and knotted off, leaving her pussy and bumhole showing. Her arms were stretched up above her head and had been tied off on the bedstead. Her face was set in an expression of agonised consternation.

That was hardly surprising. There were three other women in the picture, all in what were clearly nurses' uniforms, although like none I'd ever seen. Two had stood back, hands on hips, their hair and clothing a little dishevelled, suggesting they were the ones who'd tied her to the bed. Both were gloating over the woman's plight. The third wasn't; she looked serious, and angry, as she poked the nozzle of an enema tube at the bound woman's exposed anus. Immediately I found myself thinking of how the victim would feel, and wishing it was me.

'Wow!'

'Good, eh? I knew you'd be into it. What do you reckon, Gabs?'

Gabrielle just shook her head. Her face was flushed pink, her mouth a little open. If it got to me, I could only imagine what it would be doing to her. My arm was behind her back, out of Jeff's sight, and I gave her three quick nudges to indicate that I was ready to play if she wanted to.

'And for my next trick,' Jeff announced, and turned the page.

The second picture was equally rude, and maybe more disturbing. It showed a young girl, kneeling on the floor of an old-fashioned kitchen. She was naked save for the torn remains of a nightie and her hands were tied behind her back. Her bottom was well stuck out, the cheeks open to show the tiny brown pucker of her bumhole. A second girl, somewhat older, had the kneeling girl by the hair, face pulled tight between a pair of slim yet cheeky buttocks, grinning in wicked delight as she made her victim lick her bottom. A third woman, much older, stood by, casually preparing an enema bag, the nozzle of which was quite clearly going up the bound girl's bottom.

'If think it's supposed to be a mother with her two daughters,' Jeff remarked.

'In your imagination, no doubt it is,' Gabby responded.

She reached out to turn the page as she spoke, her fingers trembling ever so slightly. Jeff quickly shut the book and hugged it to his bear-like chest.

'Uh, uh, no you don't.'

'You brought it to show to us, yes?' Gabby queried.

'No, I bought it for you, but one good turn deserves another, don't you think?'

'It does, I suppose,' Gabby sighed.

'It gets a lot dirtier,' Jeff assured us. 'It's nearly all about enemas, and some are very imaginative, the situations too. You'll love it.'

Gabby shrugged, and spoke.

'You would like me to suck your penis?'

'I'd like to fuck your cute little arse.'

'Jeff . . .'

'I know, I know, you can't really handle it up the bum. What you need is practice, to get your ring a bit looser. You should wear a plug, like gay guys do so they can take more.'

'Thank you, Jeff. I am very well as I am.'

'Suit yourself. But I get to fuck you, yeah?'

'I'll make a coffee while you two talk it out,' I offered.

'Hey, I'm not going to leave you out, Pops!' Jeff answered quickly. 'What sort of a git do you take me for? No, I want you to pose that fat little arse of yours for me. Here, bung this on.'

He pulled something from his bag, a bundle of cloth with a diamond pattern in brilliant red and green. I didn't need any more to know what it was –

a clown costume. I caught it as I stood up, shaking my head. Jeff just grinned, but spoke as I made for the bedroom.

'It might be a bit tight.'

It was. I'm not big, by any standards, but the girl it had been made for must have been tiny. Holding it up, I wasn't even sure if I could get it on, and being small wasn't the only problem. It was like a body suit, except that there were large holes at the chest and the bottom. I like looking girlie, but this was straight out of a men's magazine.

I hesitated, not sure the book was worth it. Posing or sucking cock was one thing, but being made to look completely ridiculous another. Unfortunately I knew that Gabby would have done almost anything to own it, and it was hardly fair to leave her on her own. So off came my clothes, all of them, and I tugged the clown suit on, feeling increasingly ridiculous as I felt first my bottom left bare, then my boobs.

With it on, I went to the mirror, to find that I looked every bit as ridiculous as I felt. I also looked very rude, with my boobs sticking out at the front and my bum at the back, both looking absolutely huge. Maybe it was the costume, maybe I was just being self-conscious, but I looked and felt at least two stone heavier, and all of it on my bum and boobs.

I was making a bit of a face as I left the bedroom, but at least I wasn't going to end up with a mouthful of Fat Jeff's spunk. Gabby was, and she hadn't wasted any time. She was on her knees between his open thighs, her head moving slowly up and down on the shaft of his cock. He'd made her show off too. Her top and bra were up, to leave her little titties swinging under her chest as she worked, and her jeans and knickers had been pulled right down at the back, showing her bum and pussy. Jeff looked up.

'Nice! Turn round.'

I gave him a twirl, showing off my bum. He answered with a satisfied grunt and took hold of Gabby's hair, easing her head down further on to his cock.

'What do you want me to do?' I asked.

'Whatever comes naturally. Dance around; play with your tits; make it good and dirty.'

I nodded, wondering if he thought dancing for perverts while dressed up as a demented clown was really what came naturally to me, or any woman. It didn't matter; I was doing it for his benefit. I began to dance, wiggling my boobs and bum to imaginary music, and putting myself into increasingly rude poses, taking care not to let him see between my cheeks.

He watched, his eyes moving between my body and Gabrielle's face as her lips moved up and down on his cock. She wasn't really sucking any more, but having her head fucked, Jeff controlling both how fast it went and how deeply he penetrated her throat. After a while he adjusted himself, leaning forwards to press his huge belly into her face and reach under her. He began to play with her breasts, one after the other, bringing her nipples to erection before he sat back again. He moaned, and spoke, his voice hoarse with passion.

'I'm going to do it, Gabs, right in your mouth. Get dirty, Pops.'

I began to dance faster, feeling sillier than ever as I jiggled my boobs, then turned, to push out my bum, finally letting my cheeks part to show him what I knew he really wanted to see. He moaned, louder, and again as I reached back to take hold of my bottom-cheeks, ready to pull them wide. He grunted and spoke again, fast and urgent.

'That's right, Pops, show me your arsehole . . . stretch it wide . . . Oh, that's my girl, you dirty bitch . . .'

I'd done it, hauling my cheeks wide to show him the little hole between, and my pussy into the bargain. As I looked around to watch the final moment I realised he was already coming. His mouth was wide, his face set in glazed ecstasy, his hand twisted hard into Gabby's hair. She was pop-eyed and red in the face, her cheeks bulging as she struggled to take what he was pumping into her mouth.

It all came out, the instant he let go of her hair, all over his cock and balls in one great, spasmodic belch. She rocked back, gasping, her face set in utter disgust, with sperm dribbling out over her lower lip and hanging from her chin in a creamy white curtain.

'Good one,' he sighed. 'Thanks, Gabs . . . you too, Poppy.'

I stood up, still feeling ridiculous, but also more than a little horny, with the smell of spunk in the air and my body exposed. Jeff blew out his breath, sinking back into the chair. Gabby had taken the tissue box from the coffee table, and held it out to him as she started to clean her face. He took a bundle.

'You two going to lez up?' he asked, wiping his cock.

Gabby was still attending to the mess on her face. It had gone on her top too, and she didn't look best pleased. I was game, if she wanted to, and with her nearly naked after a man had come in her mouth it was hard to imagine her being indifferent. I had to at least offer.

'Later, Gabby? Or do you want to?'

She hesitated a moment and then she was peeling off her top, and I knew she was up for it. Jeff gave a satisfied grunt as he sat back to take his wet cock in hand.

'Yeah, clown action, cool! Sit on her face, Pops, make her lick your arsehole.'

Gabby stood up, to push the tangle of material around her legs off, along with her shoes. Nude, she gave me a despairing look, but came into my arms willingly enough as I reached her. We began to kiss, and I took her neat bottom into my hands, stroking her cheeks and along her crease. She was shaking a little, from what she'd done to Jeff, and I could taste his come in her mouth, bringing my submissive feelings up very quickly.

I didn't want to dominate her. I wanted punishment, and exposure. She gave no resistance as I led her gently down to the floor, kneeling, and over the sofa. I stuck my bottom up, feeling my meat bulge from the absurd clown outfit as I assumed a spanking position. Gabby did the same, still kissing me, still trembling in my arms as we offered ourselves.

'Spank us, Jeff, while we cuddle.'

He gave another loud grunt as he pulled his chair close. I pulled Gabby to me as my other arm went back, between my spread thighs, to find the plump, wet bulge of my pussy. I was soaking, swollen and open, and slipped two fingers into my hole. Jeff was right behind us, staring up our open pussies, a fat red tongue sticking out from the corner of his mouth as he admired the view. I closed my eyes, kissing Gabby deep as Jeff took a pinch of the fat of my bottom.

He began to fondle, molesting us as we masturbated, one hand on my bum, one on hers. I let him, revelling in his lewd, dirty exploration of my bottom. He was going to punish me, and my girlfriend, finger us, touch our bumholes up, pinch and slap our cheeks. My fingers slipped free of my hole and I began to rub myself. Almost as my fingers came out, they were replaced by one fat, male finger, then a second and a third, squelching in my open hole. It wasn't going to be long, my muscles already starting to twitch and my bumhole winking behind.

'Spank me, Jeff, hard!'

'Tart!'

'I know. Go on, do it!'

There was a wet sound as he pulled his fingers out of Gabby's sex, then a slap. I felt her body jerk to the impact, but his fingers were still in me.

'Spank me, you bastard!'

'Temper, temper . . .'

His fingers came out. My hole closed with a long, windy fanny fart. Jeff laughed and I felt the blood rush to my face.

'Spankies time, girls!'

He caught us hard, a double swat across both our bottoms. I jumped, and so did Gabby, and again as the second smack hit. I began to rub faster, and he caught the rhythm, slapping our cheeks in time to our contractions. As my bottom started to bounce I was already coming, rubbing hard and fast at my burning clitty as Gabby and I mashed our mouths together.

Climax hit her first, in a long moan of ecstasy as her muscles tightened against mine. I pulled her in, as she did me, our bodies held tight as she came, surrendered to his lewd punishment, our bottoms flaunted for spanking and groping, nothing hidden, our mouths full of the taste of his spunk.

I was coming too, gasping into Gabby's mouth as Jeff rained slaps down on my naked cheeks. I wanted more, needed more, and harder, the belt or cane, a real thrashing as I squirmed in orgasm, utterly exposed in front of him. I was wishing he could fuck me, bugger me, whip me, all at the same time, spunk up me, then piss all over my hot bottom.

That last, filthy thought brought me right to the top of my climax. My whole body was jerking in orgasm, and my bottom felt wonderful, a huge, hot ball, with my sex a squashy wet centre. I held the thought of hot pee cascading down over my smacked cheeks, filling my hole, splashing out around my fingers, dripping from my pubic hair and running down my thighs. It was wonderful, really dirty, and I held it until I could bear no more.

What happened with Fat Jeff was just one of those things. Normally I keep men at arm's length. Men are a pain. They won't accept that Gabby and I are an item, or they get funny about lesbians, or whatever. I don't need it. Some are different, just a few, the kinky ones. They know that it's nothing but tutti-frutti, just play between friends. Jeff was one of them and, even if I didn't share his bizarre fantasies, I knew he had a knack of making me feel rude. That way, if Gabby needed a Daddy for her grown-up-baby play, or if I needed a really sound spanking, we had someone we could call on. He might be crude, he might be dirty, but he was safe. He didn't judge either, just as he expected us not to judge him.

Gabby had an endless string of appointments on Thursday, so I got out of the flat early, had breakfast in Victoria Station of all places, then took a train on the spur of the moment, south, as far as Uckfield. From there I walked aimlessly out into the country-side, just enjoying the warm summer's day and thinking about my life. Inevitably my mind turned to what had happened with Stephen Stanbrook, and peeing in my knickers. There were very few people about, and as I walked I began to tease myself that I was going to wet my knickers and go home like that, with my bum all soggy as I sat among the other passengers. Of course I chickened out, but when I could hold on no more I just did it in the middle of the path, which felt deliciously naughty.

That put me right in the mood for the evening's entertainment. Gabby had managed to convince herself that it was legitimate for me to try to help Stephen dispel his doubts about female sexuality, and didn't protest. So after a light supper I got into a baby-doll, white this time, and sat down to the computer.

I was early and spent nearly an hour discussing the making of punishment implements. Having had to make canes and tawses for my own discipline while I was with Anna Vale, my previous girlfriend, I knew a great deal more than most of them. Soon I was giving advice on everything from where to get the best skins to which types of oil to use to keep things in good condition. The various Masters' comments had begun to take on a slightly awe-struck tone, which was pleasing to say the least. I stopped addressing them by title and not one tried to put me in my place. When Black Knight joined in I was trying to answer a barrage of questions, and he said nothing for some while, so, when he did comment, it came as a shock.

Black Knight: 'Getting a bit above yourself, aren't you, Poppet?'

My instinctive reaction was annoyance, but I quickly swallowed my pride.

Poppet: 'Sorry, Master.'

Black Knight: 'I think a tawsing would do you a great deal of good.'

Poppet: 'Yes, Master.'

Black Knight: 'Turn your chair around and bend over it.'

Poppet: 'Yes, Master.'

I did it, quickly swivelling my chair and kneeling up on it. To get at the key board I had to bend over the back, sticking my bottom up. Gabby laughed and gave me a swat across the seat of my knickers. I grinned at her, already shaking a little, and ready for a punishment that was clearly not going to be all virtual. Fresh words had come up on the screen.

Black Knight: 'What are you wearing, Poppet?'

Poppet: 'My white baby-doll, Master.'

Black Knight: 'Pull down your pants.'

Poppet: 'Yes, Master.'

I obeyed, reaching back to tug my baby-doll knickers down and show off my bare bum to Gabby, who gave an appreciative smile. Most of the other people in the chatroom had stopped posting, and I imagined them thinking of me in my rude, vulnerable position. The girls would have butterflies in their stomachs and feel acutely conscious of their own bottoms; the men would be cool and dominant, or just plain lecherous.

Black Knight: 'I am behind you. I have a tawse in my hand, three-tailed, heavy brown leather.'

Poppet: 'Not that, Master, please!'

Black Knight: 'Do not resist. It is your nature to submit your body to me.'

Poppet: 'Yes, Master.'

The name Boots appeared on the list of people in the chatroom, giving me an added thrill at the idea of June witnessing my punishment.

Black Knight: 'Twenty strokes.'

Poppet: 'Yes, Master.'

A box began to flash on my toolbar. I clicked on it hurriedly, making Gabby laugh again at the awkwardness of my position. The screen came up. I began to type, telling her to hang on, but her message appeared first.

Boots: 'Hi, Poppet, I am so glad you're here! Are you OK?'

I had to answer.

Poppet: 'Hi, Boots. Sorry about last week. I got a bit carried away.'

Boots: 'Carried away?'

Poppet: 'After I wet my knickers. I wasn't upset or anything.'

Boots: 'Promise?'

Poppet: 'Promise. I got so turned on I just had to finish off.'

Boots: 'Naughty, naughty! We wondered what had happened to you.'

Poppet: 'I should have come back. I got distracted.'

Boots: 'So you really wet yourself?'

Poppet: 'Yes.'

Boots: 'We thought you were only playing!'

Poppet: 'I was. I play hard.'

Boots: 'I bet you do, bad girl!'

Poppet: 'It was nice. I like to be told to do it. Your Master is good.'

Boots: 'The best.'

Poppet: 'Hang on a minute. I'm supposed to be being tawsed by Black Knight.'

Boots: 'Whoops! Sorry, didn't realise.'

I closed the little window and turned my attention back to the main screen. They were talking about implements again, but I was still up for my virtual punishment, and typed in an apology as quickly as I could.

Poppet: 'Sorry, I got a whisper.'

The response was quick.

The Keeper: 'You shouldn't have done that, Poppet.'

Stern: 'Read the chatroom rules, stupid.'

Black Knight: 'Poppet, if you want to whisper, you

must ask permission from the Master and from myself, on the main board.'

Poppet: 'Sorry!'

Black Knight: 'Poppet, if you want to do this you must learn to follow the rules. Also, while you are here you must be respectful of all Masters.'

Poppet: 'I said sorry. Give me a break!'

Black Knight: 'Never speak to a Master like that. That is your only warning. Do not do it again.'

'How arrogant can he be!' Gabby put in from behind me.

I had climbed down out of spanking pose, now feeling pissed off. The guy was so far up himself he must have been able to see his own tonsils. Fat Jeff, however crude, however dirty, would never have spoken to me that way. I spun my chair back round and put my fingers to the keyboard, intending to give him a short, sharp lecture. Thinking of Boots, I hesitated. They were now discussing different types of cane, but I no longer wanted to give them the benefit of my experience. She wasn't commenting, so I clicked on her name to bring a whisper window up.

Poppet: 'What an arsehole!'

Rules or no rules, she responded.

Boots: 'He runs the Group, so we have to follow his rules.'

Poppet: 'I see you don't!'

Boots: 'Usually I do. If I don't, I take care not to get caught.'

She followed the sentence with one of the little yellow smilies, this time winking. I began to feel better. I prefer honesty between playmates, but I could see her point. When I was with Anna Vale I'd been the same, a model of obedience on the surface and sneaky underneath. I changed the subject.

Poppet: 'So what's up?'

Boots: 'What is up, bad girl, is that Knickers and I are going down to The Master's house in Dorset. We can stay all summer and, when he comes down, he's going to take complete charge of us. How cool is that?'

Poppet: 'Wow! You lucky thing.'

Boots: 'He is so good, and he is so rich he just does not give a shit about money. He's getting us uniforms, and all sorts of gear.'

Poppet: 'Neat!'

Boots: 'Have you heard of pony-girls?'

Poppet: 'I've been a pony-girl.'

Boots: 'Oh my God! You're going to have to tell me about it!'

Poppet: 'Sure, any time.'

Boots: 'The Master is going to get all the harnesses we need, and special boots, and all sorts.'

Poppet: 'Tails?'

Boots: 'I'd love a tail, but the only ones I've seen just stick straight out of your bum. They look stupid, and I know what I want. I've got a picture of a girl with a gorgeous swishy black tail that looks like it's growing out of her spine.'

Poppet: 'What does she look like? Who else is in the photo?'

Boots: 'She is dead cute; pretty, curly black hair, lovely cheeky bum, boobs to die for. All she's got on is the harness, and her reins are being held by this really hard-looking domina.'

Poppet: 'What's the domina wearing?'

Boots: 'An old-fashioned cape, green I think, riding boots. She's got a whip.'

Poppet: 'The pony-girl is me.'

Boots: 'You are never serious!'

Poppet: 'Sure I am. The woman is my ex, Anna Vale. I can get the tails too.'

Boots: 'Pretty, please!'

Poppet: 'OK. They're quite expensive, and they have to be handmade.'

Boots: 'The Master will pay. He's seen the picture.'

I didn't answer for a moment. I was feeling very smug indeed and thinking of how it had felt to run without a stitch on besides my harness and the plug of the tail moving up my bottom. When she typed again it was a direct request.

Boots: 'Can we meet up?'

Poppet: 'OK. Where are you?'

Boots: 'Beaconsfield. Knickers will want to come too. The next munch is in Central London.'

Poppet: 'I'm in Central London, but I don't want to go to the munch, not with people like The Keeper and Black Knight there.'

Boots: 'It's best to meet at munches. Safe.'

Poppet: 'No thanks. How about the Lord March-mont in Bloomsbury Street?'

Boots: 'I can find it. Sorry to be a pain, but how can I be sure you're for real?'

Poppet: 'Easy, bring the pony-girl picture.'

That was what I wanted, to meet with June and Nicola and not to play sub to some arrogant shits who thought they knew it all. We agreed a time; I made my excuses and dedicated the rest of my evening to playing nurse for Gabrielle.

Three

I was meeting with Nicola and June, or Knickers and Boots to use their play names. Gabby accepted my decision after a moment of hesitation, and I played nurse for her all weekend to make up for it, not breaking role once. Stephen wasn't going to be there, so there wasn't really a conflict of interests, and I promised to let her know if either of the girls really did suffer from low self-esteem.

The Lord Marchmont is perfect for that sort of meeting. It's big and crowded, but there is a cellar bar with little alcoves. It's easy to stay in the background and see who comes in but, once settled down in an alcove, you can guarantee that you won't be heard. Anna Vale, always very secretive about how she earned her money, and suspicious of every man who came to her, had always used it, and never once slipped up. Not that I had to worry, because I had Stephen's unwitting guarantee that both Nicola and June were the real thing.

When I got there on the Saturday evening it was a bit less crowded than usual. The other reason that Anna had liked it was that it looked prewar. The building certainly was and, if the décor wasn't all original, it looked the part, including a huge polished propeller above the bar, photos of men in uniform with big moustaches and a framed IOU from the artist Augustus John.

I was a little wary in case Anna might actually be there, but as she'd seldom visited more than three or four times a year it seemed unlikely. Her style had always been to keep a handful of established regulars, and I was sure it wouldn't have changed. Sure enough, after sneaking in by the side door and hiding in the shadows for a few minutes I decided that she wasn't there.

Knickers and Boots were there, quite unmistakable from Stephen's descriptions, and I spent a while just watching them. As he had said, Nicola was petite, my height or maybe not even that, and very slim. Her face was delicate, elfin I suppose, with high cheek-bones and large, bright eyes. Straight, tawny hair hung almost to her bottom, and her skin was pale and smooth. She was in a crop top, obviously without a bra, and seemed to have as much nipple as tit. Her bottom was lovely, round and cheeky in a pair of cream-coloured slacks.

June looked quite chunky by comparison, although she was below average height and far from fat, with just a little bulge of coffee-cream flesh showing above the waistband of her low-slung jeans. Her knickers showed, deliberately, a scarlet thong pulled tight between two meaty bum-cheeks, and she had a tattoo, a maple leaf, its shape designed to enhance hers. Like Nicola, she was in a crop top but, unlike Nicola, hers was bulging with chubby female flesh. She was mixed-race, perhaps with a touch or Indian or Iranian, with straight black hair longer even than her friend's.

They were both drinking: June a vodka mixer straight from the bottle; Nicola a tankard of stout, which was wonderfully eccentric. I bought myself a cider and moved close, feeling a little shy and wondering how best to introduce myself. Breaking the ice is always the hardest part and, if having met online made it easier, it wasn't by all that much, and I was determined not to be inhibited. So I worked my way through the crowd, came up behind them, put my glass down and took a firm pinch of each bottom.

Both jumped and turned, their angry looks fading immediately they saw me. I grinned and hugged both of them, kissing June, then Nicola. It was noisy, and I had to shout and make gestures to get the idea across that we should go downstairs. Both nodded agreement and a moment later we were in the comparative quiet of the cellar bar. A few alcoves were still empty, and I chose a corner one, leaving us almost completely shielded from inquisitive eyes.

'Great place to meet,' June said as she slipped on to the bench. 'We should hold munches here.'

'It's full of office workers on weekday lunchtimes,' I answered her, 'but pretty empty at weekends.'

'They're usually on Sundays,' Nicola told me. 'I'll get Master to propose it.'

I couldn't help but giggle.

'Do you always call him Master, even when you're together?'

'Yes, we don't know his real name!' June laughed.

'It's a lifestyle thing,' Nicola added.

'You're really getting in deep then?'

'All the way,' she answered.

'Most of the way,' June put in. 'I'm more a masochist; Nikki's more submissive. How about you?'

'I used to think of myself as purely submissive. I was, I suppose. Punishment and pain came with the territory, but both turn me on. I've changed though, slowly, coming to express the dominant side of my nature and, really, just to be more flexible. To be honest, UK Masters and Slaves seems too rigid.'

Nicola answered me.

'I like it that way. It helps me to understand who I am.'

'I used to think that way. It wasn't until I felt secure in my sexuality that I began to want to experiment with my own fantasies, never mind switch. At first I just let my Mistress lead.'

'Mistress?'

'I generally prefer girls, but I'm bi.'

Both nodded, Nicola slightly solemn, June with a naughty grin that made my pussy tingle.

'So what are you into now?' June asked eagerly.

I hesitated, having promised Gabrielle that I wouldn't bring her into it. But, then, the gap between her professional and personal lives was so great that there was no risk of even Stephen realising, and I knew he hadn't spoken to them.

'As you know,' I answered, grinning, 'wetting my knickers, and pony-girl play of course, and being a piggy-girl, plenty of spanking and other CP, bondage, exhibitionism, all sorts.'

'You seem to know everything!'

'Believe me, I had the best teacher.'

'I do believe you. How come we haven't come across you on the net?'

'I've only had access to computers for a year and a bit.'

'How come?'

'I was in a pure SM lifestyle relationship for years, one based on the thirties, with Anna Vale.'

'Anna Vale?'

'Haven't you heard of her?'

'No.'

'I thought everyone into SM had. She has to be the most fanatic lifestyler out. I was her girlfriend, maid, slave, pony-girl, everything.'

'Wow! Sounds great! Master will love it. He's really into fantasies of girls being lifelong slaves, you know, traded between one master and another, sold even.'

'This was no fantasy, believe me.'

'So what happened?' Nicola asked. 'That's what I dream about.'

'I was just out of school, seventeen. I hadn't done badly, but I hadn't done well either. The careers office had me down as a secretary, and I could see a life of boredom and mediocrity stretching away in front of me. I already knew I didn't really fit in. Being bisexual and submissive is not easy among a normal teenage peer group, as I'm sure you know.'

'Tell me about it.'

'I tried lesbian groups because, while I don't mind hettie sex, I'm not really into men as such. That wasn't perfect, and I sometimes had to pretend to be pure lesbian, but there was no shortage of attention.'

'I bet!'

'Most of them were very political though, and SM was a big no-no. A few were different, and there was a club I used to go to, dedicated to dressing up in historical styles, Victorian mainly. I met Anna there, and she spanked and caned me in front of everyone. I was in love with her before she'd finished with me. Two weeks later I moved in with her, to live the full lifestyle. It was romantic, and great fun. We used to dress in styles from the last century, thirties mainly, but also elegant twenties dresses, or fifties style, with tight jumpers and circle skirts and lots of big, restrictive underwear. One of her favourites was wartime uniform. She would be WAAF Section Officer Vale, always immaculate, and so stern. I used to love getting the cane like that, with my blue woollen skirt rolled up and my big panties down.'

'Wow!' June cut in.

'Just perfect,' Nicola agreed. 'That is just how I want to live, only with a man ... or not, anyone really if they have real certainty of who they are.'

'It was great, yeah, for a while. In the end I just couldn't take it. I changed, she didn't. There were no modern conveniences ... I had to dry the washing in a mangle, for God's sake! The most recent magazine in the house was dated nineteen fifty-eight. We had an old black and white telly and valve radios. Even our food had to be authentic, or what she reckoned was authentic. I tell you, I never want to see another pork chop again as long as I live. That wasn't the real problem though. I was under discipline, twenty-four seven, real discipline.'

'You couldn't take it?' Nicola queried.

'I couldn't,' June agreed.

'When Master dominates you,' I asked Nicola, 'do you have a stop-word?'

'Of course. I wouldn't want to use it, because ideally I'd be able to place complete trust in my Master, but it should always be there, in case of accidents if nothing else.'

'I didn't. I had to take what she deemed right. Like you, I wanted that, and I gave her my trust. When she broke it I left, after she caned my bum and legs for going off to play with another woman one weekend.'

'Ow! I hate it on the legs!' June squeaked.

'Over a hundred strokes of the heavy cane, with me tied down over a chair.'

'Bare?'

'Yes. She tricked me. She said I was getting thirty. I was used to being tied for punishment, so I didn't think anything of it, but she wouldn't accept my count, and just kept on thrashing me, like she was demented, even when I was screaming ...'

'Poor thing!'

'So I walked out.'

'I'm not surprised! What did you do?'

'Went to stay with a girlfriend, the only one I had whose address Anna didn't know. It was all I could do. I had no money, no qualifications, nothing. By then I even talked as if I belonged in the thirties! Not like Anna, because it was me who had to do all the shopping, and anything which involved going out into the "mundane world" as she called it. Still, people kept giving me odd looks, even after I'd got some modern clothes.'

'I wouldn't have guessed. You sound a bit posh, maybe, but you don't speak funny.'

'No, but only because I've put a lot of effort into it. When I was with her I used to tune in to commercial radio and such. If I got caught it was six of the best, bare.'

'Ouch! What about the telly?'

'We only ever watched old films, that sort of thing. One of my jobs when I went out was to buy a paper and make a list of all the films on offer from before nineteen sixty, then throw the paper away.'

'So how did you live?'

'Frugally.'

'Yeah, but what about council tax and shit. Was she rich?'

'Not really, no. She owned the house, because it had been left to her, but her money used to come from pro dom work.'

'With men?'

'Sure.'

'But you said she was lesbian?'

'She is. She despises men. That's what makes her such a good dom. She used to cater for the ones who want to be treated like dirt and beaten really hard.

With Anna they got it, believe me! You see, that's what you've got to remember with an SM lifestyle. In the end you still have to interact with the real world.'

I finished with a shrug and a sudden twinge of regret. What I'd said was true, but so often I'd wished it wasn't. Nicola seemed to be the same, June more playful.

'Enough of me, anyway. What about you two?'

Nicola hesitated, looking thoughtful as she toyed with her glass, and June waded in before she could speak.

'I just think it's great, so much more intense than vanilla sex. Not that I mind a good bonk, but with SM games you can go on for hours, and all the attention's on me. I like the people too. Sometimes they can be a bit up themselves, like you said, but I don't get put down for wanting a lot of sex. I always did, and I'm sure you know what straight men get like.'

'Not really. I hardly know any.'

'Oh you know, they want you to be a slut for them, then because you are they don't trust you, or . . . Fuck that, anyway. I want to be me.'

'How about switching?'

'I might . . . not with men I don't think. Perhaps I could dom another girl. In the Groups and stuff most people make out that you can't really get all the way in as a switch. Maybe that's bollocks?'

'It is. Believe me, switching opens whole new horizons.'

'Not for me,' Nicola put in. 'I need to feel that I am somebody's, completely. I couldn't bear the thought of Master submitting, it's like . . . insane.'

'That's just how I felt once,' I answered her, 'but you go with what you feel. So what's with the pony-girl play?'

'Master wants us as his ponies,' Nicola answered. 'In the garden in Dorset. There's a lawn, he says, which you can't see from anywhere, and an old shed we can use as a stable.'

'He wants us to sleep on straw and everything,' June added, 'and pull a cart he's going to buy, and he's going to train us to walk properly, and everything.'

'That's just a part of it,' Nicola went on. 'He wants us to live as if we were his slaves, not just while he's there, but all the time. If we're not in the stable, we'll sleep on mats at the foot of his bed, and he's making rules for us to follow, with punishments if we break them.'

'How will he know?' I asked.

'I'll tell him,' Nicola answered earnestly.

June made a face and I hid a grin behind my glass. Nicola had a little learning to do, but I didn't want to spoil her fantasy.

'It sounds great!' I said happily. 'You've got to have tails, but why not give your Master a surprise? Come with me tomorrow and we'll get them ordered. How long till you go down to Dorset?'

'A week, when our colleges finish.'

'That's not enough time, really. But they can be posted. We'll meet up here tomorrow, yeah?'

Both nodded.

Sunday was the hottest day of the year so far, with no breeze at all and the sun burning down from a rich blue sky. I was in the best of moods, and threw on a light dress over a pair of big white panties, sure that it would all be coming off before the day was over. After getting thoroughly plastered at the Lord Marchmont we'd walked up to Great Portland Street tube arm in arm, with me in the middle. We'd said goodbye with a long cuddle in an empty alleyway, and I'd let my hand stray to both their bums, stroking and squeezing their cheeks. Neither had minded and, while Nicola had taken it passively, June had returned the favour and even let her hand slip a little way down the back of my jeans.

I'd been walking on air as I made for home, and had a wonderful session with Gabby when I arrived, both naked in the shower, taking turns to pee over the other's hair and face as we masturbated. Afterwards I told her everything in detail, and persuaded her to come with us the next day. Buying tails meant going to Amber Oakley's place in Hertfordshire, and like me she was under no illusions about how we were likely to end up.

We met up at the Lord Marchmont. Being pretty sure that the last thing Stephen Stanbrook was going to do was admit to his lifestyle slaves that he was in therapy, I introduced her as Gabrielle. She and Nicola hit it off immediately, both being serious on the surface and thoroughly dirty underneath. I stuck with June and quickly realised that the key to her submission was that it allowed her to indulge her filthiest needs without taking responsibility, as usual. Nicola seemed more complex, with something of that, but also a need for protection.

I'd called Amber, and she was expecting us, but in our hurry we had managed to catch the earlier train. When we got there she was standing at the door to her perfectly ordinary tack shop in full riding gear, just passing a horse over to another woman. Big and buxom, with her tawny curls spilling out from under her hard hat and a vicious-looking riding whip in one hand, she looked every inch the dominant woman. It made me want to just crawl across her knee for a good whipping, something she'd given me several times before.

Her eyes lit up as she saw us, but she greeted me with a gentle peck and ushered us all inside before turning to speak to the horsy girl. Inside, her girlfriend, Kay, was minding the shop. Tiny, very slim, tawny-haired with small apple-like breasts and a cheeky, spankable bottom, she might have been Nicola's sister. She greeted us with a bright, slightly embarrassed smile, which grew suddenly warmer as Amber came in behind us. A couple were looking at Wellington boots in one corner, and I quickly pulled June away from a display of carriage whips and pressed my finger to my lips before she could say anything.

'I need a shower,' Amber announced. 'Take everyone over to the forge, would you, Poppy?'

She tossed me her keys, which I caught. Kay gave me an arch look, which I returned as the others filed out of the shop. The forge was across a little, high-walled yard, completely cut off from prying eyes. I led them across, unlocked the high, arched doors and threw them open. We stepped inside.

I'd seen it before, and was prepared for the whips and canes, the harness and bits of furniture designed for punishment and bondage, and the overwhelming smell of new leather. The others weren't, and stared, both fascinated and frightened. June moved in, giggling as she half bent across a whipping stool with her bottom pushed out. Nicola went to a line of hooks, from which pieces of pony-girl harness hung, to finger the leather with a look of reverence on her face. Gabby stayed at the door, looking a little concerned. I knew why. Just about everything there was designed to take girls beyond her personal tolerance of pain.

'And she sells all this stuff?' June asked.

'Made to order,' I replied, 'anything you like.'

'I like it all. I want it all. We should bring Master here, Nikki.'

Nicola nodded in agreement. I wasn't at all sure what Amber would make of Stephen Stanbrook, but I felt it was my duty to pitch her spiel.

'You should,' I agreed. 'Everything she does is custom-made, to your own design and to fit properly, and it still costs less than you'd pay in Soho or somewhere. Compare this to anything you've seen before.'

I took down a head harness, a basket of straps designed to fit the human head and made in textured leather, thick yet soft and pliable. The fittings were solid brass, each double-headed rivet hammered just so, each end trimmed. Nicola took it.

'Beautiful. I would love to be in this.'

She looked as if she was about to come, with her eyes bright and her mouth a little open as she stroked the leather.

'You will be,' I assured her, 'and with a tail, right up your bottom.'

I'd reached for the album showing her designs in use as I spoke, and opened it at random. Inevitably I got the pictures of Penny Birch and I as piggy-girls, naked in a pool of mud with nothing on but our leads, with rubber snouts on our faces and curly pink tails sticking up over our bums.

'What are you doing?' June exclaimed, crowding close with Nicola.

'Being a piggy-girl,' I explained, my face warming more than a little.

There were four pictures on the page. One was of Penny rolling in the mud. One showed me face down in a trough with my mouth full of potato peelings and bits of cabbage. The third showed us together, tethered in a pen as if for sale. In the fourth I was nuzzling her bottom, with my tongue visibly in contact with her anus.

'You dirty bitch!' June crowed in delight. 'Who's she?'

'My friend Penny, Amber's ex.'

'And the other?'

It was Anna, inevitably, in the third photo, standing by the pig-pen beside Amber. She was in immaculate prewar tweeds, her glossy brown hair up, her face set in the expression of stern disapproval I remembered so well. An odd feeling hit me – regret, sadness, mixed with a little fear.

'Anna Vale,' I answered, 'my ex.'

'She looks the part,' Nicola stated, June nodding agreement.

'She is,' I answered, quickly turning the page. 'That's more like it. Pony-girls.'

Both of them let their breath out in gasps. The pictures showed a tall, dark-haired girl. In the first she was naked but for her harness, with the headgear, a body harness and calf-length boots with the soles designed to resemble horses' hooves. She was looking back over her shoulder, and her bottom was quite bare. Amber stood beside her, a tail in one hand, a tube of lubricant in the other. The next photo showed the girl bending, her cheeks pulled apart and her anus glistening with jelly. The third was a close-up, and showed the tail-plug going in, with the girl's bumhole a taut pink ring of shiny flesh as she accommodated it. In the last the tail was in, and she was standing, proud and beautiful, with the tail sticking up over her bum as if it was really growing from the base of her spine. Gabby had come to look too, but not one of them spoke, each no doubt imagining herself in the same state.

'Is that what you were after?' I asked brightly.

'That's me,' June agreed, 'me, me, me.'

Nicola nodded, and I saw that her fingers were shaking as she reached to turn the page. The next set were of the same girl being exercised, and showed various types of reins and whips. They took it in, and more, Nicola speechless in fascination, June with exclamations of delight, Gabby amused and maybe a little turned on, but always cool. We had nearly finished the album when Amber came in, now in jeans and a loose blouse, with a towel around her wet hair.

'Sorry about that. How are you doing?'

'I think they want everything,' I answered, 'but most of all, tails.'

'No problem at all,' she assured us. 'All I need is a tiny piece of hair to match your colour, a few measurements, an idea of how big or small you'd like the plugs, and two weeks.'

'Two weeks?' June queried. 'We were hoping they'd be ready sooner. We're going down to Dorset, you see, and we'd like to have them ready as a surprise for our Master.'

'Oh. When are you going down?'

'Less than a week, Friday evening.'

'That's not possible, I'm afraid. Each layer of rubber has to set. The middle of next week would be the earliest I could possibly have them ready.'

An idea hit me, an idea far too good to pass up.

'I'll take them down,' I offered quickly, before Amber could suggest posting them.

'Great!' June answered instantly. 'You too, Gabby, come and stay the weekend, yeah? You do men, yeah, 'cause Master . . .'

She trailed off, looking hopefully at Gabrielle.

'He would not suit me,' Gabby replied, 'but I would come if it was not for my work. Sorry, but Poppy may go.'

I nodded, suddenly feeling insecure at the thought of submitting myself to a man without Gabby there. Yet there was no way she could possibly go. I told myself I was being silly and nodded in agreement.

'Perfect,' Amber stated.

'Only we mustn't tell Master,' June put in. 'It can be a surprise.'

Nicola gave an appreciative smile as Amber reached for a tape measure on her workbench, along with a notebook and a stub of pencil.

'Measurements first,' she said. 'If you could stick your bottoms out, ladies.'

Nicola obeyed, leaning on the bench and pushing out her little round bum at once. She was in loose cotton trousers and looked so spankable I could barely keep my hands to myself. What with the pictures and the smell of leather and the all-pervading atmosphere of kinky sex I was fully turned on and determined not to leave without at least a little play.

'Do we need to be bare?' June asked.

'Only if you want to,' Amber answered.

June hesitated only an instant, and then she was squeezing her jeans down. Her thong came too, quite deliberately, and with it all down she stuck her bum out, making her chubby cheeks flare. Amber gave an appreciative glance and made the measurement, anus to base of spine, along the deep cleft of June's bottom.

Amber made a note in her book as June pulled her things up, then measured Nicola, who had waited patiently with her bottom ready, just trembling ever so slightly.

'I can do without hair, as it goes,' Amber stated. 'You can have black, June, or the darkest natural brown. For Nicola I'd think Kay's shade would be perfect, or maybe one darker.'

'Whatever you think best,' Nicola answered.

'Plugs then,' Amber went on. 'I can do any size you like.'

'I'm not sure,' Nicola answered cautiously. 'Small, I suppose. Master might want –'

'It's a question of what you can take,' Amber went on casually, 'and what you like to take. You have to choose, and never, ever, let a man make the choice for you.'

'Master says we need to learn to take things in our bottoms,' June stated.

'Mainly his cock, I expect,' Amber answered. 'I take it you've both had anal sex?'

'No,' June admitted.

'Not even a finger?'

'A finger, sure. Who hasn't?'

'Me,' Nicola admitted. 'Not inside.'

Amber made a face. I closed my eyes, thinking of two anal virgins and how it would feel to bend them both over and push a nice big strap-on up each tight little bumhole in turn. It was killing me. My nipples were painfully hard, and my pussy so wet I could feel the stickiness in my knickers.

'I'll go for an inch and a half,' Amber said thoughtfully, 'but maybe you should practise a little. Always use plenty of lubricant, water soluble, and take it slowly, never force yourself. If it hurts, you're not doing it properly.'

June giggled. Nicola responded with a nervous nod. Again I imagined them with their bumholes stretching to the head of my strap-on, their cheeks held open behind, breathless and shaking as their bottoms filled for the first time. I exchanged a glance with Gabby, who nodded meaningfully. If she wasn't thinking the same, it was pretty close. I was going to burst if I didn't get to play.

'And that's all I need,' Amber stated. 'How about lunch?'

'How about spankings all round, then lunch?' I countered.

'Well, I can see one person who needs one.' She laughed.

'I do, badly. You haven't spanked me in ages, and you do it so well.'

'Thank you, Poppy. Well, as you ask so nicely . . .'

As she spoke she sat down on the plain wooden chair in front of her workbench. My tummy began to flutter as she patted her lap, and I felt that lovely little tremor of fear that always comes before a spanking, however badly I want it. June giggled and moved back, making space for me, Nicola too. Gabby sat down on one of the pieces of bondage furniture to enjoy the show, as poised as ever.

I stepped forwards and she took my hand, to guide me gently down into place, with my bum stuck up in the air. My hands found the floor and she tucked her arm around my waist, firm but gentle, keeping me in place. Then her other hand had closed on the back of my dress and it was being pulled up, in front of all of them, showing my thighs and my big white panties. I had closed my eyes to concentrate on being stripped, but they came open again at a sudden noise.

'Oh!'

Kay stood in the doorway, upside down from my perspective. She looked a little flustered, but she was smiling as she quickly closed the door.

'I just came to say that I've locked up for lunch,' she announced.

'Just spanking this one,' Amber told her. 'It won't take long.'

Kay gave a nervous smile as she backed against the door, and Amber went back to dealing with me. No sooner had I closed my eyes again than her fingers caught hold of the waistband of my knickers, and down they came. Suddenly I was bare, my bottom showing to all of them and feeling very big indeed. That wasn't all I was going to have to show either.

Amber has very clear ideas about spanking. When a girl is punished, she should have a bare bum, and she should be made to show off every detail of her sex and bumhole. She would make me I knew and, sure enough, she took the time to pull my panties off one leg and slap my thighs apart, then lifted her knee to make sure everything was showing.

I was shaking hard and thinking of the four of them, all feasting their eyes on the intimate details of my body. I needed punishment, badly, and I wanted to show it all and leave them all turned on, over my naked flesh and my submission. Then they could be spanked, one by one, in the same lewd position, showing me what I'd been made to show them.

Amber pulled me close, her hand settling on the meat of my bottom; it had begun. It stung, my mouth coming open at the very first slap, and in a moment I was struggling to keep myself under control. She was hard, and my bottom was bouncing, with my cheeks spreading wider still at every spank. It was just right though, the heat coming straight to my pussy.

Soon I was pushing my bum up for more, panting in reaction. She began to spank harder, and harder still, bringing me more and more on heat. As my bum warmed I let my legs slip apart until they were as wide as they'd go, with my pussy a warm, wet patch at the focus of my whole being. Still she spanked, ever harder, my whole bottom bouncing in time and the slaps ringing out loud around the forge. Suddenly it was time.

'Take me there, Amber, please!'

She didn't answer, but her arm curled around me, her hand slipping under my tummy to my sex. I moaned aloud as she began to bring me off, handling my body so well, rubbing me even as she beat me, harder than ever, full on the fattest part of my bum, slap after furious slap as my clitty twitched and jumped under her fingers. Then I was there, all of a sudden, screaming and writhing over her lap as she pounded at my bottom with all her force yet bringing only a glorious extra heat to my long, tight orgasm.

I might have come, but I was still a spanked girl. She gave me a moment to catch my breath, then hauled me up by my hair to make me kiss her. I was more than willing, mouthing at her lips and cuddling on to her full, firm chest as the delicious after-spanking feeling of contentment and gratitude went through me. I wanted to return the favour, to get down at her knees and lick her to orgasm, or let her sit on my face. She pulled me off, gently but firmly.

'Later maybe, slut. For now, up against the wall with you, and keep your dress up and your knickers down.'

I went, rubbing my bum, unable to keep the smile from my face. I adjusted my dress, lifting it to show my bum and leaving my knickers around one ankle, then pressed my nose against the door like a good girl, for about five seconds.

'Who's next?' I demanded, giving up the unequal struggle against obedience and turning my head.

Anna would have caned me until I howled. Amber just gave the four girls a questioning look. Kay looked shy, blushing slightly and fidgeting in her lap. Gabby looked cool and poised. June was clearly excited, with perky nipples showing under her top. Nicola was biting her lip in uncertainty.

'Well?' Amber demanded.

Gabby stood up, very calm, but I could imagine what was going through her head. Spanking is discipline to her, something her nurse gives her if she's been naughty. She'll take it, and she needs it, but she hates the pain. So many times I've made her cry, and I'm a lot smaller and less forceful than Amber.

She took off her glasses and lifted her own dress, up and off, revealing her little braless breasts and a pair of waist-high panties decorated with roses in pink and blue. Amber gave her a quizzical look and patted her lap.

'Over you go, young lady.'

'Gently, please.'

'OK, but I warn you, if you wet yourself down my leg again . . .'

Gabby nodded as Amber trailed off. I giggled, thinking how Amber would look with my girlfriend's pee trickling down her jeans. I knew the nature of the warning too, not a threat, but a bargain.

I watched sidelong as Gabby's knickers were peeled slowly down and pulled off one leg. Like me, she got spread, her thighs slapped and Amber's knee lifted to make very sure her wrinkly pink bumhole was stretched out for our inspection and that every detail of her shaved pussy was on clear view. She'd done it that morning, and she was clean and pink, with traces of powder and the lube she uses on her bumhole glistening slightly in the light. Amber noticed, gave a low chuckle, put her finger to Gabby's anus and very slowly pushed it up. Gabby sighed, and began to make little whimpering noises as her rectum was fingered.

Amber was grinning in sadistic glee and, when she at last pulled her finger from the now sticky hole, it went straight to Gabby's mouth. There was no hesitation, and Gabby's face set in bliss as she let the finger in and began to suck. Nicola gave a subdued gasp. June giggled. Amber pulled out her finger and lifted her knee higher still, bringing Gabby's little round bottom up and spreading her still more rudely, with her wet anus a soft pink spot between her cheeks.

For a long moment Amber held Gabby like that, just to let the exposure really sink in. Then she began to spank, just little sharp taps with her fingertips, delivered to the very crests of Gabby's bum-cheeks. Gabby began to whimper immediately, a sound full of misery and contrition. In response Amber began to smack a little harder, to make the little buttocks quiver and bounce. Gabby's whimpers immediately grew more urgent, more pained. Amber went on, patiently building up the heat in Gabby's bottom until the whimpers turned to moans.

Amber changed her technique, now spanking properly, with the whole of her hand, slap after rhythmic slap landing across Gabby's now red bottom. Gabby began to kick, one leg pumping, then both as the pain broke her will to hold herself back. I love to spank her; I love to watch it, and I felt warm and ready. I knew what would be in her mind too, with the urge to pee growing as she came on heat and fought against the pain.

She did it, suddenly, her leg cocking up like a dog's and yellow piddle erupting from her spread pussy as Amber paused. June gasped in delighted shock; Kay made a little choking noise in her throat; I stifled a giggle. Amber gave a cry of disgust, but stopped spanking, holding her raised hand over Gabrielle's reddened bottom as she waited for the pee to finish.

It was coming in a great, thick gush, most splashing on the floor, but some going on Amber's thigh, to soak into the blue material and pool on the chair. Amber waited, stern-faced, watching the pee run from Gabby's sex until it died to a trickle and at last finished in a series of little spurts.

'Right, Miss Gabrielle, don't say you weren't warned!'

Gabby gave one choking, despairing cry as Amber's grip tightened on her waist, then screamed as the first hard swat caught her bum. Then she was thrashing and kicking and squirming, her hair flying, her fists thumping on the concrete floor, screaming and screaming as Amber spanked her, as hard as I'd been done, maybe harder.

Amber kept on, ignoring her victim's pain, face set in furious determination, slap after slap delivered to Gabby's now blazing red buttocks. Even when Gabby burst into tears she went on, spanking with all her force despite the agonised howls of protest and great wracking sobs that came with every blow.

At last it stopped, leaving Gabby blubbering freely across Amber's lap. Gabby made no move to get up, but spread her legs, wide and inviting. Amber responded, still holding Gabrielle in place as she put her hand to the wet must of pussy flesh, and began to rub. It took just moments; Gabby's bottom-cheeks started to tighten; her anus set up a lewd, winking rhythm, and she was there, coming with a long sigh of ecstasy that held until Amber at last stopped rubbing.

Only when Amber applied a meaningful pat to the little red bottom stuck up over her leg did Gabby finally get up, slowly, clutching her spanked bottom, her tear-stained face set in utter misery. She kissed Amber, and came to stand beside me without having to be told, eyes shut as she pressed her nose to the hard wood of the door, her body still shaking in reaction.

I took her hand and gave her a squeeze. She responded with a weak smile and opened her eyes, blinking to clear her tears away. Her knickers had come off during the spanking, and she was bare below the waist but for her shoes, looking sweet and vulnerable as only a spanked girl can.

Amber had stood up to take off her boots and her wet jeans, which she hung over a half-finished whipping stool. She was in blue cotton knickers, quite big and half-hidden beneath the tails of her blouse. I could see the muscle beneath the smooth flesh of her thighs, and the gentle bulge of her stomach, both adding to her impression of power.

'June?' she asked.

June stepped forwards, bright-eyed and giggling, to lay herself straight across Amber's lap with her bottom pushed up. She looked plumper than ever in spanking position, with her bum a fat ball of blue denim, yet still small and vulnerable beside Amber. Her tattoo showed, and the top of a pair of brilliant green knickers, which Amber pulled up and let go to smack the elastic back against flesh. June squeaked, and then purred as Amber began to fondle her bottom, weighing the big cheeks and stroking the taut blue denim.

The waist of June's jeans was elastic and, when Amber pulled at them, down they came, baring her ripe cheeks. Nude, her bottom was even more delightful than in jeans and, once her little green thong had been peeled down, it got better still. Amber spread her, to show off a very rude rear view. Her pussy was shaved, save for a neat triangle of crinkly black fur at the centre of her mound. Her lips were plump and pouting, a real split fig, with the flesh a rich olive brown to either side of a mushy, bright pink centre. She was wet, not surprisingly, and her hole showed. Her bumhole was the same colour, a rich brown, as if she was dirty, and every bit as pouty as her pussy.

Amber spent a moment inspecting June's bottom, with the plump cheeks spread to stretch both pussy and anus wide. I caught the scent of excited female, so familiar, yet forever appealing. Amber let go suddenly, making June's bottom wobble as the cheeks returned to their normal shape, and began to spank.

The smacks were gentle, delivered with a cupped hand to make it noisier, a good way to test a new girl. June simply sighed in pleasure, then moaned as it got harder.

'This is nice, soft. I love girlie spankings.'

Amber's eyebrows rose a fraction and she began to lay in, smacking easily as hard as she had with Gabby. June grunted and began to pant, her bottom still lifted obligingly, her legs and arms braced on the floor. Amber's face set in determination and she began to spank harder still, sending ripples across June's fleshy bum-cheeks with every slap.

'That's it, nice and hard,' June gasped. 'Under my cheeks . . . get the heat to my cunt.'

Abruptly Amber changed her grip, snatching up June's arm to twist it high. June cried out in pain, then again as the spanking doubled in pace, Amber landing smack after smack on the fat, bouncing bum-cheeks. June's legs began to kick, and her head to shake in pain, but when she at last found her voice again it was no plea for mercy.

'Spank me . . . harder . . . harder! Harder, you vicious bitch!'

'I shall!' Amber grunted, and laid in, spanking with all her force and as fast as she could, the way she'd done me as I came under her fingers.

June lost control, her kicking growing frantic and her legs starting to scissor, straining out her lowered jeans and thong to show off pussy and all, closing, then spreading once more. She was clutching at Amber's leg, and tossing her long hair, which was trailing to the floor. There was spit running from her mouth, and when she began to scream I thought she'd finally reached her limit. So did Amber, and slowed down.

'Don't stop!' June yelled. 'Just do it, you stupid cow! Spank me, beat me, really hurt me . . . come on, you fat bitch!'

Amber stopped, keeping her grip as she swivelled around to snatch up something from her workbench, a big wooden paddle, the handle still half-finished. She didn't pause, or ask, but applied it straight to June's bum, hard. June screamed, and gave one hard buck, but Amber clung on, face set in real anger as she laid in.

June went absolutely crazy, screaming and thrashing and calling Amber a bitch over and over. She couldn't get away, even when Amber changed her grip, to tuck June's body beneath one muscular arm, hand to pussy, as she'd done with me. June gave a choking scream as the paddle struck home, and began to speak again, babbling.

'That's it, you bitch, my cunt . . . bitch . . . frig me off . . . fuck me, someone, fuck my cunt . . . harder, bitch, harder!'

Her words were punctuated by the smacks of the paddle as Amber belaboured her bottom and, at about the tenth, she broke. Screaming, struggling, with spit flying from her lips and juice splashing in her pussy as Amber frigged her, she hit climax, her whole body going into convulsions. Amber kept on, spanking and rubbing, never once relaxing her grip, even when June's anus opened in a long, loud fart. That was it though, and as June collapsed across Amber's lap the paddling finally slowed, and stopped.

June's bum was purple, much worse than mine, let alone Gabby's. She was going to be bruised, badly, but there was a big grin on her face as she finally pulled herself up. She was a mess, her hair plastered across her face, her lips red and wet, spittle hanging from her chin.

'Nice,' she sighed as she reached for her thong.

'Uh, uh,' Amber said, 'keep it all down and up against the wall with you.'

'Yes, Mistress,' June answered, and her voice held just a touch of mockery.

'I hope you behave better than that with your Master?' Amber asked sweetly.

'I don't know.' June giggled. 'He's never spanked me! Sorry about the name calling, Amber, that's just me. It was nice.'

Amber gave a single stern nod of acceptance. She was flushed and breathing hard. Her face was set in determination, and when she patted her lap again it was not a question, but an order.

'Nicola, over,' she snapped.

Nicola came forwards, her head hung, her fingers working in her lap in desperate embarrassment. That didn't stop her doing as she was told, bending meekly across Amber's lap and lifting her bottom in submission. Amber wasted no time, tugging Nicola's trousers smartly down and taking a pair of diminutive pink panties with them. She was a sight: her firm, cheeky bottom was already open, with her little pink pussy quite bare. Her bumhole was a tiny knot of pink flesh, no more, pretty and virginal. June might have been virginal, but she looked ready for a horse cock. Nicola was the opposite.

She waited, trembling and silent as Amber began to explore her bottom, squeezing the muscular little cheeks, tickling the tiny anus with a fingernail, and suddenly slipping a finger deep into the wet pussy hole. Nicola stayed quiet, even as she was finger-fucked, utterly submissive. Amber made an appreciative face, and briefly put her fingers to Nicola's clitty, rubbing until the little bum-cheeks at last began to tighten.

'Spanking time,' Amber stated suddenly. She took a firm grip on Nicola's waist and laid in.

Nicola took it without a sound, her little bottom bouncing rhythmically, with the muscular cheeks barely changing shape to the slaps, but moving as a whole. It got harder quickly, and after a while Amber changed to the paddle to spare what must have been a very sore spanking hand. Still Nicola stayed quiet, just jerking slightly to the impacts as the red flush of her bottom grew darker and purple welts began to appear.

'So we've got a tough egg, have we?' Amber asked. 'Let's see how serene you stay like this, Miss Nicola.'

I thought Amber was going to masturbate her, but she made a sudden move, pulling at one of Nicola's legs to spread her, thighs open, little pink pussy squashed out, flesh on flesh, and went back to paddling. Nicola's jerking became a little more pronounced, but no more. Amber gritted her teeth and laid in, landing a cascade of hard paddle strokes on Nicola's spread bottom. At last Nicola began to whimper, and her anus to twitch. Her odd little jerking motions grew urgent, then frantic and she was masturbating on Amber's leg, in perfect time to the paddle smacks. She gave the sweetest little cry and I realised she'd come, but that was the only sound she made through a paddling that had left her bottom the same rich, bruised purple as June's.

When Nicola's pussy had finally stopped contracting the beating finished. She got straight down, to the floor, to kiss Amber's bare feet, then scampered over to join the three of us at the door, her bum bare behind. Amber put the paddle down, then sighed and stretched. She had to be turned on, and I was wondering who was going to be made to lick her pussy, but when she spoke it was with casual good humour.

'What a pretty picture, four little maids, all in a row, and all with their spanked bottoms on show.'

She sang it, making it rhyme, and still sounding so taunting, so superior that I felt myself melting again.

One word and I'd have been back over her lap, or a whipping stool, or tied helpless to a frame with a big dildo stuck in each hole.

'All very different too,' she went on. 'Two tough eggs, one baby and one very rude, Miss June, but each with her own style. Well, that was very enjoyable, girls, but it's made me hungry, so one last detail, then it's panties up and we'll go in to lunch, shall we? Except for you, Miss Gabrielle. You need a shower, and so do I.'

I turned, immediately jealous, to see her half-standing, in the act of pushing her knickers down her thighs. Kay is shy, and looked relieved to think that she was going to get away with it, but jealous too. Her expression changed to shock as Amber beckoned, then pointed to the puddle Gabby had made on the floor.

'Strip.'

Kay went pink, but she obeyed, scrambling out of her clothes as quickly as she could. I watched, admiring her embarrassment as much as her cheeky little bottom and firm, apple-sized breasts. She might easily have been Nicola's sister, in looks, and her attitude wasn't so very different either.

She got down, in the pee puddle, first on her knees, then rolling on to her back, with her big blue eyes looking up at Amber in timid expectation. Amber nodded and stepped forwards, to set her feet at either side of Kay's head. Kay swallowed hard, then opened her mouth. I thought Amber was going to pee on her, but she sank down into a squat and Kay's face disappeared under the big, muscular bottom.

'Oh my!'

It was June and, like me, she'd seen how Amber was sitting, not to make Kay lick her pussy, but her bumhole. Kay was doing it too. I could hear the wet slurping sounds and Amber's expression had changed to bliss. When she spoke, it was hoarse and urgent.

'You four, hands on your heads, keep your bottoms showing. Kay, stop, until I tell you.'

I obeyed, tucking my dress up before putting my hands meekly on top of my head. So did the others, all four of us with our smacked bottoms on show for her enjoyment. I had to look though, and stayed half-turned. She said nothing, and had taken her breasts in hand, stroking them through her blouse with her eyes closed in pleasure as she rubbed her bottom in Kay's face.

When the pee came it was completely unexpected, spurting from Amber's pussy to splash over Kay's breasts and belly. Immediately Kay's thighs came up and open, to show off her sex, with trickles of pee running down to either side of her pussy-lips. She began to masturbate, rubbing herself in her Mistress' pee as it splashed out across her naked body. Amber watched with an affectionate smile, waiting until her stream had died before her fingers went to her own pussy. Her eyes fixed on our naked bums and she began to masturbate.

'Lick,' she ordered, 'well in, and don't stop.'

The slurping sound started again as Kay began to tongue Amber's anus. She was dripping pee, and masturbating hard, with one finger in the mouth of her bumhole and the other attending to her pussy. It took just seconds, her bum tightening and her back arching, one leg jerking briefly and her bottom splashing in the pee puddle as she went into spasm. Then it was done, and she'd taken Amber by the hips, her full attention on licking her Mistress' bumhole.

I had to come again and, sliding a hand down, found my pussy warm and welcoming. Amber shook her head, but her mouth was already slack and her eyes were glazing in pleasure. She moaned and I saw the muscles of her thighs and tummy tighten. Then she was coming, full in Kay's face and wiggling her bottom on the willing tongue pushed so well up her hole, a thought I held as my own orgasm hit me.

Four

If I'd got on well with Nicola and June before going to Amber's, afterwards it was just perfect. After taking a giggling shower one after another, lunch stretched out all afternoon, with bottle after bottle of wine and increasingly dirty conversation. I had to admit my real age, after it became obvious just how long I'd known Amber, but it made no difference. By the time we left we were all drunk and, if there were any naughty secrets left to share, it was because there'd been no time to get them in.

Except for one thing. We kept firmly quiet about Gabrielle's professional relationship with Stephen. He was coming again on Monday but, as his opinion had barely changed, Gabby was hoping he'd give up and leave her free to be open with the girls.

I felt the same way, only I was going to get it, in Dorset. Both of them had begun to defer to me, not because they were any more submissive, but for my age and experience. They both had strong personalities though, whatever Stephen thought, and kept to their outlook on SM, June as a masochist and playmate, Nicola as a wannabe lifestyle slave.

Neither denied she had some learning to do. With June it was just a case of practice; but with Nicola it was more – if she wanted to be a perfect lifestyle slave for Stephen, she needed a little training first. Dominants, and dominant men in particular, never really understand the sensations they inflict on their partners. They can't, when they haven't experienced it themselves, no matter how much they've done or how much they've read, while the ones who claim to have some sort of deep empathy are usually the least understanding. Nicola could take the inevitable whippings, but she was definitely going to have her bumhole stretched, and I was determined to make that my job.

They were going down on Friday, in his car, and I just had to pray he wouldn't decide to bugger her over the weekend. It seemed all too likely but, with her finishing up at college and living with her parents in Sevenoaks, there was nothing I could do.

Stephen came for his normal appointment, and as before I stationed myself in the bedroom with my ear glued to the keyhole. It had become personal, with Stephen likely to be dominating me for real, and I was all attention as they settled down to the session. There was the normal preamble, then as usual he launched straight in, explaining that the relationship between him and the girls had intensified before going into a long self-justification as Gabrielle listened patiently.

'. . . they are so enthusiastic,' he finished, 'June especially, but there's a sweetness to Nicola that just makes me . . . makes me want to sing.'

'Yet you still believe that their sexuality derives from low self-esteem?'

'I'm not sure. I don't know what to believe any more. I've been reading up on the psychology behind SM, and most authorities seem to agree that the desire to submit one's will to another derives from insecurity and an inability to relate within a normal sexual relationship. The ones who disagree are mainly into it, so presumably they have something to gain.'

'While it is notoriously difficult to make an objective analysis of oneself, I do feel that those who practise SM might be expected to have insights unavailable to those who do not. Remember that we are still emerging from a society in which sexual pleasure was considered a negative thing, to be suppressed, or avoided. Could your reaction simply be an echo of this?'

'I don't know. Rationally, I understand what you're saying, and I want to accept it. It just doesn't feel right.'

'Precisely. Your feelings derive from the subconscious, but it is a mistake to confuse them with basic human instincts, such as fear when confronted by a potential predator. These feelings derive from things you have learned, Stephen. They may be examined rationally, although discarding them is not always easy. Again, it may prove best to allow your libido to be balanced by your conscience.'

'You're right. I'm sure you're right. Believe me, it is all too easy to be led by my libido. In fact, I have been. I've done something really stupid.'

'And that is?'

'We have a holiday cottage in Dorset. I've been talking to the girls, and Nicola was describing how she would like to live as my slave. One thing led to another, and I've set her up in the cottage, June too, for the whole summer.'

'And this presents difficulties with your wife and children?'

'Not my children. Both are away all summer. With Kate it's impossible to predict. She loves the place and tries to get down every year, but this thing in Korea is dragging on endlessly, and I was sure it was safe. It is, probably, but I just know I'm going to be living on my nerves all summer.'

'A difficult situation. It is not my position to give advice, Stephen, but I must ask if you find taking this risk stimulating.'

'No, not the risk, not at all. It's Nicola and June I find stimulating. I'm forty-eight; when am I going to have another chance to have two beautiful young girls ready to answer my every sexual whim? How many people get the chance at all for that matter?'

'Very few, I imagine.'

'I have to do it. You understand that, don't you?'

'I certainly understand the temptation. I am not in a position to advise you how to act.'

'No, and I wouldn't take your advice anyway, or anyone else's, unless they told me to go for it.'

'My concerns are more with your uncertainty as to what drives the girls' sexual needs. Did you communicate with the third girl again?'

'Poppet, her real name is Poppy. No, I didn't, but Boots did . . . June. Apparently everything was OK but, again, how can I be sure? Nicola and June met up with her, and she turns out to be more experienced than any of us. She and her girlfriend showed them the best place to buy SM gear, and I've put an order in for all sorts of things, just this morning.'

'I see. Tell me, how will they behave while at the cottage?'

'We've agreed that at length and signed a sort of contract. We do have what's called a stop-word, but that's only to be used in case of accident. Otherwise, they have agreed to be my slaves, both sexually and practically. Nicola in particular wants to waive the need to consent. That seems very important to her. With June I feel it's more a game, but she's very keen.'

'And if the third girl should become involved, or others?'

'I'll talk it through with them, but from the sound of things Poppy is much the same. I don't pretend to understand it, but these women have a genuine need to be told what to do, and to be punished.'

'But you seek to understand it?'

'Yes. Once I do, and if I can feel right about it, my only problem will be my wife!'

He gave a hollow laugh, not hysterical, but hardly cool and dominant. He'd got in too deep, and couldn't help himself. The answer would have been not to marry a straight woman in the first place, but it would hardly have been a useful suggestion.

The conversation was less juicy than I'd hoped for, and I moved back from the door. I could see his point about not wanting to reveal his insecurities to Nikki and June, but it made it easier for me. After Anna, I prefer my dominants a little less certain of their right to control and punish me.

The rest of the week passed painfully slowly. Gabby was busier than ever, with all her appointments shifted to accommodate a conference, and I found myself at a loose end. Normally I'd have gone out to the country, or just spent my time wandering around London alone, which still gave me a buzz after so many years of being at Anna's beck and call. Now it had lost its savour, and I constantly found myself thinking of Dorset and what might happen.

My one concern was not to upset Gabby. I wanted her to come with me and, while she obviously couldn't stay the weekend and risk running into Stephen, that still left the best part of two days to play. She appreciated my concern, but work pressed, with half her clients expecting her more or less constant attention.

Saturday we went out, but in a big group that included the self-obsessed Jo Warren, who monopolised Gabby for most of the evening with her insecurities about men. Sunday was better, with Fat Jeff and his friend Monty turning up in the hope of some kinky sex. We gave in, and let them masturbate into our mouths and give Gabby a sperm facial, most of which went on her glasses. She looked a picture, with the come dripping down her lenses and a big blob hanging from the tip of her nose, and I ended up getting my bottom roasted for laughing at her.

That left us in the mood, and once we'd got rid of them we went into the bathroom for some extremely wet and dirty sex, which kept us occupied until well into the evening. I felt a lot better for it, and better about abandoning her the following weekend, and that night we slept together in the playroom, both in nappies.

Stephen had been with Nicola and June at the weekend, and I couldn't wait to hear what had happened, even if it was the version abridged for therapy. I listened as usual, to discover that the girls were safely installed in the cottage and were behaving like perfect little slaves. He was less worried about his dominant feelings, mainly because he was finding it impossible to accept Nicola's sheer devotion as anything but genuine. On the other hand he was both guilty and anxious about his wife, who was apparently considering handing over her Korean business to somebody else once the initial deal had gone through.

Amber rang on Wednesday to say both tails were ready. There was a lot of other gear too, and I decided to alter my plans and hire a car. The last one I'd driven had been a 50s vintage Morris, chauffeuse being one of my many duties for Anna. After that the brand new Renault I picked up from a car-hire place in Wembley was a piece of cake, and I managed to get to Hertfordshire without any disasters.

The day was glorious, hot and sultry, and I was up for fun, hoping that Amber would have time to put me through my paces in the paddock or at least give me another of her lovely firm spankings. I'd dressed in anticipation, a loose dress over knickers and no bra, a combination that had drawn more than a few lustful looks at the car-hire place. By the time I'd parked I had the whole thing worked out in my head. I'd be done in front of Kay, as before, but more casually, just upended in the kitchen and told off for being a slut as I was beaten by hand, and with a wooden spoon.

It was not to be. The shop was closed for lunch, but the gates to her yard were open. I went in, and stopped dead. There was a car there, an all-too-familiar car, Anna Vale's ancient Morris, and beside it, Anna Vale herself. She was immaculate, as ever, in a 30s day dress and neat black heels, also a hat, all in tones of russet and black. I just froze. The last time I'd seen her I'd been running from the room, naked and streaming tears, my bottom and the backs of my legs a mess of cane welts.

Amber was there too, in jodhpurs and boots, talking earnestly to Anna. My first instinct was to back away quietly and wait in the pub, but Amber saw me immediately, looking up in concern. Anna turned. I shrugged and walked forwards, my face going pinker with every step. Anna looked me up and down, her expression cool and haughty, as if I was something the cat had dragged in.

'Hello, Poppy,' Amber greeted me quickly. 'Why don't you wait in the kitchen, or you'll find Kay in the shop, I think. I just need to sort a few things out.'

'Pray don't trouble yourself. I was just leaving,' Anna stated and gave me another of her looks, this time as if I was something the cat had decided was beyond use.

'Sorry,' I managed. 'I'm early, I know. I'll go and talk to Kay.'

I hurried indoors, blushing to the roots of my hair, and caught Anna's voice as the door swung to behind me.

'I see brassieres are out of fashion again.'

I was shaking my head as I made for the shop and struggling to rid myself of all the feelings seeing her had brought back so quickly. Kay was about to open the door, so I waited a moment before greeting her with a hug and a kiss.

'You're shaking, what's the matter?' she asked.

'Anna's here, outside. I virtually ran into her!'

'Shit! But that's all over, isn't it, ages ago?'

'Yes, but I haven't seen her since. I just wasn't ready for it.'

'Poor thing! Do you want a coffee or something?'

'Yes, a strong one.'

'Call me if anyone comes in, yeah?'

She went out and I was left to try and calm down. My hands were still shaking and my stomach felt weak, a reaction far stronger than I would have expected. Then again, after so many years completely under her command, and her discipline, perhaps it wasn't surprising.

When Kay came back with the coffee Amber was with her, and a moment later Anna's Morris went past the window. I took the coffee gratefully and almost spilled it as I put the cup to my lips.

'Sorry,' Amber said, 'I should have mentioned that she was coming up, but I didn't –'

'I know, it was my fault,' I broke in. 'You didn't tell her where I'm living, did you?'

'Of course not, but I wouldn't worry. I think she's accepted that you're not coming back.'

'Thank God for that! Is she with someone then?'

'No.'

That was not reassuring. After our split she had been desperate to find me, and even after she seemed to have given up I hadn't felt entirely secure. All the while I'd been hoping she'd find someone new to distract her.

'She bought a tawse,' Amber went on, 'for use with her clients, I suppose. It's heavy duty, from a bull's hide I picked up. That guy Stanbrook took one too.'

'Ah, yes,' Kay put in, 'Mr Stephen Stanbrook. He wanted Amber to call him Master. Not good.'

I laughed, the picture of Amber's face at such a suggestion enough to override my shock.

'He's an idiot,' Amber stated. 'First it was that and, once I'd explained that he wasn't my Master, he didn't want to use his real name. Fine, only he didn't have enough cash to pay for everything. So he was going to use a card but suddenly got in a state about his wife wondering why he was paying several hundred pounds to a saddlery. So in the end he had to go all the way to Broxbourne to get some more cash. Idiot.'

'He's quite a good dom, in his way.'

'Idiot,' she repeated firmly. 'Anyway, he paid up in the end, and I've got everything ready. He thinks it's coming down by courier, so I've packed it all in a big parcel with the address of the cottage on it.'

'Great, thanks. What did he buy?'

'Lots. The tawse, a dragon cane, a heavy paddle, a flogger, a riding crop, a dressage whip, two full sets of pony gear, with tails of course . . .'

'I get the picture. How does he think he's going to hide it all, never mind a pony cart?'

'There's an outhouse, apparently, which is full of junk.'

'Sounds risky to me.'

'Probably. He's been clever with the cart though, I'll give him that. He's bought an old handbarrow, and reckons it can live outside the back door with a couple of pots of geraniums in it.'

'What, one of those things like a huge wheel-barrow?'

'No, a proper two-wheeled one. I imagine it'll be pretty heavy to pull.'

'Maybe I'll volunteer to be groom if he's only got two sets of gear. He's quite a big guy, apparently. Do you know I've never actually seen him?'

'Oh. Well, he's maybe six foot tall, slim, quite military, with short grey hair and a beard.'

'I quite like the sound of him. He's not as big a dignity dom as he makes out, you know.'

She gave a shrug of indifference, then abruptly looked up as the shop bell went. It was a trio of teenage girls, all three blonde and all three looking slightly smug. They went to the display of saddles and Kay tapped me on the arm.

'I'll get your stuff.'

I followed her, watching her bottom move in her tight jeans, but with none of the easy lust I'd felt earlier. After seeing Anna I just didn't feel like it, and I let the opportunity pass, despite knowing that playing with her would undoubtedly lead to a double punishment from Amber.

My package was in the old forge. There were others, but mine had a slip of paper with my name pinned to it, and the address of the cottage. It was also the biggest, a huge thing wrapped in brown paper and tied with string. Kay and I managed to get it into the back of my car with some difficulty, but even with her bent over the seat and her beautiful bottom in perfect spanking pose I didn't feel tempted.

She had realised I wasn't my usual self, and took my arm as we walked back to Amber's shop.

'Cheer up, you can't let exes get to you, or you'd always be miserable!'

'She's my only ex, and . . . sorry, Kay, but it was a long time, and a very serious relationship.'

'I know.'

She gave me a squeeze as we came into the shop, where the girls were still looking at saddles. I didn't even want to stay any more, half-convinced that Anna would come back, and left with simply a peck for Amber and for Kay, very different to what I had anticipated.

I was so paranoid I even drove back into London on the A10, doing eighty-five to make absolutely certain that Anna couldn't be following me in her cranky old grid. There was no sign of her, but I didn't feel safe until I'd lost myself in the maze of London's streets.

I set off early on Thursday to get clear of London before the rush hour. By nine o'clock I was eating breakfast in a café on the A303 and trying to work out the best way to get down to the coast near the cottage; not long after ten I was there.

It was one of the most beautiful settings I had ever seen. There was a gentle valley running down to the sea, with a cluster of houses and a pub set around a shingle beach with fishing boats pulled up above the tide mark. Beyond, a high cliff cut into a hill, the crest golden-green where the morning light struck. Woods covered the valley, little fields just visible among them, and what had to be the cottage. Just the grey slate roof was visible, with a curl of smoke rising from the chimney.

I drove over, doubling back in the little village and following a rough track, as I'd been instructed. Twice the track split, both times my route being the rougher and more overgrown, until at last I reached a decaying gate with a sign nailed to it – Golden Acre. The cottage was immediately beyond, a low, white-washed building surrounded by beds of fern and bright orange mombresia. I got out to open the gate, but on a sudden mischievous impulse climbed it instead, as quietly as I could, to sneak close and peer through the windows.

June and Nicola were in the second room I looked into – a kitchen. They were washing up, side by side, and one look was enough to tell me that they were taking their role seriously. They were in uniform, but a uniform that would have had any army martinet locked up for indecency. They were in overtight white cotton knickers, with their bottoms bulging out from beneath the hems of the sweetest little tailored jackets, vaguely military, in bottle green, tightly belted at the waist and flaring at the hips. Both were in calf-length, high-heeled boots, making their bottoms tighter still, with the shapes of their cheeks quite clear under the knickers. They had pinnies on too, long ones with a trim of lace. As June turned to put a plate in the rack I saw that it left the full depth of her cleavage showing, almost to where her jacket buttoned at the front. She was bare under the jacket, and I knew Nicola would be too. Immediately I wanted to be dressed the same way.

I went to the door and knocked boldly, now keen to get in. Nicola opened it a moment later, her pinny in her hand, with a little slice of tummy and the front of her knickers on show where her jacket flared, also what cleavage she had. I gave her a big grin, hugged her and stepped back.

'My, do you look cute!'

She smiled and gave me a twirl, showing off her bottom. June appeared, also showing her knickers and a little bulge of tummy. I hugged her and she responded with even more passion, kissing me open-mouthed for a moment before we broke apart.

'Stephen got these for you?' I asked, and realised my mistake even as the words came out.

'Stephen?' Nicola queried. 'The Master?'

'Whoops,' I responded, searching frantically for a viable explanation and finding one just in time. 'Sorry, he had to give his real name to Amber, so he could pay. I've got all the stuff in the car.' I jerked my thumb back to where the car was visible beyond the gate.

'He has to be Master here,' Nicola said firmly.

June just shrugged and gave Nicola a pat on her bottom to send her out into the garden.

'I want to see,' she demanded, 'everything.'

'Patience. Those uniforms are so sweet; I want one. So what else has he bought for you?'

'These are daywear,' Nicola answered proudly. 'There's nightwear too, little blue baby-dolls that only come to our tummies. That's thanks to you, that is, and your panty-wetting fetish.'

'Only you can't now, because they don't come with panties,' June added. 'And there are the punishment fatigues too.'

'Punishment fatigues?'

'Yeah, shirts cut a bit like the jackets, only in this really rough material, and with straps at the back to fasten our arms. There are no panties with those either; we have to be nude from the waist down. There's a punishment book we fill in, and punishment drill, when we have to wear the fatigues.'

She was at the gate, and swung it wide. I went to the car and parked, then pulled the package from the back seat. They followed me in, to a neat little living room with a parquet floor and a big picture window looking out across the garden towards the sea. Trees hid us from the village and from higher up the hill, while it ended at a big hedge beyond which I knew would be a couple of hundred yards of rough, bramble-covered ground, then the cliff edge. Nobody was going to see us by accident.

'We can do pony play on the lawn,' Nicola said, following my gaze, 'and he's going to put some straw down in the shed for a stables.'

I could see some of the shed, a low, red-brick structure with cobwebbed windows and a door fastened with a heavy padlock.

'What else has he got?'

'A lot of imagination. There's the kitchen, two bedrooms and the bathroom, along with a sort of covered yard. We have to keep a routine, and clean every day. He'll inspect when he comes down at the weekend. Then there's punishment.'

I nodded. There was bound to be punishment, there always is. June had been pulling at the package as Nicola and I spoke, and was spreading it out on the floor, her mouth open in shocked anticipation as she gazed at the harnesses, bondage straps and punishment implements. I picked up the tawse, a huge, triple-tailed thing a good half-inch thick and two feet long. My hand just about held it comfortably, and it weighed maybe three pounds. The bull it came from must have been a monster.

'Ouch! This is going to hurt!'

'It's terrifying, just to look at it makes me feel weak,' June agreed. 'I can't wait!'

'Don't then.'

I smacked it against my palm, and nearly ruined the effect by wincing. It stung like crazy. She stood up, her face working between serious worry and expectation.

'Oh you wouldn't!'

'Oh I would. I switch.'

'I'm not sure you should,' Nicola put in as June began to back, giggling, towards the settee. 'Master might not want us to.'

'Then he can beat me,' I said happily. 'For now, over the settee, both of you, bums in the air.'

'Poppy!'

'Come on, Miss Knickers, get it up.'

She swallowed, and I could see her doubt as her desire warred with the way she'd learned about SM roles. I smacked the tawse on my palm again and gave her my toughest look. She went, slowly, reluctantly, twice looking over her shoulder before she reached the settee.

'Over, and get that bum up,' I ordered.

After a last moment of hesitation, she bent, her jacket lifting to show off the full expanse of her knickers as she went over, with the tight white cotton absolutely bulging with muscular female bum. June giggled.

'And you, Miss Boots, over you go.'

She scampered over, taking little, quick steps in her awkward heels, and bent, sticking out her lovely plump bottom. The white knickers were straining to hold in her flesh, which bulged from each leg hole to make her bottom look fatter than ever.

'Knickers down, naturally,' I announced, stepping close.

I touched Nicola's bottom, feeling the warmth of her flesh through the soft cotton of her panties. Her cheeks were wonderfully firm and resilient, and I could feel her trembling as I stroked them, making my heart hammer. I ducked down, her beautiful bottom just inches from my face as I took a firm grip on her knickers and peeled them down. She came

88

bare, right in my face, her tiny pink bumhole and neatly shaved pussy showing between slim bum-cheeks and thighs. A few marks showed on her pale flesh, slight bruising, maybe from the weekend, maybe from Amber's paddle.

She moved slightly and I caught her scent, rich and female, and had to fight to stop myself burying my face between her cheeks to lap up the taste of her sex and bottom. June was watching, and I managed a disapproving look as I moved behind her. Her bum was stuck right out, her legs a little apart, leaving her chubby sex-lips as a little pear-shaped bulge within the white cotton of her knickers. A little wet spot showed at the centre, and I could smell her arousal, stronger even than Nicola's. I knew if I touched I would lose control.

'Pull your knickers down, Boots,' I ordered.

Her hands came back immediately to take hold of her waistband and peel them slowly down off her bum, letting her soft flesh bulge out into its natural shape. Bare, her rear view, just made to be licked, was plump and enticing, with her deep crease, olive-brown sex-lips and pouting, dark anus. Another moment and I'd have had my tongue up her.

As I stood up, my face was set in what I hoped was a look of amused contempt. Inside I was boiling, but I was determined to hold my poise. I was in charge; I was the girl holding the tawse, the girl who was properly dressed. They were the ones with their bums bare and their pussies and bumholes on show. They were the ones about to be beaten.

'Spankies first,' I announced, 'just to get you warm.'

'No, do it. I want to be tawsed.'

'Best to warm up –'

'Just beat me, you little bitch!'

'Mind your language, Miss Boots.'

It meant she was scared, I was sure, but also excited. Abandoning the idea of warming her bum, I hefted the tawse, trying to get a feel for its weight and suppleness. It was perfectly made, the edges smooth, the leather soft and pliant, yet heavy and almost rigid. I couldn't have asked for better, but there was a trace of fear for my own bottom as I tapped it to June's ample cheeks.

'Twelve, I think, then perhaps I'll teach you how to say thank you to a lady.'

Her response was a giggle, and I thought of Amber, red-faced and angry as she applied a wooden paddle to the same big bottom. June liked to taunt and, whatever the reason, that carries its consequences.

'Funny is it, Miss Boots?' I asked as I lifted the tawse over her bottom. 'Eyes front, girl!'

She had looked round, to stick her tongue out at me.

'Right!'

I struck, bringing my arm around and down as fast and hard as I could. The tawse smacked into her meat, drawing a gasp of pain out of her and setting her cheeky bottom wobbling.

'Oh, you bitch!'

'Don't start that, Miss Boots. Lesson one: take a warm-up before a proper beating.'

'Yes, but –'

'Shut up!'

Again the tawse smacked on her exposed flesh, a lovely meaty sound that set me grinning in delight as she went into a little dance of pain, hopping up and down on her toes. Only when I'd brought the tawse back up to the ready did she speak again.

'You really are a bitch, Poppy. You know that?'

'And you, Miss Boots, should learn to show some respect during punishment. Did Stephen beat you? I bet he did, and I bet you swore.'

'He spanked us. Nikki got spooned. Do you know what he's going to do to you when he sees the state of our bums?'

'Shut up and stick that fat bum out!'

She did, still smirking, until I brought the tawse down again with a crack that shook the windows and made her scream. By the time she'd finished jumping up and down her expression had turned to a sulky pout, and I saw that she had begun to sweat.

'Enough?'

'Yes . . . I think so. Red.'

I laughed.

'That thing hurts, Poppy. It's worse than the fucking paddle, and you spank hard!'

She got up, rubbing her bottom, on which I had drawn three thick red lines.

'That was no harder than your paddling,' I pointed out. 'It just hurts more on a cold bum. Amber spanked you first, and you should have let me too. Now, let's see how Knickers performs.'

June sat down, not bothering to pull up her knickers, but curling herself into an armchair so that her bum showed, with the lips of her pussy peeping out between her thighs. I promised myself I would find an excuse to lick her just as soon as I'd tawsed Nicola's bum.

She had stayed perfectly still as June was beaten, bent down with her head hung and her bottom well up. I came behind her, to stroke her silky smooth skin and run a teasing finger up the wet cleft of her cheeks.

'So, Miss Knickers, do you need a warm-up?'

'Whatever you see fit, Mistress.'

'That's better. You should learn from your little friend, Boots.'

'That's what Master said.'

'I bet he did. Now, let's see about warming this sweet little bum.'

I took her around her waist and began to spank, slapping quite hard at her cheeks. She took it in silence, only the slow deepening of her breathing betraying her reaction as her flesh gradually turned pink. I got harder, smacking under the tuck of her bum to bring the heat to her sex, until the goose pimples had started to rise on her flesh. She was breathing hard, and shaking a little, clearly ready, with a little blob of cream forming at the entrance to her pussy.

'Enough. Let's get you beaten.'

She didn't even flinch as I tapped the tawse to her bottom, right where her cheeks tucked down to her thighs. I lifted and hit, a rush of pure sadism coming through me as the thick leather strap smacked into her little cheeks. She gasped, no more, but as I lifted the tawse again a muscle in one of her thighs began to twitch.

'Go on, make her squeal!' June urged.

I looked round. June was as before, pussy on show, white panties halfway down her thighs. Her hand was on her bottom, stroking one smacked cheek. Her eyes were glittering with pleasure at the sight of her friend being beaten.

'Do you want those knickers taped into your mouth?' I threatened.

She just stuck her tongue out, and I went back to my task. Nikki took the second as well as the first, barely twitching as her little bottom took the impact. With the third the bead of fluid at the mouth of her vagina broke away, to trickle slowly down between her lips. The fourth left her bumhole winking; at the fifth I paused.

'Rub off if you want. I'll keep it up till you come.'

Immediately her hand was on her sex, two fingers splaying her pussy-lips wide to let a third to her clit. She began to do it, flicking at the tiny swollen bud of her clitty with her fingertip. I measured up – and smacked. She gasped and jumped. Again I hit, and again, keeping a steady, even rhythm as she masturbated, my tawse cracking down on the fat of her cheeks. She was soon panting, then gasping as I picked up the pace, bringing the leather down across her dancing bum with firm, regular smacks. I'd given her twenty, maybe more, when she came, dancing and jumping on her legs, crying out in pain and ecstasy, and snatching at her swollen sex. Still I beat her, now with all my force, to leave thick red welts across her ivory skin with every blow, stopping only when her knees gave way. She sprawled on the sofa, panting. I stood back, feeling well pleased with myself and impossibly horny.

'That is the way to tawse a girl,' I announced. 'Now, Miss Boots . . .'

She didn't need to be asked. I knew she'd been stroking her bottom and sex as I beat Nikki, and as I turned to her she flipped herself over, sticking her bum up with her fingers already working in the wet mush of her pussy-flesh. I didn't know whether to beat her or lick her, but I did know that I had to get some attention to my own pussy. I cracked the tawse across her bottom, once, hard.

'Down, on the floor. I want a cuddle.'

I dropped the tawse, my hands going to my dress, to haul it high, and off. My knickers followed, pushed down and kicked away with my shoes, to leave me naked and ready. June had got down and was sitting on the floor, her arms open to receive me. I squatted to take her in my arms, kissing her forehead with my face buried in her thick, scented hair, her nose, her mouth. Her lips came open and our tongues met as I fumbled for her jacket button. It came open and an instant later I held one of the plumpest, roundest little titties I have ever had the joy of feeling in my hand.

She responded in kind, holding me to her, by my back, then my bum. I pushed her jacket back and she paused to shrug it off her shoulders, then lay back on it, arms once more open in welcome. Her large, dark nipples were quivering and hard at the tops of her boobs, her tummy soft and plump and bare with a green glass gem showing in her deep belly button, her thighs wide to show off the fat, moist lips of her sex.

'Lick my cunt, Poppy.'

I was going to, and more. I spun around to cock a leg over her body and stick my bum full in her face even as I went down on her. She took hold of me, around my hips, pulling me down as my hands cupped her bottom-cheeks and my tongue found her pussy. Then I was licking, even as I felt the soft, muscular end of her own tongue start to probe my hole. She tasted so good, and I buried my face in her, slurping up her juice and squeezing the meaty cheeks of her bum. I could feel her welts where the tawse had caught her. I could see them too, red and blotchy against her coffee-cream flesh, also her bumhole, dark and juicy where a trickle of her juice and my spit had run down between her cheeks. I stuck a finger in, feeling her soft little ring give to my pressure, then the warm, mushy inside of her rectum. For one instant her tongue left my pussy-hole.

'Dirty bitch, deeper!'

Her tongue found my sex again, now right on my clitty. I obliged her, pushing my finger all the way up her bum and easing two more into her pussy-hole. She had hold of my bottom, my cheeks spread wide to Nicola, and I was praying she would return the favour and penetrate me, pussy and bumhole too.

What she did was start to spank, slapping hard at my bottom as she licked me, and all the time nuzzling and lapping at my sex. I was going to come pretty soon, but so was she, with her holes already tightening on my fingers. Her thighs came up, trapping my head to her. She moaned, her licking and spanking became desperate, unco-ordinated, and she was there, coming full in my face with my head clamped hard to her pussy and her anus sucking at my fingers in spasm. I gave what she needed, licking hard at her clitty and wriggling my fingers up her juicy, sloppy holes as she bucked and squirmed under my body, all my concentration on her needs until she had finally come down.

It was my turn. I sat up, pulling my fingers from her holes, to stick them in my mouth and suck up the thick taste of girl and earth. She took my thighs, licking more slowly now, on my pussy, as I rode her face. I made myself relax a little, then wriggled down, spreading my cheeks over her face to get the tip of her nose to my bumhole. There was a moment of protest, but I locked my thighs around her body, forcing her to submit to the queening.

'Good girl, Boots. Have you ever licked a bum before?'

She shook her head, her nose wiggling deliciously in my bumhole.

'Well, you're going to, right now.'

Her licks became a little more urgent, but her tongue stayed on my pussy.

'Come on, Boots, you're already brown-nosing, you may as well . . .'

She shook her head, making her nose wiggle in my bottom again. I was getting slippery, and it felt so good, too good to miss what I knew she could do.

'Pretty please, Boots! I'll do yours . . . any time.'

Again she shook her head.

'If it's any consolation, I can taste you in my mouth.'

One more shake.

'Just a little! Please . . . please . . . please . . . please . . . Just lick my bum out, you little slut, or I'll take the tawse to your cunt!'

She was licking immediately, her tongue deep up my bumhole. I sighed, my mouth coming open, and took my boobs in hand, caressing myself as I squirmed my bottom in her face. Now I could come, a good, dirty orgasm, but I could do more, and I wanted to.

'Lovely . . . thank you, Boots, that is so good. You are such a sweetie. Keep it in, and I'll piss on you, all over your little fat tits . . .'

I just let go, all over her, just as Amber had done to Kay. I'd had a big orange juice for breakfast, and hadn't been since, so there was plenty of it, spraying out in an arc of golden droplets, all over her tits and her tummy and her spread sex. Her body jerked in shock as my hot urine pattered down on her skin, and for one instant she stopped licking my bum, only to start again, harder than before. She was gripping tighter too, holding me tight by my thighs, with her body squirming beneath me in my rapidly growing puddle.

My fountain was still a full one, spraying over her and on the floor beyond, trickling down either side of her tits, filling her bellybutton to make a little yellow pool around the gem at the centre of her tummy, running into her pussy and down between her bum-cheeks. I had to come though, and I put my hand to my pussy, to spray pee on to my thighs, up my tummy and all over her tits.

It was going in her mouth too. I could feel it, hot and wet on my bumhole, and she was making sweet little gurgling noises as she struggled to swallow and lick me all at once. The thought settled in my mind, as my pee began to die down, of how she would feel, her body dripping with my pee, her face smothered between my cheeks, her mouth full of the taste of my bottom.

I started to come, expelling the last of my pee in little squirts down her neck. My bumhole tightened on her tongue; my mouth went wide and I heard my own cry of ecstasy. I rode it, my eyes tight shut, everything focused on my burning clitty and the little muscular tongue pushed up into my pulsing bumhole. For one glorious moment nothing mattered at all but my pleasure and the state of the girl whose face I was sitting on. Then it was over and I was giggling as I dismounted, my leg shaking hard. June came up, her eyes unfocused, her mouth wide with spittle and pee and pussy juice running out over her lips, her wet hair plastered to her face. She shook her head, gasping.

'You . . . you dirty little bitch.'

I just smiled.

Five

The next morning the cottage looked as if a herd of angry and slightly incontinent cows had been let loose in it.

The girls were supposed to stay indoors, in their uniforms, and use what Stephen had provided. I was less than impressed, especially at the drink, and had persuaded them to come to the pub for lunch. June had readily agreed. Nicola hadn't, despite having turned submissive to me and cleaned up the puddle I'd had June in. So we'd simply sat on her to get her jacket off and put her in my dress, then carried her out between us. She'd been a bit sulky at first, but soon cheered up once I'd put a pint of stout in front of her.

We'd got drunk, completely wrecked, spending the whole afternoon outside the pub, where some tables had been set out overlooking the sea. By the time the landlord finally suggested we leave I had barely been able to walk, and nor had they. We'd had to support each other as we staggered up the track in the warm evening sunlight, and before we'd even got out of sight of the houses our hands had started to wander. I'd been feeling horny again, and so had they, June especially.

Back at the cottage we'd just had Nikki, then and there in the hall, after stripping her naked and making her lick our pussies. She'd been eager, and that had made us worse. June had pushed her down on the floor and pissed on her, laughing as she'd directed the thick yellow stream over her friend's body. It had gone everywhere, but it had just seemed funny, and before June was finished I'd gone down on Nikki.

June had joined us, the three of us rolling together in the wet, groping and licking at each other's bodies, kissing and sticking fingers into willing holes, slapping at eagerly thrust-out bottoms and pinching at tight nipples. We'd come, all three of us, Nikki under her own fingers, June and I with help from her tongue.

That had sobered us up, a little, and we'd tried to have a bath. It had been a disaster, because we hadn't been able to keep our hands off each other, or stop giggling. By the time I'd tried to wash June's mouth out with soap for all the times she'd called me a bitch and she'd retaliated by sitting on my back and spanking me with the bath brush, the floor had been awash, the towels had been soaked and the head of the brush had come off.

Dinner had been worse. Nikki had tried to make a stew with some frozen chicken legs, carrots and potatoes. Somehow she had managed to burn the potatoes while leaving the chicken uncooked in the middle. She'd then dropped the lot. We'd given up and retired to bed, all three of us together.

I woke to the wreckage and a vile taste in my mouth. There were vague memories of sex before going to sleep, and the bedclothes were badly stained. All three of us were nude, our clothes strewn around the cottage. My head ached.

June's bare bum was sticking out from under the covers, and I slapped it to wake her up. All I got was a groan. I gave up and staggered to the kitchen.

There was orange juice, of which I drank as much as I felt I could hold, and coffee. I made a pot, treading carefully among the mess of stew and pottery on the floor, and took it outdoors.

I hadn't bothered to dress, but grabbed my sunglasses from my bag on the way out. It was cool, with the sun not yet over the woods and a fresh breeze blowing in from the sea. That felt glorious, especially naked, and I went to sit in the middle of the lawn, drink coffee and think. It had been a good night, a real riot, and if I couldn't remember exactly who had done what to whom, a few details stood out, and a few discoveries or, rather, confirmations.

Nikki liked to be at the bottom of the heap, always. It didn't much matter what happened, as long as it happened to her. She liked to be beaten, and pissed on, and made to do degrading tasks, and would lap it all up, often literally. What did matter was that what was done to her was for a reason, however contrived. June was very different, and more like me, a playful little slut, self-aware and eager to enjoy her body every way she could. Neither liked to dominate, but June had a vengeful streak. Neither had much experience. I did.

That was satisfying. They were deferring to me and, if Stephen was any good at all, I was going to be in switch heaven, with two gorgeous girls to boss about and punish and a stern Master to see to my rear end. Despite my weariness and my aching head I was soon smiling.

Stephen was driving down that evening, straight from work. He was due to arrive around nine, by which time the girls were supposed to be in their smart little uniforms and ready to serve his dinner. Obviously we had to tidy up, but I really couldn't face starting, and had done nothing more than leave the door open to get some fresh air into the place.

I sipped coffee as the sun climbed slowly into the sky, making the complicated tree shadows shorten, then disappear altogether to leave me in a blaze of sunlight. The wind had died, and I realised it was going to be a baking hot day. The sea beckoned, and lazing on the beach with a book, maybe finding somewhere quiet and just dozing away my hangover, anything but housework.

Sneaking off was more likely to cause genuine ill feeling than to get me whacked, but I was still considering it when Nicola came out of the house. She was in a plain white sundress, a broad straw hat and flip-flops, with sunglasses on and the carton of orange juice in her hand. She came towards me, to sit down by my side, her legs crossed beneath her. I was glad to see that she wasn't in uniform, showing that there was a limit to her submission after all.

For a while neither of us spoke. Thinking she might not be completely at ease with what we'd done the night before, I let her take her time, waiting for the guilty question or embarrassed denial. When she did speak, it showed at once that she had no such doubts.

'Are you going to take charge of us, while Master's not here?'

I took a swallow of coffee, not sure what to say. She wanted something I simply could not give, dominance outside of sexual play. I did have something to give though.

'I might. I'm certainly going to try and teach you a thing or two.'

'I need that. Thank you.'

There was another pause as she took a swallow of orange juice, then she spoke again.

'Will you punish me, like you did yesterday?'

'Yes.'

She gave a delicious little shiver, making her tiny breasts shake under her dress. I smiled to myself, thinking of how well she had taken the tawse, and how accepting she had been of our cruelty and discipline. I tipped the last of my coffee down my throat. She turned to me, her elfin eyes looking right into mine.

'Even though Master will punish you?'

'Yes.'

She nodded, then spoke again, thoughtfully.

'I crave punishment, but at the same time I'm terrified of it.'

'That's just the way it is. I'm the same. I love a good spanking, even the tawse or cane, and I know it'll make me come. I still get butterflies in my stomach when I know it's going to happen.'

'But you do it for fun. For me it's punishment, it has to be.'

'You come pretty readily.'

She just shrugged. I went on.

'You can't expect your feelings to make sense, Nikki. I mean, do they ever?'

'Sometimes.'

'Do as you feel you should, but I have to tell you, it's not all roses being a full-time sub. You get security, sure, and emotional satisfaction, but there's a big world outside, and if things go wrong it's not very sympathetic.'

'I know, but I have to try.'

'I understand. I felt the same, and I'm glad I did try. So you think Stephen is the one?'

'Yes. He makes me feel right, dominated and protected at the same time.'

I didn't answer, thinking of Stephen's high-powered wife. To him it was ultimately a game, and one he had allowed himself to be drawn into without really thinking out the consequences at that. I wanted to tell her, but I didn't have the courage to just come out with it and she spoke again before I could find the right words.

'He makes me feel complete, liberated too. Just a few years ago I could never have imagined a relationship in which I could express my submission ... my bisexuality too, and without criticism.'

'It's really just a question of knowing the right people.'

'Maybe, but I need a master. What do you think I need to know then? Surely as long as I'm obedient, and can take my punishments?'

'A little more than that. For one thing, when Stephen was here last weekend, did he have your bum?'

'No. He is going to, and I am ready, but I've never done that.'

'You said.'

I'd wanted to explain to her, and to coax her into letting me give her her first anal experience. A part of me still wanted that, but I felt too drained to do anything about it. So I said nothing, but lay back on the lawn, wondering if I'd be able to manage it later, or keep Stephen despunked all weekend to stop him buggering them. I was on the edge of sleep when June called from the house, calling us a pair of lazy cows and demanding we help her clean up.

It took hours, mainly because Stephen, in his masculine wisdom, had failed to provide washing powder, or conditioner, let alone anything to deal with the floor properly. I had to drive into Bridport, and by the time I got back it was past noon. I put a wash on and went back to bed.

I woke, feeling a lot better, to find the girls in their smart uniforms taking in the sheets. A cup of coffee and I was ready to face the world, and Stephen, but it was gone seven before we finally had the cottage perfect save for the absent casserole dish. All that remained was to deal with dinner and we would be ready for inspection.

'There we are, not a thing out of place,' June said proudly, 'and with a bit of luck he won't notice that the pot's missing.'

'We ought to confess,' Nikki pointed out.

'You confess, you broke it.'

She nodded, tight-lipped. June picked up the book of instructions, turning the pages until she came to the right date. Her expression changed suddenly.

'Shit! That chicken was supposed to be his dinner. We've got to make *Coq au Vin!*'

'That was the only chicken!' Nikki exclaimed.

'Well, we could get it out of the bin . . .'

'June! Don't be disgusting!'

'Well, what else are we supposed to do?'

'Not that! Have some respect!'

June shrugged and made a face.

'It'll be crawling with flies,' I pointed out. 'We'll just have to do something else. Who's supposed to be cook?'

'We both are,' Nikki answered.

'I'm no good at cooking,' June protested. 'It's all very well giving us these menus, but all we ever eat at home are ready meals.'

'I can follow a recipe,' Nikki put in, 'but that's about it.'

'Something else you'll have to learn if you're to be a lifestyle sub,' I pointed out.

'How about you?' she asked.

'I'll do you a mean bangers and mash, steak and kidney pudding, spotted dick maybe. Not *Coq au Vin*, filthy French recipe. Anna wouldn't have it in the house. One thing I do know is that you can't make it without a chicken.'

'Very funny. It's six of the cane if dinner isn't up to standard.'

'So we get caned,' June put in, grinning.

'No, I want to do this properly,' Nikki answered her. 'Come on, we've got to be able to think of something!'

'Serve me,' I suggested, 'as his surprise. He'll forget all about the chicken.'

'Neat!' June agreed. 'Help me get her, Nikki. Stuffed and trussed, with an apple in her mouth like the little pig she is!'

Nikki hesitated only a moment, then nodded her agreement but went to the freezer.

'So what have we got?' June demanded.

'Spare ribs . . . burgers . . . steaks . . .'

'We could barbecue her.'

'What do you mean barbecue me!?'

'Not stick a stake up your bum or anything, silly. There's a barbecue in the shed, and charcoal. Nikki and I can cook and serve the food on to your body.'

'Ouch!'

'We'll make sure it's not too hot, or if you lie on the outdoor table we can put sauces and pickles and stuff on you, salad maybe.'

'I can do salad,' Nikki volunteered.

'OK,' I agreed, already trembling slightly at the thought of a strange man eating from my body. 'I'll move the car first, down to the village.'

I went and, by the time I had taken a quick shot of Dutch courage in the pub and walked back, they had the barbecue set out and going. There was a big steak ready beside it and the potatoes already on, while Nikki was adding dressing to a bowl of salad. Both were still in their smart jackets and tight white knickers, June in her trademark boots, Nikki bare-foot, also in pinnies.

'I hope you like blue cheese?' Nikki asked.

'Sticky, yum!' I answered. 'Pour some on my pussy and maybe he'll lick it off.'

'Master doesn't lick cunt,' June replied. 'I tried that, after my first spanking. Anyway, you're a bit hairy, aren't you?'

'Good point, I'll shave.'

I went back in, first to push my bags out of the way under the bed, then to the bathroom. There were no razors, which was a bit odd as they both shaved, and I was just about to go back and ask when I realised that a squat, pale-blue box was a waxing kit. There was another behind it, of a different make, and that was all. Anna had liked me bushy, Gabby too, and, while I'd shaved before, I'd never waxed. Just reading the instructions made my pussy twitch.

Bare was best, and I was still hopeful that Stephen might not be able to resist a nice sauce-covered pussy, that or he'd make one of the girls eat me. So I reread the instructions and carefully applied the strips, coating my pussy in waxed cloth. Ready, I spread myself out on the loo seat and tried to jerk the cloth off in one quick motion, as recommended in the instructions.

A moment later I was clutching my pussy and gasping for breath, after pulling off about the first ten hairs. It stung like crazy, and just that little bit had left my hands shaking, but I told myself to stop being a baby and that, if Nikki and June could do it, then so could I.

I tried to make it sexual, imagining myself held down by a group of prison warders so that I could be waxed for the sake of hygiene. It was a good fantasy, and I got back in position, took hold of the end of the cloth and let my mind wander.

It would be part of the routine on arrival at prison. I'd be made to strip, or stripped by force if I resisted, and put in a room with a load of other naked women ... No, in a huge wire compound, like a cage, in which the wardresses and the women already there could see us. We'd be taken out, one by one, washed in a tub of cold, dirty water and scrubbed down with carbolic soap. Then it would be on to the table, pinned down, spread-eagled in the nude, a massive wardress on each limb, or strapped in place. The other prisoners would be laughing at me as my turn came, joking about what they were going to do to me when they got me alone as hot wax was rubbed into my pussy mound. I'd squirm, begging to be spared, maybe wetting myself to cause more laughter and dirty jokes at my expense. The wardresses would take no notice. One, the biggest of all, would lean down, gripping my pussy cloth in fat, rough fingers, and pull ...

I did, hard, and screamed as my pussy hair tore free, all at once, to leave me clutching myself and jumping up and down on my toes in the middle of the bathroom floor. It stung so much, but I already felt puffy and sensitive, my fantasy having got me ready for more than just having my pussy denuded.

Now feeling horny and very submissive, I showered and dried. June was in the kitchen, collecting cutlery and a plate, while I could smell the scent of burning charcoal from outside. Suddenly I felt extremely hungry, remembering that I hadn't eaten all day.

'By the way, June,' I asked. 'What do we do, eat at his feet or something?'

'No, we eat after him, and what we get depends on how well we've served, and on how cruel he's feeling. Last Saturday he had me blow him while Nikki ate his leftovers out of an old dog bowl he'd found in the shed.'

'And what did you get?'

'Spunk.'

'Spunk? Just spunk?'

'Yeah, only I sneaked into the kitchen late and pigged a can of beans.'

'I hope he lets me eat properly, I'm ravenous.'

'Don't count on it. I've got to lose two pounds a week or I'm on punishment drill. Come on, he just rang and he'll be here in less than half an hour.'

We went outside, where they already had the table set out, with a red paper cloth over it. I climbed on and made myself comfortable on my back, reasoning that as a dom he'd probably rather eat off my tits than my bum, and that I'd stand a better chance of a lick.

'Great! He's going to love this,' June stated as she came over to me with the bottle of blue cheese sauce. 'Spread it then.'

I pulled my legs up, offering her my pussy. She was grinning as she stepped close, to upend the bottle over my sex and squeeze out a long worm of thick blue cheese sauce. It was warm from the sun, and felt lovely and sticky as it trickled slowly down over my pussy and between my cheeks to my bumhole.

'Bad girl,' she chided as I sighed in pleasure. 'No touching now!'

She gave the bottle another squeeze, to make a blob of sauce on the crest of my pussy mound. I nodded, although the urge to masturbate in the sticky mess covering my pussy was pretty strong.

'Something up the cunt,' she said thoughtfully. 'Put the salad on her tits, Nikki, and I'll see what I can find.'

She went in, leaving Nikki to spoon salad carefully on to my chest. The expression on her face was so serious I almost laughed, but my feelings turned back to sex as she carefully topped my nipples with the blue cheese sauce.

'Have a taste,' I offered.

'That's for Master,' she replied, completely earnest, and stepped away, leaving me hornier than ever.

June came out again, and she was holding a pot of gherkins, fat green ones like they always have on the counters of chip shops. My pussy was already spread, and full of sauce, while my bumhole felt moist and sticky. I rolled my legs up, offering both holes.

'One in each, please, June.'

'You are such a dirty bitch, Poppy,' she answered me as she twisted the lid free to add the scent of vinegar to the tempting cooking smells.

She pushed her fingers into the jar, to rummage among the gherkins until she had found the fattest. It was as thick as a cock, and knobbly, making my pussy twitch in anticipation as she put it between my legs, only to have the round, wet tip touch my bumhole instead.

'Hey, not that one, it's huge!'

'This goes where you made me stick my tongue yesterday, Poppy, and no crap.'

I sighed, wanting it, but not at all sure about having my bumhole stretched so wide or penetrated so deep, when I was sure to be made to eat the gherkin for my own dinner. She pushed anyway, the sauce squelching out around my hole as I let myself go loose. I felt my ring open around the head of the gherkin and it was going in, past my ring and into my rectum. The vinegar stung a little, making me wince, but June just giggled as she slid it up me, until my bumhole was stretched wide around the middle. It felt as if I had a good-sized cock up my bum, and I couldn't resist wiggling a bit to get the feel of it.

'How does it feel?' she asked.

'Up the bum? Lovely.'

She made a face, slightly doubtful, and dipped her fingers back in the jar, to pull out the second largest of the gherkins.

'Better than this?' she asked as she put the fat end to my pussy and pushed.

I sighed as my hole filled in one smooth motion, easily accommodating the fat gherkin. Now I felt as if I was being taken in both holes at once, the only thing missing being two men to do the fucking. I wiggled again, wishing I really did have a pair of cocks inside me.

'No,' I answered June, now a little breathless. 'Different. Not so ... so sweet. It feels ruder up the bum, but you still feel full.'

She pursed her lips, perhaps thinking of Stephen's threat to take her anal virginity, then smiled brightly.

'Trussed, you must be trussed. I'll get some twine.'

The shed was still open, and she ran over, bringing back a big green ball of twine. I crossed my hand over my tummy and she quickly twisted some around my wrists, then cut it with the steak knife she'd put out for Stephen. One knot and I was bound. In the distance I caught the sound of a car's engine.

'Shit!' June swore. 'That's got to be him. Get the steak on, quick! Poppy, use our nicknames, and call him Master. Hell!'

'What?'

'Open wide.'

I obeyed, and had a apple thrust into my mouth, hard, so that I was left mumbling and struggling to close my aching jaw.

'Sh!' she urged. 'Just be good.'

Nikki had scurried to the barbecue, to throw the steak on and quickly pat down her pinny and jacket. June was snatching for the various utensils she'd left out, and ran in with them as we heard the car draw up at the gate. It was Stephen, and the fluttering in my tummy came back, stronger than before as I thought of how I was, nude and penetrated, an offering for him.

June didn't come back, and Nikki followed her, pausing only to tuck a chair beneath my table. I heard the gate open, and the car pull in, then the slam of its door and the crunch of footsteps on gravel. The next thing I heard was Nikki's voice, now meek and quiet.

'Welcome, Master.'

'Welcome, Master,' June added and, if she sounded a touch less humble, there was none of the slightly mocking tone she'd used with me, and with Amber.

Stephen's voice came next.

'Hmm, not bad, not bad at all. Smart, certainly. Turn around.'

I realised he was inspecting them, and thought of the way their bums bulged out from under the tails of their jackets. That would be what he could see, with just the thin cotton of their knickers to stop him from fucking them, or jamming an erection up either tight, virgin bumhole.

'Very neat, Knickers, but why no boots?'

'Sorry, Master. I forgot to put them on, Master. I was cooking, Master.'

'No excuses. Put that in the punishment book.'

'Yes, Master.'

'I'll think of something to make sure you don't forget them next time. Boots, your panties are a little out of line.'

There was a meaty slap, presumably June catching his hand across her bum. She didn't squeak though, or speak. Stephen did.

'Is everything in order then?'

'Yes, Master. Dinner is served, Master,' Nikki answered.

'Umm, it certainly smells good, but it does not smell like *Coq au Vin*, which is what I ordered, wasn't it?'

'Yes, Master . . . sorry, Master,' Nikki stammered.

'We have a surprise for you, Master,' June added quickly.

'Disobedience, punishment book,' he responded. 'So, let me see this surprise.'

He stepped from the door and, if his eyebrows rose slightly at the sight of me spread naked as his dinner and stuffed with gherkins, that was all. Nikki scampered quickly to the barbecue to turn his steak as he came towards me.

'Long pig, I see,' he remarked. 'Shouldn't you have cooked it? Punishment book.'

'Master!' June protested.

'Speaking out of turn, Boots?' he answered her. 'Punishment book. In fact, you'd better fetch it and fill it in while Knickers sees to dinner.'

June ran in to the cottage, looking worried and a bit sulky. Nikki was busying herself at the barbecue.

'A pretty creature,' Stephen remarked, his eyes lingering on what could be seen of my breasts among the salad as he sat down. 'Where did you get her?'

'That's Poppet, Master,' Nikki answered. 'We thought she'd make a nice surprise for you.'

'Our little panty-wetter from UK Masters?' he queried. 'Ah yes, I recognise her from the pony-girl photo.'

'Yes, Master.'

'Excellent! So, three little sluts for my amusement. How long is she staying?'

'Just the weekend, Master.'

'A shame, but I suppose I'll just have to make the

best of her. That should be about right now, I think. Never overcook a good steak.'

'Yes, Master,' she answered and slid her spatula under the steak, lifting it on to a plate and adding potatoes.

'On her belly,' Stephen ordered.

My muscles jumped in reaction at his words, and again as the hot steak was slid on to the bare flesh of my stomach without a murmur of protest from Nikki. It hurt, and I found my eyes bulging in mute protest and my arms twitching in my bonds. The potatoes followed, put on the salad between my boobs, but still unbearably hot. Stephen saw the pain in my face and chuckled, but quickly snatched the potatoes down on to his plate. He picked up the steak knife, and for one moment I really thought he was going to cut the thing on my tummy, but he flipped it neatly off and on to his plate again.

I was left with the hot juice running down my skin and pooling in my tummy button. Nikki passed him a pair of salad forks and he began to serve himself from my chest, making a point of scraping the blue cheese sauce from my nipples. I'd hoped he'd suck it off, and was shaking with frustrated reaction by the time he started to eat.

He ignored me, tucking in, then calling for beer, which Nikki ran to fetch. I could only lie still, with the sauce and the steak fat slowly congealing on my body, hoping he'd pay attention to me once he'd eaten. June came out, holding a big red book, but said nothing, simply standing a little way behind his chair with it clasped in her lap.

Stephen ate slowly, indifferent to our needs, with the delicious smell of steak and baked potato strong in my nostrils. I didn't know if I wanted to be fed, or fucked, or both. I did know it was coming to me, something, and was praying that the conscientiousness he'd shown in front of Gabrielle meant that he would take us all to orgasm before he'd finished.

Nikki had brought the beer in a pint glass, half of which he'd swallowed at a draft. The apple in my mouth was hurting, and I was desperate for a drink, adding to my woes. It was getting to me though, exposure and submission combining to bring my need slowly up, until the temptation to push my hands down to my sauce-smeared pussy and frig off was close to unbearable.

I'd begun to lose my sense of place and time when I heard him click his knife and fork together on the plate. Nikki came forwards to clear away, and as he sat back he put his hand on her bottom, fondling her cheeks and stroking the seat of her knickers, then abruptly jerked them down. He slapped her to send her off, her bare bum wiggling behind her as she ran into the cottage with his plate. I waited, hoping he'd start on me, and, sure enough, a moment later I heard the soft purr of his zip being pulled down. Not to look round would have taken more resistance than I had.

He had begun to masturbate, a thick, pink cock rearing up from his open fly, already close to erection, with the wet helmet appearing at the central hole of his wrinkly foreskin with each tug. I found myself hoping it was for me, to fuck me, perhaps push it up my bum as well, so he could amuse himself with my sloppy, sticky holes while I was made to eat the gherkins that had been in my body.

'Punishments,' he announced suddenly, and snapped his fingers.

June quickly passed the red book to him. He opened it, scanned down the page, then spoke.

'One broken pot, tut tut, Knickers. Spunk dinner for you, I think. You can get sucking while I read all this stuff about Poppet.'

I wondered what he meant for a moment, then realised that they had confessed to everything we'd been up to the day before. My tummy contracted hard at the thought of what would be coming to me if Nikki was made to eat nothing but his spunk for her dinner just for breaking a pot.

She didn't object, but hurried to do it, and to what was obviously an established ritual. As he pushed back the chair to let her get at his cock, she went straight down, kneeling at his feet. A single quick motion had the button of her uniform jacket open and her little tits were showing, and then she had taken his cock in her mouth, sucking on it with her big eyes lifted for his approval. He didn't even bother to look down, but took a swallow of beer and began to read. He had barely started when he stopped and moved the book aside to look down on Nikki as she mouthed on his now fully erect shaft.

'You let yourself be beaten by Poppet with my new tawse?'

Her head bobbed on her mouthful of penis. He grunted and went back to the book, only to speak again almost immediately.

'Licking each other, and up Poppet's arse! Pissing on each other!'

He began to read again, shaking his head repeatedly as he followed the story of our escapades. I could see that he was amused, and turned on, as his hand occasionally strayed to his balls or Nikki's head. Some of that showed in his voice when he had finished and passed the book back to June, but more dominance – certain, commanding dominance.

'Tomorrow morning you will parade on the lawn in punishment fatigues and I'll decide what's to be done with you. That will be for your drunken orgy. We'll deal with your little tawsing games now. Knickers, you may stop sucking.'

Nikki moved her head back, but only a little way, to leave her lower lip joined to the head of his penis with a strand of saliva. Her eyes were big and round, her neck and chest flushed rich pink. He looked down and slowly shook his head.

'So, whatever is to be done with you?'

'Whatever you wish, Master,' she responded.

'Exactly, Knickers, whatever I wish.'

He stood up, Nikki scrambling hastily out of his way. He undid his trousers, to push them casually down and off, taking his pants, shoes and socks with them. At the click of his fingers June ran over to retrieve his discarded clothes and he was looking down at me with amusement and a trace of contempt as he nursed his erection.

'Kneel there,' he ordered Nikki, pointing to the ground at the end of the table. 'First you can watch me fuck your little friend.'

So it was going up me, at last. I lay back, watching and waiting, but rather than go to my feet he came to my head. I had to quickly change my expectations, and then he had pulled the apple from my mouth and stuck his cock in, to fuck my head with short, sharp thrusts. I kept my thighs up, sure he wouldn't waste his spunk down my throat with three of us to play with, and the spunk supper was reserved for Nikki.

It only lasted moments, really just long enough for him to be able to say he'd had his cock in my mouth. He pulled out and walked slowly down the table, ruffling Nikki's hair as he passed her. Reaching the end, he took my legs, to pull me forwards with my bum sticking out over the edge of the table. His fingers found the gherkin in my pussy and it was drawn slowly out, leaving my hole to close with a wet sound. Immediately his cock was there in its place, pushing into my sticky, soppy hole, and up.

I couldn't help but purr as my pussy filled with cock, all the way, until I could feel his balls pressing between my cheeks, to the head of the gherkin lodged up my bum. He began to fuck me, easing his cock slowly in and out, penetrating me each time, and each time pushing his full length inside, right up to his balls. Nikki watched, waiting for orders, her face passive, only her slightly open mouth and erect nipples betraying her arousal.

He was in no hurry to come, playing with my pussy by penetrating me over and over, then by rubbing his cock head to my clitty until I was gasping and wriggling below him. My passion drew only a cruel chuckle and more torment; his cock popped back up me as his thumb was pressed to my sex. He began to masturbate me, and I relaxed, letting my body rise towards orgasm, even if I knew it was being done merely for him to feel my hole contract on his prick.

I didn't even get that. He stopped and pulled out once more, his fingers still between my legs. I felt him grip the gherkin up my bum and moaned aloud as it was pulled from my anal passage, from the sensation, and from what it meant. I was to be buggered. I was open, my hole gaping and slippery, an easy tube for his rigid erection. It still made me gasp when I felt his helmet push into my ring. He took no notice, pushing himself firmly up into my rectum as the mess of blue cheese sauce and pussy juice squashed out around his shaft.

'Tight, aren't you?' he grunted as he wedged the last inch or so in, to press his balls between my cheeks.

'Yes, Master. Thank you, Master,' I managed weakly, hoping it was the right thing to say.

Some men, the real sadists, like girls to hate it up the bum. Not Stephen, all he seemed to care about was how it felt to have his cock in my rectum, and his eyes were shut in pleasure as he buggered me to a slow, lewd rhythm. He was easing his shaft in and out to make my ring pull, and pushing as deep as he could with each thrust. It put me in a mellow, slightly breathless ecstasy, and I decided to come with his cock up my bum. Stretching my bound wrists out, I started to stroke at my pussy, only to have my hand slapped.

'None of that, Poppet, my eager little slut. Master comes first, something you will have to learn, across my lap if necessary.'

I nodded my head in submission. He chuckled and took a firm grip of my thighs, to help him pull his cock out of my bumhole. I relaxed, feeling more than a trace of regret as the thick, hard penis slid out from the dirty cavity where he had lodged it. I looked down, and saw it bob up as he left my bumhole, the shaft wet and glistening with my juices, a ring of sauce trapped below the helmet. He was smiling, a truly wicked grin, and I braced myself as I imagined being made to suck him clean, only to see him turn to Nikki.

'Right, Knickers,' he said, pushing his filthy cock down towards her face. 'Open wide.'

She gaped, pop-eyed and slack-mouthed, staring at what she was about to have to suck. I could see her shaking, and she was twisting her fingers together in agitation, yet she never so much as hesitated, leaning forwards in meek submission to the filthy act.

'Supper time,' he announced, and stuck his cock into her mouth.

Her cheeks bulged as it went in, and her eyes screwed up, to suck first with her face set in disgust, and then in meek resignation. I could imagine the taste, all too easily, and found my stomach twitching in rebellion even as I wished it was me. He was going all the way too, this time, watching her pretty face as he jerked the stem of his erection into her mouth. Then his hand had locked in her hair, forcing his cock in deeper. She began to make odd little gobbling motions with her cheeks, and suddenly he was there, moaning in ecstasy as he fed her, cock to mouth, pouring her spunk supper straight down her throat.

Some of it anyway. Too high to care, he had jammed his prick so deep she started to choke. He kept it in, even as spunk started to bubble from her nostrils and her arms began to flail in panic. At last he pulled back, but it was too late for her to keep even the tiniest trace of her dignity. Mess exploded from her nose as she bent double, coughing and retching. Her mouthful came out, in one thick clot of whitish muck, all over her little boobs as she struggled for control of herself. Sperm bubbles had started to froth from her nose and around her lips, but disappeared as she sucked back, only to emerge once more as her breath came out.

Stephen finished himself off in his hand, milking the last of his spunk into her hair as she fought for breath. When at last she came up, gasping, with spunk and spit and blue cheese sauce and mess dripping down her face, he merely nodded and wiped the end of his cock on her nose.

'Sorry, Master,' she managed.

'You must learn to take me in your throat properly,' he answered. 'Clean up, and you'd better eat it, because that's all you're getting.'

For one instant she looked shocked, but no more. Then she began, using a finger to scrape the slime off her face and popping it quickly in her mouth as soon as what she'd collected began to run over the sides. Some was hanging from her chin, and more was splashed over her breasts, with one piece of stray spunk hanging from an erect nipple. She ate it all, until nothing more than a slimy smear was left where her skin was soiled and, if the look of disgust never left her face, she never hesitated either. Only when she'd swallowed the last of her disgusting meal did she look up at Stephen.

'Thank you, Master,' she said, and hung her head.

He didn't bother to answer, but turned to look down at me.

'So, a suitable punishment for Knickers, and for Poppet too. We're just left with Boots then, aren't we?'

'Yes, Master,' June answered.

She looked worried, but her knickers were damp at the front and the skin of her throat had begun to flush. He pointed to my sex.

'Clean her up, then you two can tidy the patio up and eat whatever scraps you can find. Knickers, you're a disgusting mess. Clean yourself up and get into your nightwear; I expect a glass of whisky in five minutes sharp. Then I'm for bed; it's been a long day. You're on breakfast duty, Poppet.'

He walked into the cottage and that was it. He'd come, and we no longer mattered. We hadn't, but Nikki hastened to obey, running into the house behind him. June waited until they were gone, gave me a conspiratorial wink and quickly stripped her jacket and knickers off. She climbed on to the table, settling her pussy over my mouth as she began to lick the mess of blue cheese sauce and juice from between my thighs.

Six

I awoke to Nikki shaking my shoulder, bringing me to with a jerk. She looked worried and for a moment I thought something was seriously wrong, only to find it was trivial.

'Don't forget you're on breakfast duty!'

'Oh, God . . . All right, fair enough, just let me get a coffee down. What am I supposed to do anyway?'

'You're to wake him at ten, with his breakfast on a tray. He likes toast done at number three, eggs sunny-side up, three rashers of bacon and coffee with cream and two sugars. He likes his morning erection sucked too.'

I groaned, not at all sure I could really face cock sucking first thing in the morning. Nikki was in her little white baby-doll, and the sight of her bare bum peeping out from beneath the hem as she left the room made the prospect just that tiny bit easier. I was still wishing he'd picked on someone else as I dragged myself out of bed and followed.

Nikki had slept with him, fetched from the warmth of her bed at some unknown hour of the night, presumably for a fucking. June and I had been together anyway, having decided to have a cuddle after licking each other and showering together. We'd gone to sleep in each other's arms, only to be woken by Stephen ordering Nikki into his bed. Sex had followed, head to tail again as she seemed to like that and we fitted so snugly together.

June was now fast asleep, and it seemed cruel to wake her. So I made my way into the kitchen and threw breakfast together with Nikki's help, managing to reach Stephen's bedside at three minutes past ten. I reset his radio clock, shook him gently awake and picked the tray up, so that the first thing he saw was me standing over him, stark naked, with the breakfast tray in my hands. For a long moment he watched me, bleary-eyed with sleep, then abruptly pulled himself up in bed.

'That sulky look will cost you, Poppet. Put the tray down, and get your lips around this.'

'Sorry, Master,' I managed, wishing I'd had the sense not to let my true feelings show.

He pushed the bedclothes down, exposing his cock, lying fat and heavy along his thigh, stirring as the blood pumped into it. I held the tray as he adjusted himself up, and put it down carefully. He smacked his lips in appreciation and began to butter a piece of toast. I climbed on the bed, curling up to make myself as comfortable as possible.

'No, not like that. Straddle my legs and stick your bum up.'

'Yes, Master.'

I obeyed, getting into the rude position he demanded, with my sense of submission rising despite myself as I spread my bottom to the air. There was a mirror behind me, a big one attached to a wardrobe door, and from the smirk on his face as he glanced up I knew that I was making a prime show of my pussy and bum. I kept it up in the air, obedient, and wondering if I could really manage to enjoy my task after all.

He was growing hard quickly, and I picked his cock up, feeling the weight of it and the firm, rubbery flesh. He'd been in Nikki, I knew, from the smell of her on his helmet as I rolled his foreskin back, but not up her bum. She was still virgin anally, and with that happy and lewd thought I took his cock in my mouth.

I rolled his foreskin back with my lips, to suck quickly on his helmet and clear the taste of stale sex. He gasped and told me to take it slowly, but I was already sliding my mouth down the thick, hot shaft. Outside the room I could hear Nikki and June going about their morning business quite normally, as I sucked on their Master's penis. He went on eating, more normal still.

By the time he'd finished breakfast, my jaw was aching and my head was spinning from the taste and smell of cock and my own sex. He'd barely seemed to notice me, the straining erection in my mouth and hand the only evidence that he was aware of me. That changed when he'd swallowed the last of his coffee to wash down the food.

'Breakfast?' he asked mildly.

I knew what my breakfast was, the same as Nikki's supper – spunk. I tried to look innocent as I came off his cock, opening my mouth as if waiting for a treat. He put the tray aside, then held the plate out. There wasn't much, just a smear of grease and egg yolk, but as I stuck my tongue out to lick it up he shifted position, going higher in the bed to let him push his cock to the plate. I watched as he moved his fleshy helmet around the edge of the plate, scooping up the greasy yellow paste.

'Eat up,' he ordered, taking my hair to force me down.

In it went, my mouth filling with the taste of bacon grease and egg in addition to cock as I began to suck again. Twice more he did it, until the plate bore only a glistening smear and my lips and nose were dirty with what he'd left. He chuckled as he put the plate on his tray again, and back went his cock, deep in my mouth.

'Boots, tray!' he ordered.

June came in almost immediately, nude. She giggled as she saw the position I was in and took the tray. I kept on sucking, and as his hand closed in my hair I was thinking of the way he'd made Nikki choke, forcing her to suck even with spunk bubbles coming out of her nose. He'd made her eat it too, and as he began to fuck my head I was expecting the same rude, callous treatment.

'Get that big arse round a bit,' he ordered suddenly. 'I can't see your cunt properly.'

I shifted, the crudeness of his words and their implications adding to my feelings as he worked his cock in and out of my mouth, ever faster. Suddenly I wanted fucking, from behind, in the rude position he had made me adopt, the rudest a girl can get in, her boobs dangling, showing everything, pussy and bumhole available to be plugged with thick, hard cock, or anything else.

From the corner of my eyes I saw that Nikki and June had come to watch, arms around each other as they stood in the doorway. Both looked thoroughly pleased that I was the one gagging on the Master's penis, and June laughed as he jammed his helmet deep in, to block my windpipe, and came at the same instant.

Spunk erupted down my neck and I went straight into a coughing fit, my throat in spasm on his cock. He moaned in pleasure, his fist locked in my hair to force me to take it as the agonising spasms of my muscles milked more and more spunk into my gullet.

My stomach heaved, burning, egg-flavoured fluid rose up in my throat, to explode from my nose behind a great gout of spunk, and I'd been sick on his cock.

I managed to swallow, just, as he finally let me pull my head up. Then I was gasping, breathless, unable to speak. There were two great streamers of dirty yellow muck hanging from my nose, spunk and mucus and the grease from his breakfast. My mouth was full of it too, a salty, slimy, burning mess.

'Swallow it, Poppet,' Stephen growled, his eyes fixed hard on mine.

For one moment I was going to rebel, or just be sick all over his cock. It passed as I shut my eyes and forced myself to behave as I'd decided I would. With an effort I swallowed my revolting mouthful.

'And the rest,' he ordered.

Again I hesitated, then sucked up what was hanging from my nose, swallowed and went down on him once more to lick up the mess in his pubic hair and suck his cock clean.

'Good girl,' he remarked as I swallowed for the third time. 'D'you know, you're not a bad little cock sucker.'

'Thank you, Master,' I managed as I came up.

He'd done it on purpose, dobbing me and making me sick on his cock, to get off on my distress as much as the sensation, I was sure. Not that he was the first man to treat me that way. That honour, and my introduction to the dirty practice of dobbing – making a girl eat food off a man's cock – belonged to Fat Jeff Bellbird. Someone had been boasting in the office and, if there had obviously been no names, I found my face going red at the thought.

'Ah, she's embarrassed!' Stephen laughed. 'Never mind, Poppet, these things happen. It's all part of being a girl.'

I nodded, unable to find words, and climbed down off the bed. Nikki and June put their arms around me as I reached the door. I immediately found myself wondering if there was time to turn what had been done to me into a fantasy as one or other licked me to ecstasy, only for Stephen to suddenly clap his hands.

'Punishment drill in half an hour. Knickers and Boots, into your fatigues, Poppet can go nude. Look sharp or there'll be extra!'

Nikki immediately scampered for the bedroom, June following at a more leisurely pace. I made for the bathroom, getting rid of the taste in my mouth well worth whatever punishment he might decide on for not jumping to obey his command. He followed, and gave my bottom a firm swat as I bent over the sink but no more, doubtless satisfied for the moment.

By the time I'd washed and dried, Stephen was getting dressed in his room and the girls were outside. It was cloudy but warm, which was just as well. They were in their punishment fatigues, tailored shirts made of some coarse brown stuff like sacking, and less smart than the green jackets. Straps at the back showed where their arms could be put in restraint. Nikki's fitted perfectly, but June's was too tight at the front, squashing her big breasts and leaving the single button at the front straining, with a generous slice of cleavage on show as well as her round little tummy. She turned as I came to join them and I saw her wince as the coarse material moved over her nipples. As they came to attention the tucks of their bottoms came on show, peeping out beneath the hems of the shirts, quite bare. They were also barefoot. I hastened to join them and came to attention just as Stephen emerged from the cottage.

He was in white trousers and an open-necked sports shirt, completely informal, but he carried a swagger stick, army style. As he came behind us he disappeared from view and I found my bottom-cheeks twitching in anticipation of his touch, a pinch or a cut of the stick. Sure enough, strong, male fingers found my bottom, squeezing the flesh of one cheek, then taking a hard pinch. I winced despite myself, but he merely chuckled and moved on to June. From the corner of my eye I saw him use the stick to lift the tail of her fatigue shirt, showing off the full expanse of her bare bum.

'Very fetching,' he said casually, 'although, as I have said, your bottom is just a little porky. Have you lost your two pounds since last week?'

'No, Master.'

'No? We'll have to do something about that then, won't we?'

He laughed, gave Nikki a swat as he passed her and came to stand in front of us, his eyes flicking over our exposed pussies before he spoke.

'Punishments in a moment. First I have an announcement. Does the Capo System mean anything to you?'

'No, Master,' Nikki and June chorused.

'Yes, Master,' I responded.

'Then perhaps you would care to enlighten us, Poppet, after you have touched your toes for being a smart-arse.'

I went down, only to catch his stick across my bum as he stepped forwards; once, twice and a third time, leaving me wincing and shaking my head against the sudden sharp pain.

'Go on,' he demanded, 'but stay down, and stop wriggling.'

My cheeks stung and I wanted a rub, but I held still and was about to speak when something round and smooth pressed against my bumhole. I gasped as he eased the swagger stick up into my rectum, leaving me with it pointing up in the air from my hole. I heard June bite back a giggle. Slowly the effect of the sudden and unexpected penetration of my unlubricated bumhole faded and I managed to speak.

'The Capo System, Master, is when one or more of a group of prisoners is put in charge of the others to save trouble for the guards.'

'Hardly save trouble,' he answered, 'more avoid tasks inappropriate to their status, or, at least, that is the case here. I have decided that it is demeaning for a Master to have to issues mundane orders. So, from today, we shall have a Capo. Poppet, I trust you will be joining us again?'

I hesitated only briefly.

'Yes, Master.'

'Good. One of you three will be Capo then, or Lance-Corporal as I've decided it will be, and to show that you're Lance-Corporal, you get to sew single chevrons on to your uniforms. The Lance-Corporal will then be responsible for general order. She may spank the others whenever she sees fit, and generally keep them in order, but she may not use implements. If she fails to meet the standards I require, she will be demoted and someone else will take her place.'

He had pulled a brown paper bag from his pocket and took out a set of bright-pink chevrons.

'The question,' he went on, 'is ... Who will be Lance-Corporal? First I thought a bit of responsibility might do something to improve your manners, Boots. When I discovered what a little bully Poppet is, I was going to pick her. Then I thought of how amusing it would be to put both of you under Knickers.'

He paused to pull the swagger stick from my bumhole.

'Stand up, Poppet, to attention! Open your mouth.'

I obeyed, snapping to attention and letting my mouth come open despite myself. He pushed the swagger stick straight in and watched as I sucked on it, then nodded.

'Good girl, you're learning. What I decided was that it would be best to have a little competition, and the winner gets to be Lance-Corporal. That way it's fair. That will be today.'

He paused to look thoughtfully up at the low cloud above us; a sudden breeze ruffled the leaves and I felt a spot of rain on my tummy. He frowned, then continued.

'Punishment then. I could just spank your little arses, and maybe add a dozen hard cane cuts each. You sure as hell deserve it, but I don't want you marked, for now. Maybe I'll do it anyway, in due time, but I happen to think that the punishment should fit the crime. So what did you do? You left the cottage when I had expressly forbidden it. You got drunk. I'm sure you flirted with the locals. Both are serious offences. Do you think I want the local yobs up here? One sniff of your cunts and they will be. That is not to happen again, or it's back to London for you.'

His voice changed on the last sentence. He meant it. I could understand why, and found myself looking down in genuine compunction.

'I'm glad you're sorry,' he went on, 'but you're still going to get punished. The orgy I'm prepared to forgive, mostly. After all, how could I expect three little sluts like you not to have sex together? You did clear up well too, but there will be additional punishments for the mess, the broken casserole dish and not following my instructions. Boots, Poppet, kneel.'

We got down quickly, side by side, our heads bowed.

'Chins up, bums out,' he ordered.

I lifted my head and stuck out my bum, acutely conscious of the way the position left my mouth, pussy and bumhole vulnerable. He eased his fly down as he stepped close to flop out his cock. I opened my mouth, impressed by how quickly he'd got ready again, only to shut it as he tapped the swagger stick under my chin.

'No, Poppet, no more nice, leisurely cock sucking for you, at least not for the moment, and I'd keep that little mouth shut if I were you. Boots, top off.'

She hastened to obey, popping the buttons and shrugging it free in a series of quick movements. Beneath, her big, dark nipples were hard, and looked a little irritated from rubbing on her shirt. Naked, she looked up, right at his cock, which he held firmly between fingers and thumb.

'You two pissed on Knickers, didn't you?' he said, and let go.

June shut her eyes just in time, and the full force of his urine caught her in the face. She gasped in shock and got her mouth filled, shut it and collapsed gasping, with urine spurting from her nose. He just laughed and began to spray her back, making the thick yellow stream run down between her bum-cheeks and over her pussy, then into her hair, which he left dripping and bedraggled before suddenly cutting off his flow.

I instantly shut my eyes, and not a moment too soon. He did it in my face first, against my tightly held lips, and lower, over my boobs, to leave my nipples dripping and a trickle running down over my denuded pussy, then he stopped and I heard his voice.

'I thought you were the one with experience,

130

Poppet. Don't you know it's a privilege to be allowed to drink your Master's urine?'

His words got to me, tempting me to open my mouth and let him do it, the result of years of training. His pee was just too rich, the acrid, male scent just too strong. He gave a click of his tongue in disapproval and let go again, into my hair, holding it until the hot fluid was running down the groove of my spine and over my out-thrust bum. I stayed still, full of disgust and the joy of submission too as his piss ran down my body.

It stopped. I shook my head, clearing what had pooled in my eyes but not daring to open them. He chuckled, and the stream hit me again, right up my nose, catching me completely unawares. I gasped by instinct, and then it was going in my mouth, with Stephen laughing uproariously as I jerked back with piss spurting out around my lips.

'That'll teach you!' he crowed. 'Obey your Master, Poppet, you can never outwit him, so it's always for the best! Now stay put while I deal with Knickers.'

He finished off on the top of my head as I kneeled coughing and spluttering on the ground. I stank, and I was kneeling in a pool of it, but if I didn't want to come then and there, I knew I would later, and what I'd be thinking of, but it would be with a girl. He moved away, still laughing as he stuffed his cock back into his trousers and pulled up his zip.

I knew Nikki was still standing to attention, but I couldn't look to see what she was to be subjected to. There wasn't much to hear either, just a little gasp of pain and a metallic tinkling, then Stephen spoke again.

'There, and you stay that way until I say so. Now, run and fetch a bucket to sluice these two sluts down. I want all three of you at attention by the car in five minutes, in trousers, warm tops and sensible shoes.'

131

I heard him walk off, then the pad of Nikki's bare feet as she went for a pail. I stayed down, the pee dripping slowly from my hair and the acrid scent strong in my head, until at last she came back, to pour water over June, then me. It was cold, and set me shivering and I jumped quickly to my feet.

We were going out for a purpose and I had no intention of smelling of male pee, so I snatched a shower before I dressed. June did the same, leaving Nikki to wash the patio down. She'd had her nipples clamped – her punishment – and a little bell hung from each, with a bud of flesh poking through a thing like a miniature thumbscrew. We had to inspect and take turns to hold her while the other teased her swollen teats. By the time the three of us came out to parade by the car in our jeans and jumpers, Stephen was leaning against it, tapping his fingers on the bonnet.

'That must be the longest five minutes on record,' he remarked, 'even for girls. Turn around, bums out.'

We obeyed, presenting him with a line of three denim-clad bottoms, each of which earned a dozen firm swats. I got into the car with my bum tingling, strapping myself close beside June as Nikki did the gate. It felt odd to be in the car, and normally dressed, even after so short a time, but, as we drove, the occasional tinkle from Nikki's nipple-bells kept me reminded that the situation was far from normal.

Stephen took the Bridport road, then turned inland, through a series of lanes he obviously knew. When he stopped it was at the edge of a little wood where a track joined the lane. It had been spitting rain as we drove, but had stopped, leaving the air fresh and cool, and everything very silent.

'Here?' June demanded, looking around at the wood, the piece of rough ground beside it and the fields beyond. 'What are we supposed to do here?'

'Yes, here,' Stephen answered. 'It's about five miles back to the cottage if you'd like to be pissed on and left to walk home. I could manage . . .'

'No, Master, sorry, Master,' she said quickly.

'This,' Stephen went on, pointing to the rough ground, 'is the back of Oudley Common. I'd thought of taking you pony-carting up here, but there are generally more people around than I like to take that risk. Not that many though, and it's just the place to decide who gets to be Lance-Corporal. It's simple. You three go out, and the first to come back and show me a pool of spunk in her mouth is the winner.'

I swallowed hard as his words sank in and found myself glancing nervously out across the common. The only person visible was a highly respectable-looking woman walking her miniature poodle, but that was hardly reassuring. June spoke.

'We have to suck some guy off . . . Master? And show you what he's done?'

'Exactly.'

She went quiet. Nicola looked pale, and didn't speak. My butterflies had started again, worse than ever.

'Come on,' Stephen urged, 'run along. There's a golf course to the north and west if you fancy a crusty old Colonel, and some old earthworks due west, where the main car park is. That's more wooded. There are always dog walkers or, if you're lucky, you might meet a flasher.'

Nikki was nearest, and he gave her a pat on the bum to get her going. She went, reluctantly, to the stile beside the gate. She climbed over and we followed, not talking until we were well out of earshot.

'I can't do this!' Nikki hissed.

'No?'

'No! It's one thing online, when you know what everyone's into and you can be anonymous anyway, but I can't just ask some stranger if I can suck his cock!'

'I can,' I answered. 'I've never done this, but some of my friends have. There are lay-bys the blokes know, where girls get taken to give peepshows, sometimes worse.'

'Yeah, but here?' June protested. 'I don't know . . . it's quite a turn on, and I would love to be your straw boss, Poppy, because you can be such a bitch, but what if we get caught?'

'We won't,' I promised her. 'Just be careful who you pick . . . Hang on, what am I telling you this for! Work it out for yourself, Miss Boots! Don't worry, Nikki, if you can't handle it, then don't bother. Go watch the crusty Colonels play golf or something.'

I'd moved back as I spoke, among the gorse bushes that grew everywhere on the common. June hesitated, as if to follow me, then set her face in determination and went the other way, leaving Nikki standing there looking glum. I picked up my pace, thinking of what it would be like to have June made Lance-Corporal over me. She'd abuse me, thoroughly, I was sure, and I knew how I'd react. That didn't stop me wanting to try and win.

The common was too open, the only cover the gorse, which is much too prickly to be sucking cock in, while it would be just my luck to have one of the respectable walker's dogs come to investigate. The golf course was no better, probably too crowded, while players would be in twos and fours. The car park was better, as at the very least I could get my man to stick Fido safely inside his vehicle before going down on him.

June was bold, and I knew that once she felt she had a chance she'd go for it, maybe even with a dog

134

walker. So I hurried on to where the rough ground began to slope away towards a wooded valley. I could see a stream at the bottom, with a road beside it ending at a car park set among the trees. To my right the earthworks topped an open spur. There were plenty of people, maybe too many, and as I began to scan around for a likely candidate I realised I was being stupid. The only sensible thing to do was find a dog walker, proposition him and take him back to the little wood where we'd parked. That way I wouldn't have to walk half a mile with a mouthful of spunk.

I was sure June would have thought of it, and turned back, starting to panic. Half the population of Dorset seemed to be in the area of open woodland below me, including two coach parties. It was too risky, and I hadn't seen anyone suitable on the tops either. Even as I vacillated June might be sucking away on some dirty old man's prick, or even an attractive young one's. I had to act.

A big eroded path led up from the car park, south, opposite the ancient earthworks. It had to be better, and to lead roughly towards where we'd parked. I reached it, to find it deserted. Clutching my fingers in rising panic, my stomach tying itself in knots at the thought of what I had to do, I turned left, running. Then I saw him.

He was perfect, or at least, he was going to have to do. He was about thirty, unkempt, with a mass of untidy hair framing his face and bare, skinny arms, one of which showed a faded tattoo of a skull amid a clump of roses. He wore a dirty singlet and still dirtier jeans, along with huge boots. He was smoking, the waft of cigarette sharp in the still air. A shaggy black and tan mongrel with a piece of string for a lead lay at his feet, looking at me.

To have called him a tramp wouldn't have been fair, but it came pretty close, and, if he wasn't going to let me have a suck of his cock, then nobody was. It was a pretty disgusting prospect, but there was no time to be choosy. I approached, smiling sweetly.

'Um . . . Hi.'

He looked up.

'Hi, babes.'

It's one thing at a dirty party, or with someone like Fat Jeff who always wants it. To offer a suck to a man I'd never met before and who looked like he'd been kicked out of the Hell's Angels for untidiness was something else. I was going pink, but others had done it, and so could I.

'Can . . . can we talk?'

'Sure, babes. Fag?'

'No . . . thanks. I was . . . I was, um . . . thinking of something else . . .'

'I can score you some weed . . . skunk, at my van?'

Suddenly I had a let in.

'Great . . . cool . . . but I don't have much money.'

'Who needs money?' he answered, his eyes moving to my boobs, true to male form.

I just smiled and shrugged. He was leering as he stood up and moved off, in completely the wrong direction.

'So where's your caravan?'

He jerked his thumb in the general direction of the valley.

'Oh . . . couldn't we just do it here?'

He looked at me as if I was an idiot.

'I ain't got the blow, babes.'

I was making a complete mess of it. June would have just asked, I knew. If June wasn't sucking on cock it was probably because she'd finished.

'Oh shit! Come in here.'

I glanced around. We were alone. I took his hand and lead him quickly in among a clump of gorse where it pressed to the boundary fence of the common. There was a field beyond, but nobody visible.

'Hey, what ...' he protested, and stopped as I pulled up my jumper and bra to show off my boobs.

'Nice,' he managed.

I squatted down, my back towards the fence, trying to ignore the smell of stale sweat as I grappled for his fly. The dog had followed, and watched with interest as I opened his master's trousers. He was still smoking, the smell mixing with his own to make me wince.

He had no underpants on, and his big, grimy cock flopped out into my hand as his fly came wide. I began to tug, rolling the dirty foreskin back and forth. He gave a pleased groan as I fought down the sick feeling in my throat and took him in my mouth. He tasted truly disgusting – sweat and old spunk and oil. I sucked anyway, forcing myself to swallow and make spit until I'd polished his cock and all I got was man.

For all I knew he had some slovenly girlfriend back at his caravan, but I was expecting a big mouthful at any moment. I didn't get it, and he accepted his blow-job as if it was his due, in no hurry whatever. That was not what I wanted, and I took his balls in hand, stroking them, and tickling him just an inch from his anus. He gasped, then spoke.

'Hey, slow, babes, slow, or you ain't going to get your shagging.'

I shook my head on his cock, sucking harder and making a purse of my lips for him to penetrate. He groaned, stubbed his cigarette out quickly, and I knew he was close. Swallowing my disgust once more,

I slid my hand deeper under his balls, to find his anus. It was sticky and wet; my fingertip went in easily. I began to wiggle my finger up his bottom, and to jerk at the base of his shaft, all the while fucking my own pursed lips with his swollen helmet and down to the meaty ring of his foreskin. He had to come; it was just a matter of keeping the rhythm, which broke as something firm pushed against my bum, right between my cheeks. I came off my man's cock with a squeak, spinning round to find the dog behind me, his nose pressed to my bum.

'Hey, stop it!'

The dog moved back as I slapped at him, his big eyes full of hurt. I pushed him away and, as he shuffled back, went back to my task. No sooner had I got my lips around the man's cock than once more his dog began to nuzzle me, his nose pushing to the seat of my jeans, right over my bumhole. I stopped again, looking up to find my man grinning down at me.

'Sorry, but could you stop him snuffling my bum, please?'

'He can smell your cunt, that's all.'

'I don't want . . . Hey, get off, you!'

The dog had pressed his nose in again, deeper, right against my pussy-lips. He moved back as I slapped at him again, but not far.

'Don't be mean, he'll just rub up your bum,' the man advised. 'Get with it. I was nearly there, unless you want that fuck?'

I shook my head as I took his cock back in my mouth, now determined to make him come. My hand went between his legs, my finger to his anus and in, well up his bottom. He gasped as I began to wiggle it about and once more I started to wank him into my mouth, and to fuck my lips. It had to happen, at any moment, and when the dog began to snuffle me again

I just ignored it, wanking, sucking and fingering furiously even as the firm, inquisitive nose moved down, to rub right on my pussy.

He came, my mouth filling with thick, salty spunk. I milked him, the dog still nuzzling at my bumhole and pussy through my jeans, until my mouth was full, then jumped up, slapping at the dog and hastily covering my tits.

'Geb . . . glub . . . obb! Dirby abimal!'

I shut my mouth hastily as the spunk threatened to spill from my lips.

'Whoah! Look who's talking!' The man laughed.

I gave him a dirty look and backed off, my cheeks bulging with spunk. It felt as if he'd done enough in my mouth to fill a half-pint glass, and I felt sick and flustered. He looked at the dog, put his head to his temple and tapped meaningfully as I pushed through the bushes, then called after me as he realised I was really going.

'Hey, what about your blow?'

I could only shake my head as I dashed off between the bushes. At any moment I was going to be sick, but I ran, convinced that I would have been beaten, but praying that somehow June had failed to get her mouthful. As I approached the wood I saw that she was already there, and my hopes sank, only to rise again as I saw the look of annoyance on her face and caught her tone.

'. . . just would not believe me! First he asks how much, as if I'm a fucking whore! Then, when I tell him it's for free, he takes off! What a prat!'

'Wob habbebed?' I queried, mumbling through my sticky mouthful.

'She approached some guy and he thought she was out to mug him!' Stephen laughed. 'You've got it, yeah?'

I opened my mouth and it all came out, my gullet going into sudden, unexpectedly spasm. June gave a gasp of disgust as I spewed my mouthful of thick white slime out on to the ground, right at her feet.

'Yuck, gross! Poppy!'

Nikki just stared in horror from the car window.

'Sorry,' I managed, gasping. 'Yes . . . yes, Master. I got it.'

'Good girl!' he responded. 'That's what I like to see, obedience. Seriously, we'd better go. June's guy must have thought she was working with a gang and may well have called the police. Get in, you lot.'

I hurried into the car, Stephen assisting me with a slap on the bum. There was a bottle of water, and I drank greedily from it as we started off. June took it from me, and as I settled back in my seat I realised that I simply had to come.

'Cuddle me,' I demanded, as I tugged at my zip. 'Play with my tits.'

June and Nikki shared a look, but their arms came around me as I slid my hand down the front of my knickers. I was soaking, my pussy swollen and sensitive, ripe for a cock. I hadn't adjusted my bra, and my boobs came bare as they pulled my jumper up. June took me in hand and began to suckle me, Nikki stroking a nipple, then licking.

I sighed, already rubbing at my clitty, my head full of dirty images and thoughts – the man's dirty cock, the taste of his spunk, the way the dog had snuffled my bottom and pussy, what the man had said . . . He can smell your cunt . . . He can smell your cunt . . . He can smell your cunt . . .

Then I was screaming as my orgasm hit me, and jerking at my sex, my head filled with the unspeakable dirtiness of what I'd done, and of what I might have done.

140

Seven

Saturday night was very formal, done by the rules as laid down by Stephen. I had nothing to sew my Lance-Corporal's stripe on to, so took advantage of my position to borrow June's smart green uniform jacket, ordering her to go topless for the evening. When she protested I made my move, got her down across my knee on the settee, whipped down her panties and gave her a sound spanking on the bare. There was less cheek after that, and I spent the evening organising them as we served Stephen a crab salad. I was chosen to give him his after-dinner blow-job, my third of the day, but that was all, and I made up for it by spanking June and Nikki side by side and having both lick me before bed. Stephen came in to us again during the night, this time to take me. I went, led by the hand, and was given a brief but surprisingly tender fucking, on my back with no hanky-panky.

Sunday was bright, as predicted, with just a few puffy white clouds drifting lazily across the sky. June was breakfast girl, and I watched her suck Stephen off with considerable satisfaction, leaving me pleasantly turned on and ready for the day. I knew it was punishment, and was expecting to be put through my paces, perhaps as a pony-girl. I was very surprised

141

when Stephen ordered the three of us into bikinis and dresses and announced that we were going to the beach. We obeyed, our feelings mixed, but sure that after the day before we were unlikely just to be going for a swim and a sunbathe.

We drove for several miles, west along the coast, to a village. There was a pub and a single shop. Stephen parked and we went to buy a picnic lunch; Cornish pasties, a cucumber, tomatoes, peaches and three big bottles of water. We were on quite high land and, presumably, close to a cliff, so I was wondering what he was up to, but he started down a half-overgrown footpath with confidence.

'What are we going to do, Master?' June finally asked as we reached a clump of elder trees.

'We're going to play a simple little game called Risk Strategy,' he answered. 'I offer a punishment. You can take it or leave it. If you take it, that's your lot. If you leave it, you go on to the next choice.'

'What if we always choose to leave it, Master?' Nikki asked.

'Then you must accept my final choice,' he told her. 'The first punishment is simple. To go topless all day, in just bikini pants and shoes.'

June shrugged and put down the bag she was carrying, to peel off her dress, unclip the top of the bright red bikini she'd chosen and peel it off. Topless and obviously proud of herself, she stuffed her clothes into the bag and spread her hands in a gesture of indifference.

'Big deal, Master,' she announced, and for the first time speaking to him there was a touch of mockery. 'I'm showing my boobs, so what?'

He simply grinned, and I hesitated. June was right. Going topless on a lonely beach is no big deal, but then, I didn't suppose Stephen thought it was either. There had to be a trick. He'd said all day, and if he meant it that would mean going through the village on the way back, maybe into the pub. Eventually she'd be told to put her top on, and I couldn't see that she'd care. I would, a bit, but I could do it. Then again, I might miss the fun later.

'Poppet? Knickers?'

'No, I'll move on.'

Nikki simply shook her head.

The path moved deeper in among the elders, which closed over us to make a cool green aisle, still damp underfoot. It also became ever more overgrown, and after a while Stephen had to find himself a stick to slash back the nettles that grew to either side. When we at last reached the edge of the cliff I realised why. There had been a landslip, breaking off the footpath and leaving a series of terraces of broken rock and mud leading down to a beach of grey-blue shingle and bright golden sand.

We began to pick our way down, Stephen leading at first, then Nikki as her confidence grew and her athleticism came into play. By the time we reached the beach he was well behind despite all the gear we were carrying, and arrived puffing, dishevelled and not looking best pleased.

The landslip had formed a little haven of sand, the ideal place to go bare, and to play. June walked over and began to rub suntan lotion into her skin and I went down to the edge of the sea until the gentle waves were washing over my feet. I could see for miles in both directions, along a strip of beach below undulating cliffs. Far to the west there were people and a scattering of houses where a valley came down to the sea. In the east the beach curved out of sight maybe a mile away, and not a single soul was visible.

'What a lovely place, S – Master,' I called. 'I'm going to strip off.'

'You're not here to muck about; you're supposed to be being punished,' he answered. 'You may take your dress off, but keep your bikini on.'

I was pouting as I pulled my dress over my head, but not too worried as I was sure to end up nude soon enough. June was having great fun, and had taken her bikini pants off, but he said nothing, merely slapping her as we reached the place where Nikki had set out the picnic rug. Stephen sat down on it as soon as it was ready and snapped his fingers.

'Beer, Knickers.'

Nikki hastened to obey, handing him a can of lager from the cool-box. He opened it, took a long draft, then spoke.

'Second punishment, a dozen ice-balls up the arsehole. Any takers?'

He looked from Nikki to me. She shook her head, looking doubtful. I was blushing, and thinking of some of the games Gabby and I played, but he had to know what would happen, and he was offering. I tossed my dress over a rock.

'I will, Master,' I promised.

'Good. Arse up, panties down then.'

I obeyed, the heat in my belly rising as I got into position, on all fours with my rear end stuck out towards him. June sat down on a rock, giving herself a prime view of my bottom. Nikki came to stand beside her. My fingers were shaking as I reached back, to ease my knickers down, and everything was showing.

It was sudden, from perfectly decent to flaunting my bum in a few seconds. I could see too, looking back, my spread thighs with my yellow bikini pants taut between them, and Stephen beyond, digging into the cool-box. He brought out an ice-mould, a big rubber one holding twelve ice-balls. I'd used them in drinks, and knew how big they were, nearly the size of a squash ball. He squeezed one out, smiling as he rolled it in his hand to melt the surface.

'Lubricate me, please, Master,' I managed, not at all sure if I could take them with just water.

Stephen nodded and snapped his fingers towards the picnic bags.

'Boots, grease her arse. Use the marge.'

June went into a fit of giggles as she reached for a bag.

'One for the cunt, I think,' Stephen remarked, and casually pushed the ice-ball up my pussy.

I gasped as cold, hard ice filled my pussy mouth, and was left panting, with my hole stretched. I could feel it, but not the cold, as he'd pushed it deep in until, as June pulled the tub of margarine from the bag, the first drips of icy water began to run down between my sex-lips.

June came to me, her face lit up in a truly wicked smile as she threw a leg across my body and sat herself down, her full, cheeky bottom resting on my back. I heard the pop of the margarine lid, her giggle of delight and disgust, and then her finger was between my cheeks, squashing out a thick blob over my bumhole, and up. I moaned as my rectum was invaded, June pushing the warm, greasy margarine well in, probing me, then pulling out to smear it around my ring.

Immediately I could feel melted margarine trickling down over the fleshy bar between bumhole and pussy, just as ice water was trickling down between my sex lips. I had fluid oozing from both holes, hot and cold, and there was going to be more, and worse. My breathing was deep and even, as I let my bumhole go loose, expelling a little more molten margarine. June climbed off, her face wreathed in smiles as she watched my lewd display, and even Nikki's little pixie face was bright with interest.

Stephen squeezed out another ice-ball and I closed my eyes. It touched, right on my ring, hard and round and so cold, making me gasp. He pushed. I felt my hole open, taking the ball, and it was up, in my rectum, where I could no longer feel it. A second followed, squeezed into my slimy bumhole, and a third, chinking against the one already up me. Stephen paused to push a finger in, forcing the balls deep into my rectum.

I could now feel their weight in my gut, and the slightly straining sensation. A fifth was added, and a sixth, pushed up into my now gaping bumhole. My ring was numb with cold, my pussy too where the water had run down, but in my rectum I could feel only the growing, bloating pressure. The seventh went in, and the eighth, which he had to push deep once more, with two fingers inserted into my well-stretched bum ring. They paused for June to slap more margarine on to my anus, and to finger me, giggling as she felt about among the ice-balls in my cavity.

'In her mouth,' Stephen instructed, his voice now hoarse with excitement.

June giggled, pulled her fingers free of my bumhole and offered them to my mouth, slimy and yellow and cold. I sucked, tasting myself and the cheap margarine and the cold of what was now melting up my bum. She laughed as I sucked, and gave me a resounding slap on my bum as she sat back on her rock.

'You are so dirty, Poppet! How does it feel, tell me?'

'Heavy,' I admitted.

'Like you need the loo?'

I nodded as the ninth ice-ball was pushed up my bottom. It did feel as if I needed the loo, badly. My rectum was bulging, my ring open, the balls threatening to come out, save for Stephen's thumb, which he had put in to cork my hole as he readied the tenth ball.

His thumb came out, and the tenth ball went up, squashing out a little water. I clenched, my teeth gritted against the strain, which was growing close to what I could bear. June laughed to see my distress, and reached out to wobble my bottom and pat it.

'How must that feel!' she crowed. 'Ten ice-balls up the dirt-box! Boy, am I glad I'm not you!'

I stuck my tongue out at her, but she only laughed, and then the eleventh ball was being pushed into my ring, hard, to force it in among the others. I blew my breath out as it went up, and shook my head as my ring closed behind it, but not all the way.

'I can see a bit!' June laughed. 'Look, it's going to come out!'

She was right. It was more than I could hold, my rectum bulging with solid to absolute capacity, beyond capacity, and it just had to come out.

'Don't you dare, Poppet,' Stephen chided, and slapped my bum. 'One more.'

With a rush of despair I realised that he had more, the ones he'd have needed to stuff June and Nikki's bumholes if they'd been stupid enough to volunteer. I had, and now I was suffering for it.

I waited, panting, as he extracted the final ball from a new mould. It went to my bum and I gasped as he forced it in, until my ring was stretched around it, half in and half out. June laughed at the sight. Nikki giggled, a sound quickly cut off. Stephen poked his finger in, forcing the rebellious ice-ball deeper, and wriggling it around to push them all further up.

I farted as his finger came out, but my ring was closed and I was left gasping and shaking, my head hung, my gut bloated, feeling horny and dirty and utterly sorry for myself and desperate to be used.

'Pants up, I said!' Stephen ordered. 'And then stand.'

It took a long moment before I could get control of myself and obey him, but I managed, reaching back to tug my bikini pants snugly up around my bum and clambering to my feet. Standing, the load in my rectum felt heavier than ever, and I had to keep my hole tight and my cheeks clenched to stop the ball at my hole from squeezing out. Once they melted, it was going to be harder, maybe impossible, and if so, unless Stephen let me squat, I was just going to have to do my enema in my pants.

'Should have gone topless, Poppet!' June taunted.

I shook my head, my emotions too strong to allow me to reply. My load felt awful, heavy and urgent, enough to make my head spin. I could feel the wet at my hole too, and I was sure I'd never be able to hold it, and once it was coming . . .

'May I squat, please, Master?' I pleaded.

'No,' he answered calmly, and took a swallow of beer. 'Have these two serve lunch.'

'Serve your Master,' I ordered, but there was no authority whatever in my voice, only panic.

'Yes, boss,' June answered, her voice dripping sarcasm. 'Right away, boss.'

'Enough of that!' I managed, forcing myself to be severe. 'Over that rock now! Knickers, serve the Master.'

June stuck her tongue out at me, but bent, her back dipped, her bottom well spread to show off the dark star of her anus and her pouted pussy lips. Just the pose was insolent, however exposed she might be, and as I waddled over to the tangled foliage at the base of the landslip I was determined to assuage my own distress and humiliation by adding to hers.

There was fireweed, and there were nettles. June wasn't even watching, but talking to Nikki and Stephen as the picnic was laid out. She was still bent though, as if it didn't matter. More determined than ever, I began to snatch out stalks of fireweed, choosing the longest and driest. With a good clump in my hand, I took a big dock leaf and carefully broke off some nettles, to conceal them at the centre of the bunch.

Ready, I started back. The feeling in my tummy was getting worse, and I had to walk back in tiny steps to keep the pain in my bulging rectum down as much as possible. I was leaking too, my crease warm and wet around my hole. The rest wanted to come out, badly, but I knew I could hold it, at least long enough. As I reached the rug I faced Stephen, my head hung in submission.

'Please, Master, may I squat.'

'Yes ... once you've beaten Boots,' he answered, not even looking up as he chose a tomato.

'Yes, Master, thank you, Master,' I managed.

'Stick it out, Boots, now!'

June stuck her bottom out as ordered, still looking back, as insolent as ever.

'Oh, my! She is going to beat me with a flower. Please, Master, stop her, I can't bear it!'

'Be careful, Boots,' Stephen warned, 'or I'll do it, with a proper stick.'

He was facing away from her, and she stuck her tongue out, pulling it back not an instant too soon as he turned. Ignoring the chance to sneak on her, I hefted the bunch of fireweed and thrust it at her bottom, twisting my wrist to make sure both fleshy orbs got a fair share.

'Hey, that tickles!' She giggled. 'Oh no, stop her, Master, she's tickling me! Come on, beat me, you bitch! Come on!'

She pushed her bum out still further, taunting me with her thick, dark pussy-lips and the moist oval of pink flesh between. I thrust the bunch in, rubbing it over her sex, even as the nettles began to take effect.

'Hey, ow! What have you done!? Ow! Fuck that . . . My bum's on fire!'

I just chuckled, and gave her a solid whack across both cheeks an instant before she jumped up, clutching her bottom.

'Nettles, darling,' I told her, 'nice fresh ones!'

'You little bitch! Ow! Ow! Ow!'

She began to hop up and down, slapping at her bottom, gasping and squealing, a sight so absurd I just doubled up in uncontrollable laughter . . .

. . . and squirted twelve big ice-balls' worth of water into the seat of my bikini pants.

It just came out, all at once, one huge rush of water and solid, filling my bikini pouch and exploding from the sides, down my legs and on to the sand beneath me. My laughter turned into a gasp of horror, but it was too late. I couldn't stop it, but I ran, in panic and burning humiliation with water still spurting out of my bumhole and into my bikini. More followed, now mostly solid, until I could feel the weight of it, wobbling behind me, and the wet squeezing out at the sides, to run, hot and sticky, down my thighs.

The instant I got to the water I sank down, squatting in the cold surf, my bum under water. I tried to get my pants down, but as the wave sucked back it left my bulging bikini pouch on show again, and I stopped, not wanting them to see what was left come out. I couldn't stop anyway, and I was forced to do it in my pants as the waves washed back and forth, alternately concealing and revealing the obscene bulge under my bottom as it grew fatter and heavier.

I let it come, all of it, then waddled a little further into the sea, to pull off my pants. They'd seen my bulge, knew what I'd done, and that was enough. I had to come, but the humiliation of having them know was more than I could bear. I glanced back, as if by accident, as I tugged one ankle out of my filthy bikini pants. Stephen was holding his nose in disgust, but grinning too. Nikki was staring in open shock. June was still doing her mad bottom dance about fifty yards along the beach and hadn't even noticed.

My pants came free and I was in just my bikini top. Slipping a hand between my bum-cheeks, I began to clean up, and to masturbate. I found my bumhole, to slip a finger into the slimy cavity. The flesh of my rectum felt cold, a strange sensation, and one that put what had been done to me firmly in my head. I let my legs spread, sinking into a low squat, my bum stuck out as I cleaned my crease, my other hand on my pussy, ostensibly doing the same. I had only moments before they realised just how dirty I was being, but that was enough. I focused.

In front of other people I'd been given an ice enema and made to poo my bikini pants. They'd seen everything. They'd seen me lose control, seen my pouch fill and burst as I squirted in it, seen the mess run down my legs as I fled for the sea. Worse, they'd seen me fill, seen my bulge grow as I let it all out, and I'd done it on purpose. I could have gone deeper, easily, but no, I'd let them watch as my poo filled my bikini pants, bulging behind me, fat and heavy under my bottom.

It hit me, the most wonderful orgasm, setting my thighs tight and my bumhole pulsing on the finger I had jammed up it at the last moment. I had to bite my lip to stop myself screaming, and that made it longer, lasting on and on as I slid my finger in and out of my slimy hole and stroked my burning clit.

When I finished I felt as if every last tiny piece of energy had been drained from my body. I slumped forwards, my vision suddenly red and hazy, my breath coming in long, ragged pants. Only when I heard Nikki's voice from behind me did I turn round. She was at the water's edge, the sea washing her bare toes.

'Are you all right, Poppy?' she asked, her voice low and full of concern.

'Fine, thanks,' I managed. 'Just cleaning up. Sorry about that . . .'

'Don't be, it wasn't your fault,' she answered, and stepped deeper in, to sink down beside me and put her arm around my shoulders. 'He can be a pig, can't he?'

'He's not bad,' I answered, 'just a bit inexperienced. He's OK as a Master.'

Her lips had set into a firm little line, but she nodded in agreement. I knew how she felt, wanting it but feeling she was being taken too far, too fast. I kissed her and she hugged me in return, then left as I went back to washing myself. On the beach, Stephen had a half-eaten pasty in one hand and was washing down a mouthful with beer. June was in the sea, a good hundred yards along the shore, up to her waist in water. I waved cheerfully as I got up and was given a 'V' sign in return.

Thinking I'd upset her, I quickly buried my ruined bikini pants and started to make my way along the beach, but when I got close she did nothing worse than splash water over me. I splashed back, and for a moment we were playing together before coming into each other's arms in a wet embrace.

'What happened to you?' she asked as we left the water, hand in hand.

'I let my enema out in my pants,' I admitted. 'I was laughing so much over you I couldn't hold it.'

'Serves you right, girl! Those nettles sting. My bum's still throbbing now!'

'Best not cheek me, then, Miss Boots!'

'I won't. You are well dangerous.'

'Thank you.'

We walked back together, Stephen nodding down the beach as we approached. A group of three people were coming towards us in the distance, so I quickly dried myself and slipped my dress on to cover my nudity. June wasn't going to bother, but Stephen told her to put her pants on. By the time they reached us we were simply another group of holidaymakers having a picnic. They were students, or looked like it, all male, all wearing rucksacks and holding hammers. Other than shifty glances at June's bare chest, they paid no attention to us at all.

'Fossil hunters,' Stephen explained when they had passed.

They stopped, maybe three hundred yards beyond our picnic spot, where a band of greenish rock in the cliff angled down to the beach. Stephen threw the stone of the peach he'd been eating into the sea and glanced at his watch.

'I need to leave about seven,' he stated thoughtfully, 'so that gives us maybe three hours before we have to think about starting back.'

'Plenty of time for Knickers to get punished, Master,' June said.

He nodded, looking more thoughtful still, then spoke.

'You didn't even try yesterday, on the common, did you, Knickers?'

'No, Master,' she admitted. 'Sorry, Master. I was shy.'

'Very sweet,' he answered, 'but hardly obedient. Still, you can suck cock as well as the next little slut, as I know. So, for your punishment, Boots will go and ask those three if they'd like you, nude, for blow-jobs all round.'

'No, Master, please!' Nikki squeaked. 'Not with strangers, Master. They wouldn't understand.'

'I think just about every man on the planet understands about blow-jobs, Knickers,' he answered her.

'I mean, about me,' she said, 'the way I feel . . . the way I am. You respect my submission, Master. They won't.'

He nodded again, and took his chin between forefinger and thumb.

'Sorry, Master,' Nikki said quietly, her voice barely more than a whisper. 'I do try to obey.'

'I know,' he said, 'and I know you're shy, but sometimes, with shyness, the only thing to do is to drive a truck through it.'

'Don't make me, please,' she said.

'I won't,' he promised, and I caught the flicker of disappointment beneath the immediate relief on her face.

She needed the responsibility for the dirty deed taken out of her hands, and into his, as usual. On the common she would have had to make the final choice. Here she didn't but, if Stephen had any idea what was going on in her head, he didn't show it.

'A truck, yes,' he mused. 'Come here, close to the cliff where you can't be seen. Hands on your head.'

She obeyed, looking a little frightened as he went to the edge of the landslip.

'Is it to be nettles, Master?' she asked suddenly.

'Be quiet, Knickers, or it might be,' he answered, and bent to where a trickle of water was seeping from a crack in the thick, blackish-brown clay of the landslip.

She watched, puzzled as he scooped up a good double handful of the clay and squashed it into a rough, lumpy ball. Apparently satisfied, he walked to her, pulled out the pouch of her bikini pants and dropped the ball down them. Her mystified look immediately changed to chagrin. He laughed and tugged out the back of her bikini pants. The ball fell down a little, so that it hung below the tuck of her cheeks, making a bulge just like the one he had seen in my own bikini pants, only fake.

I wouldn't have known it was fake. Her bikini was black, and while the bulge was improbably large, that only served to make it more obvious, and more humiliating. After all, who would purposefully put a load of clay down her panties to make it look as if she'd had an accident in them?

As he stepped away, grinning, Nikki craned back her head, twisting around far enough to inspect her bulge. She looked as if she was about to cry, and in the end simply hung her head and followed him meekly back to the picnic rug, her load swinging behind her in her pouch. I did feel sorry for her, but I was having to force myself not to laugh. She looked so rude, and so absurd, with the huge bulge hanging beneath her neat little bum, and her shamefaced expression making it seem all the more real.

'We'll start back,' Stephen stated evenly. 'Pack everything up, you three.'

'Yes, Master,' Nikki answered, choking on unshed tears.

As she bent to take hold of the picnic rug her load squashed to her bum and between her thighs, making it look more obscene still. She straightened up, grimacing in consternation and embarrassment, then disgust as she tugged at her bikini pants to make the clay pull from between her buttocks.

'We'll do it,' I offered, putting my arm around her shoulder, 'and don't worry, most people will feel sorry for you, and the perverts will think you look cute.'

She tried to force a chuckle at my weak joke, but she was biting her lip and kept her back firmly to the cliff as June and I quickly packed everything away. Stephen watched, his arms folded across his chest, then to my surprise began to gather up the bags.

'I'll take those,' he said, 'after all, we wouldn't want you cheating, would we?'

'How do you mean, Master?' June asked.

'I'm going back to the car by the direct route,' he explained. 'You three are going to walk along the beach to Eyles, where I'll pick you up in the car park on the front.'

I glanced towards the distant houses I had noticed earlier. There were more people there than before, maybe a hundred or so visible. Suddenly I was extremely glad I had my dress on to hide my nakedness.

'But, Master –' Nikki began, her face flushing to crimson as the implication of his words sank in.

'No buts,' he cut her off. 'You might have chosen to go topless, you might ... In fact, there's a lesson here. Never resist your Master. It is always best to obey the first order, and promptly, or it will only make things worse.'

Nikki managed a single, miserable nod. Stephen scrambled up the first of the ledges, turned to look down on us, waved and he was gone. I turned to the others. June looked a little uncomfortable despite her boasts of not caring who saw her topless. Nikki was chewing on her lip and looking anxiously towards Eyles, with one oily tear running slowly from her eye.

'Take it out, Nikki,' I suggested.

She shook her head.

'No, Poppy . . . I should do this.'

'Because he said so?' June demanded.

'Because I should,' she answered. 'I need to . . . to be me, because I've been punished.'

I nodded and held my hand out. She took it, and June's on the other side and we began to walk along the beach, slowly, Nikki with tears running down her face and the fat bulge swinging slowly in her bikini pants. It was going to look more like she'd had a shameful accident than ever with her crying and holding our hands, but it was what she wanted.

It was a long way, and slow going, with patches of the coarse golden sand alternating with rounded stones that were a pig to walk on. The fluttering in my tummy grew stronger as we went, and not only for my friends' sakes. My dress was light and the material tended to cling, making it clear that I had no pants on underneath. Bare boobs would have been better, in some ways more acceptable, but I knew my feelings were nothing beside Nikki's.

She walked on though, her head hung, her tears rolling slowly down her cheeks. I could feel the trembling in her hand, and her fingers were clenched tight on mine. When we drew level with the first group of people she gave a little sob and faltered, hesitating when a few more steps were going to leave her bulge on show. Two more paces and it was showing.

There were five of them, another group of fossil hunters, three male, two female. Most were looking at something they'd found, but one, a woman, looked around. Her expression was indifferent, even as she saw that June was topless, but changed, abruptly, to shock and sympathy, and she turned quickly away. Nikki had seen, and I heard her mutter something under her breath, more a whimper than words.

We began to walk faster, my eyes fixed to the houses of Eyles, which still seemed impossibly distant. There were others ahead, and some had seen us coming. They could see that June was topless too. Most were pretending not to look, some were staring openly. We reached the next group: three young men. One wolf-whistled and nudged his friend. Then we were level.

'Fuck me, she's shit in her pants!' one called.

Nikki just burst into uncontrollable tears, snatching her hands away to cover her face and running, her load bouncing in her bikini pants behind her. The three men dissolved in laughter, pointing and catcalling, until June rounded on them, screaming abuse at the top of her voice. One went quiet, but the other two just turned their malice on to her.

'Come on!' I urged, tugging at her.

For a moment she resisted, then ran after me, leaving them behind. Nikki was well ahead, running in blind panic, her bikini pants half down with the weight of their load, showing the top of her bum crease. Then they were right down, dragged suddenly to her thighs; her little round bum was bare and she went headlong, tripping on her pants, to her knees in the sand.

I knew it wasn't real, but I couldn't have told. Her bum was completely bare, a dirty smear showing between her cheeks, her pants around her knees, with the fat, dark ball sitting in the open gusset. The men behind us exploded into fresh laughter and jeering calls.

June turned to yell fresh abuse back at them. I kept on, to Nikki's side, pulling at my dress for all I knew it meant adding the sight of my own bare bum to the yobs' amusement. She saw, raised a hand and shook her head, then reached down and pulled up her bikini pants, lump and all, to settle them around her hips with her bulge looking as rude as ever, ruder in fact, because she had smeared the insides of her thighs.

She walked on, still crying, her face screwed up, but in determination as much as misery. I'd just flashed my bare bum at the yobs, who were laughing harder than ever and challenging June to take them on. She didn't, but hurried after us, red-faced and flustered.

'Bastards!' she panted. 'Come on, Nikki, go in the sea, take it out!'

'No,' Nikki answered, tight-lipped.

June shook her head, but took Nikki's hand again. More people were looking at us, in shock, in sympathy, in lust, in amusement, and a dozen other reactions, each to their own. I kept my eyes ahead, near to panic myself, and Nikki's hand firmly clasped in mine. Not one person offered to help.

We were level with the car park before I even realised it was there. The cliff was low, with a white-painted balustrade at the top, and suddenly there was the wine-red nose of Stephen's Mondeo, and Stephen himself, looking down on us. He waved cheerfully, as if nothing was wrong.

There were steps, another two hundred odd yards away, across sand, and the most crowded part of the beach. Every single person there was staring at us, maybe a hundred pairs of eyes, fixed on June's bare boobs or on the swaying bulge in Nikki's bikini pouch, which now hung so low it was visible from the front. As we came closer I caught whispers, sympathy again, and disgust, and disapproval.

Nikki broke, suddenly, without warning, dashing for the steps in a flurry of limbs and bouncing panty load, her mouth wide in distress and the tears streaming from her eyes. I followed, and June, overcome by panic and raw emotion, jumping over people, stumbling on bits of seaweed, to the concrete base of the steps, and up.

By the time I got to the top of the steps Nikki was in the car. Stephen had the door open and I bundled in behind her, June coming up gasping for breath a moment later. Nikki was sitting on a towel, leaning forwards, her head in her hands, her whole body shaking. Where she'd sat down the muck had squeezed up her crease and was oozing slowly from the back of her pants. Stephen got in, grinning, and started the car, glancing back only as he reversed out of his space. For one moment there was doubt in his eyes, but it didn't show when he spoke.

'A lesson learned, I trust, Knickers?'

She gave a single, dumb nod.

'Good,' he said. 'What we need now is privacy.'

He took off, driving dangerously fast along the coast road. We cuddled Nikki, holding her as the shaking of her body slowly died away, but she still hadn't spoken when Stephen abruptly pulled off the road where a great pile of asphalt chips had been left. I knew what was coming, and my butterflies started once more. There was a little wood, very dense, and no room for other cars to park, but it was still outdoors, with all the thrilling fear that brought.

'Out,' he ordered. 'Into the wood and line up at attention.'

We scrambled out and pushed in among the trees, Stephen urging us forwards with slaps and pinches. Once under the trees I realised that the wood was only fifty yards or so deep, with a wide open field on the far side. He didn't seem to care.

'Right. Poppet, dress off, top off. Boots, pants off. Knickers, top off.'

He squeezed his crotch, watching as we began to strip. I kicked my shoes off and peeled my dress high as June pushed down her bikini pants; my bra followed and we were nude. Nikki glanced at us, her tear-streaked face full of uncertainty. Stephen nodded as we came back to attention.

'I hope you all feel suitably chastised?'

'Yes, Master,' June and I answered in chorus.

'Then turn and bend, arses high, hold your knees and I'll give you your reward.'

We went, turning to present him our bums and bending down to offer access to our pussies. I felt horny, but confused too, sorry for Nikki and unsure of her reaction. Part of me wanted to use my stop-word and demand a time out, but I didn't. My pussy wanted a cock and it was so much easier to obey.

'Back in, come on, flaunt those arses,' he demanded.

I obeyed and felt my bum-cheeks spread to show off the little hole between as I caught the scent of aroused pussy. Stephen chuckled as he came behind us, to put one big hand to my bottom and another to June's, stroking and kneading our flesh. A shiver went through me as his fingers strayed between my cheeks, to touch on my bumhole, and I wondered if I was to be buggered again.

'Such a pretty view,' he remarked, 'and such a good position for a girl. I think all women should be photographed in this position, maybe on their eighteenth birthdays. It would be so good for their sense of humility. Now, which lucky girl is going to be first?'

I heard his zip come down and my pussy gave an expectant twitch. June sighed and I pulled in my back tighter still, flaunting myself for rear entry. Stephen came close, to settle his half-stiff cock between my bum-cheeks. He spoke again as he began to rub himself in my crease, at the same time fondling June's bottom.

'Yes, bare-arsed in public, that's the way it should be, and plenty of discipline, every man with the right to pull any woman's panties down and spank her, any time she needed it.'

He laughed and slapped June's bottom. His cock was growing hard, and he kept rubbing as he went on, the thick shaft swelling and growing between my cheeks until my hole was aching to be filled with it.

'Just think, at work, secretaries across their bosses knees, bare of course, and it wouldn't matter who was watching. And at colleges, students made to go over their desks, bums on show for a good whacking, one at a time, just the girls naturally. In parks too, and on the beach, any little tart who doesn't show respect for her betters, and over she goes, panties down and . . . Ah!'

He finished with a sigh because he'd sheathed his cock in my pussy. I clutched my knees, struggling to stay in position as he began to fuck me. Then he had taken my hips and I was panting out my lust to the wood in time to his grunts and the squelching noise of my sloppy hole being filled. I needed it, for all my doubts, and wanted to come, reaching back between my legs to find my pussy, only for him to pull out. Seeing my fingers, he slapped me hard, right across the meat of my cheeks.

'None of that, Poppet, you little slut, not until I say.'

I nodded and took my hand away, bracing myself once more in my lewd position. Turning my head, I watched as he got behind June and slid himself up her, her face softening in ecstasy as she filled with cock. He began to fuck, holding her by the hips as he had done me, to make her fat little boobs swing under her chest and set her gasping with pleasure.

He stopped, just as her moans had began to show real passion, pulled his cock free and got behind Nikki. I could see her bulge, hanging in her bikini pants between her thighs, and her little tits were quivering in her emotion, her nipples erect. He was grinning as he took hold of her bikini pants, and as he pulled them low he spoke again.

'You enjoyed that, didn't you, Knickers?'

She nodded as the pants were adjusted around her thighs, to leave the heavy lump of muck swinging in the gusset.

'It was not easy, was it?' he went on.

Nikki shook her head. Her tits shivered.

'Yet you are glad I made you do it, aren't you?'

'Yes, Master,' she said, her first words since leaving the beach.

He settled his cock into her bum crease and began to rut in it, talking.

'I know you are, and I appreciate both your arousal and the gesture. You are truly mine, aren't you?'

'Yes, Master. Truly, Master.'

Her voice was hoarse, full of passion, and she was crying again. He chuckled and slipped his cock lower, into her hole. She cried out in blind ecstasy, shaking her head and clutching at her legs as she was fucked.

'Which is why,' he panted, 'I've saved my spunk for you. You two sluts, you can rub your cunts.'

I was going to. I felt resentful, a little abused. He'd made us perform in public, twice, sucking off complete strangers, showing our bare breasts and bottoms, to his order, because it amused him. Now he had us bent, in a line, nude to fondle, nude to fuck, and his cock stuck in Nikki's pussy with the ball of what a hundred, maybe two hundred people had thought was her turd swinging in her bikini pants.

My hand was on my pussy, rubbing as the sheer power of what he'd done to us ran through my head, utterly debasing us, to make me come, to make June come, to enslave Nikki, because it was what we wanted, what she needed.

I didn't need him, but I needed what he was doing to me. I was wishing we could all be fucked together, repeatedly, man after man using our juicy pussies, their cocks squashing in again and again, and up our bums too, buggering us in our own juice, their own too, the spunk running down our flesh, keeping us open for cock after cock after cock . . .

My pussy was burning hot, and sloppy with juice, I could feel my bumhole winking behind, and then I was coming, and screaming out my passion to the wood, oblivious to whoever might hear. June hit her orgasm even as mine began to fade, and at the last moment I grabbed her, to kiss her hard on the mouth. My passion was returned, and we rode it together, sinking to our knees, still rubbing, my orgasm dying in a long series of delicious little shocks. Stephen grunted in ecstasy and my pussy gave a last, exquisite twitch on the thought that he had come in Nikki's sex.

She hadn't, but we saw to that, taking her in our arms as Stephen slumped back panting against a tree, his cock dripping white stuff. My hand went between Nikki's thighs as we cuddled her, to find her pussy slick with spunk and juice, and dirty with clay. I found her clit, rubbing quickly until her shivering turned to sudden, hard spasms and her gasps became helpless grunts and cries.

164

We held her, taking her all the way, kissing and stroking at her body and whispering to her, until at last her contractions died down. I still held on to her, wondering if she could really handle what she'd done, but she came up smiling, embarrassed but happy.

'Best get back, girls,' Stephen said puffing, his role breaking post-orgasm. 'And get your clothes on; I'm not really sure how safe we are here.'

I nodded my agreement as I retrieved my dress. Like him, my need had blinded me to common sense, but we'd got away with it, and that was what mattered. I didn't bother with my bikini top, and June didn't bother at all, just peeking out of the bushes to check that no cars were coming before dashing bare-arsed to the door of the Mondeo. Nikki alone bothered to cover herself, pulling her top back on and flopping the worst of the muck out of her pants before tugging them up, then running for the car with one hand clasped to her bum. Stephen gave a dry chuckle as he watched her go, and he followed.

In the car June made herself decent by putting my dress on, and we set off, reaching the cottage in time to swallow a quick cup of tea before preparing a simple dinner for Stephen. He left immediately afterwards, somewhat hurriedly, with no more than a peck and a squeeze of our bums as we said goodbye in front of the cottage. I let him out of the gate and watched the car go with a mixture of relief and regret.

Eight

With Stephen gone we all felt a bit melancholy, especially Nikki. He'd taken her deeper into submission than she had expected, perhaps deeper than she had realised she could go. It left her feeling very much his, and wanting to be treated as his. For that, he had to be there in person, the knowledge of his position as her Master was not enough. It was more than I could bear to tell her the truth, for all that I desperately wanted to, and that spoiled my mood in turn and left me angry with him. It was all very well for him to lead her where she wanted to go, but the deeper she went the more she needed his support. In the end he would be unable to give that support, and he knew it. She was strong, and in the end it would prove to be valuable experience, but that didn't excuse him.

The hire car was due back in the morning, so I had to go. I left at dusk, with a final cuddle for Nikki and June. It was a slow drive back, with a lot of holiday traffic on the roads, but my mood picked up at the thought of being back with Gabrielle. When I finally got back to Victoria, she was still up reading a journal and sipping wine. We went straight to bed, with barely a word exchanged, for kisses, cuddles, spanks and finally licks. Only when we'd both come and were lying together in the darkness did she ask about my weekend.

'So how was our friend Stephen Stanbrook?'

'Not bad, not great.'

'Yes?'

'He's new, to be fair, but for a guy of his age he doesn't know a lot. What he does is picked up from the net and Fat Jeff.'

'What has Jeff been saying?'

'Nothing too much, I'm sure, or Stephen would know about you. Just dirty talk in the pub, I think.'

'I hope.'

'Stephen dobbed me, with egg and bacon fat, and made me choke on his spunk. He put it up my bum and made Nikki suck it too, after lubing me up with blue cheese sauce.'

'Yes, I see he has been listening to Jeff.'

'The sauce was my idea, and June's. They barbecued me . . . sort of. No, the thing with Stephen is he wants to be Mr Military, with uniforms and lots of rules and regulations. There's a punishment book, and we're supposed to write down everything we've done wrong. That's great, but he doesn't dish out all the punishments for all the crimes, and he gets carried away as soon as his cock's hard. With Anna, she would make me write down everything I'd done wrong, and what I was going to get for it. I would get it too, every time, no more, no less. I used to hate it, and it made me come so hard, but if I was good I wouldn't get punished. With Stephen I know I'm going to get punished anyway, good or bad, and once he's despunked he really can't be bothered. That takes the fear out of it. I'd give him six out of ten.'

'Does his insecurity evidence itself?'

'No. He plays the Master twenty-four seven, and he's full of confidence.'

'What of his wife?'

'Not a mention, and not a hint of her presence at the cottage. He's thorough, I'll give him that.'

'Will you go down again?'

'Yes, in the week, and you're coming with me.'

She couldn't, of course, but I did manage to persuade her to keep a few days clear the following week and she promised she would. I got up early to avoid the parking restrictions, and was back from Wembley before Stephen arrived for his appointment. I quickly installed myself at my listening post, this time with a coffee and a slice of mushroom quiche left over from Gabby's supper.

It was odd hearing his voice in such a different context, and as they went through the preliminaries I kept expecting him to tell Gabby to strip or bend over for a whipping. As it was, his most commanding statement was to ask for more milk in his coffee. Once that had been sorted out she bided her time, waiting for him to get his thoughts in order. After a bit of coffee slurping, he spoke.

'I've changed my opinion.'

'In the matter of your friends' self-esteem?'

'Yes. I realise now that it must take immense inner strength to cope with the sort of things that excite them, to do things I would find utterly degrading, and to feel happy with it.'

'I see. And this has come about by spending more time with them?'

'Yes. All three girls were at the cottage. Nicola and June had brought Poppet down as a surprise for me. They behaved as my slaves all weekend.'

'And you, as Master, felt able to accept this without misgivings?'

'I played my part, yes, and I enjoyed it. What misgivings I had quickly went. You remember I said

I'd always felt that women . . . that female sexuality was essentially passive, a giving thing?'

'I do.'

'I was wrong. All these years with Kate thinking it was something she gave . . . something she enjoyed, sure, but could give or take. Not these three. Their needs are as strong as mine.'

'This is an important understanding.'

'It is? Now I feel I've been cheated my entire life!'

He gave a bitter laugh. I shook my head. There is no pleasing some people.

'Once I'd realised that,' he went on, 'I thought their submission might be like a drive, a hunger, something they needed to express, but wouldn't be happy with afterwards . . . once they'd come.'

'A somewhat masculine perspective.'

'If you say so. It's not true anyway. They do it, then laugh about it and tease each other afterwards.'

'So you have come to accept that they are secure in their own sexuality?'

'Yes, and I wish I was! No . . . I am; I have never experienced anything like the pleasure of having the three of them as my slaves. It's not just physical either, the whole thing gives me this enormous sense of wellbeing.'

'And thus you feel your relationship with Kate is unsatisfactory?'

'Yes, frankly. I mean, don't get me wrong, sex with her is great, physically, and mentally too, really, but it doesn't make me feel . . . feel . . .'

'More masculine?'

'I don't know. It does, in that I've satisfied her, but it always leaves me feeling as if it was something she did for my benefit more than her own, as if I'm taking charity, perhaps. It not like that with the girls. They make me feel they need me, that I'm giving as much as I'm taking, maybe more.'

That was news, after his 'spunk and go' attitude, to use one of Fat Jeff's pet sayings. Still, what he was saying gave hope for Nikki, even if it was at Kate's expense, or so I thought until he spoke again.

'Not that I could ever leave Kate. I'm not going to be one of these bastards who gets into a mid-life crisis and goes off with some girl half his age. There's the house too, which is in her name. So's the cottage, and I can't see myself getting much of a divorce settlement after setting myself up with three young girls in an SM relationship.'

He gave another bitter laugh. It was a bit pathetic, feeling sorry for himself over a situation that was entirely of his own making. Gabrielle responded, as professional as ever, her voice neutral, as I picked up the piece of quiche.

'There is conflict here, clearly . . .'

The end of the quiche broke off, falling right down my cleavage.

I spent the next three days being very, very sweet to Gabby. I wore my blue nurse's uniform as a matter of course, and took her in hand after work each day, putting her into a routine. First I'd have her strip and bath her, then dry her, powder her and put a little jelly on her bumhole. Then it would be into the playroom, where I'd get her in a nappy and let her suckle at my breast before putting her in bed and going to eat. When she wet herself I'd clean her, spank her gently and put her in a fresh nappy, by which time she'd be ready to come. I'd masturbate her, cuddling her head to my boobs with one hand down the front of her nappy, which would leave me in need of my own orgasm. I'd take it sitting on her face, as she licked my pussy and bumhole, a slight deviation from her fantasy, but one she was always happy to indulge.

It kept her in the best of moods all week, calling me her 'Bobonne' and coping with the most demanding of her clients with never so much as a flicker of irritation afterwards. I'd decided to go down first thing on Friday morning, by train, and hopefully introduce Nikki to the joys of anal play before Stephen could get round to sticking his cock up her bum, perhaps June too.

I knew the girls wouldn't be in the UK Masters and Slaves chatroom on the Thursday night, and Stephen might be. I wanted to see how he'd react to me without them there, also what he'd say about his weekend. So after putting Gabby to bed and eating I settled down at the computer with the rest of my wine and logged on. Sure enough, he was there, and immediately put up a whisper box for me. I responded, expecting some rude demand, but only swapped messages to say that he'd bought uniforms for me and to confirm I'd be at the cottage all weekend. He then said that the managers had been complaining about too many people whispering in chat and suggested we move back to the main board. I did so, hastily replying to the greetings.

Poppet: 'Hi all. Sorry, distracted there.'

Black Knight: 'Not whispering, I hope, Poppet?'

Poppet: 'No, Master.'

Black Knight: 'Good, don't.'

Poppet: 'Yes, Master.'

His next post was to answer somebody else, a question from a newcomer about etiquette in the Group. Gabby was tucked up in bed with a dummy in her mouth and a tube up her bum. Her enema bag was on a slow feed and I wasn't worried, so I took a while to work out what the conversation was about, then joined in. They were discussing piercings and tattoos, so I didn't have much to say and for once had more questions than answers. After a while there was a lull in the messages, then the one I'd been hoping for.

Black Knight: 'No Knickers and Boots this week?'

The Master: 'They're away.'

There was another pause, which somehow seemed expectant.

Mr Big: 'How about some virtual?'

Black Knight: 'Yes, a virtual piercing.'

The Keeper: 'Let's do Poppet's cunt lips and put her on a chain.'

Black Knight: 'Masters, we shall vote.'

Poppet: 'I don't want to be pierced. How about a nice spanking?'

Black Knight: 'Silence.'

The Keeper: 'This will be an important lesson for you in true submission. You would be better to accept it meekly.'

I was about to tell him what I thought of him when a blue flash caught my eye at the bottom of the screen, signalling a whisper. I clicked on it, bringing up a small window. A message appeared.

Mr Big: 'Hi there, Poppet. Don't worry about those arseholes. Talk to me.'

I felt an immediately wash of gratitude.

Poppet: 'Sure.'

Mr Big: 'So you don't fancy virtual piercing.'

Poppet: 'I'm not really into it.'

Mr Big: 'How about something else?'

Poppet: 'Maybe.'

Mr Big: 'Show a bit of "respect" then.'

Sometimes a pair of inverted commas makes all the difference.

Poppet: 'Please, Mr Big, sir, don't hurt me, sir!'

I was wishing there was a sarcasm symbol available, if only to tease him, but he seemed to get the point.

Mr Big: 'Mind your manners, young lady, or it's straight over my knee.'

Poppet: 'Sorry, sir.'

Mr Big: 'Apology accepted.'

Poppet: 'Are you going to spank me, sir?'

Mr Big: 'No, I've something else in mind for you.'

Poppet: 'Yes, sir?'

Mr Big: 'Yes. You're the girl who likes to piss in her panties?'

There was no point in denying it.

Poppet: 'Yes. How did you know?'

Mr Big: 'Boots told me.'

That was going to cost June, big time. Not that I minded, and his knowing had piqued my sense of submission, and his manner my naughtiness.

Poppet: 'What are you going to do about it, sir?'

Mr Big: 'Make you do it. What are you wearing?'

Poppet: 'A nurse's uniform.'

Mr Big: 'Really?'

Poppet: 'Yes, really.'

Mr Big: 'You're a real nurse?'

Poppet: 'Sort of.'

Mr Big: 'Nice. Describe your uniform.'

Poppet: 'OK. It's pale blue gingham, with a white collar and a belt. There's a little white hat too.'

Mr Big: 'Cute. How short's the skirt?'

Poppet: 'Just below my knees.'

Mr Big: 'What panties are you wearing?'

Poppet: 'Big white ones. I have stockings on too.'

Mr Big: 'I think I'm going to spunk in my pants.'

Poppet: 'Get your cock out then, silly.'

Mr Big: 'I have now. Are you ready to piss your panties?'

Poppet: 'Not quite. Tell me who you are, and what you like to do.'

Mr Big: 'I like pretty nurses who piss in their panties.'

Poppet: 'Tell me.'

There was a pause. I took a big swallow of wine. I could pee, just about, but there was no splash mat. I wasn't sure if I cared. A mess would be good. I'd have to get down on the floor and mop it up, still in my wet knickers . . .

The message flashed up.

Mr Big: 'I'm wanking now, Poppet. If you were here I'd stick my big cock right up your cunt. I'd tie you to your chair, backwards, so your arse sticks out. I'd pull up your skirt. I'd make you drink water, loads of it. I'd wait, until you pissed in your panties. Then I'd fuck you with the piss still coming out of your cunt and all down my balls.'

Poppet: 'You wouldn't need to tie me up!'

Mr Big: 'I want to tie you up. I want you helpless. I want you to hate it. I want you to struggle and swear at me and call me a bastard as my cock goes up your pissy hole.'

I began to type in a gentle rebuke, hoping to get back to my own fantasy, then changed my mind.

Poppet: 'But you can't, can you, Mr Big. All you can do is sit there with your little willy in your hand and imagine me, and what you could do to me if you were here. But you're not, so bye bye!'

I finished with a little yellow smiley, winking, and closed the box down. The others were still hard at it, Stephen included, but I couldn't be bothered. I was feeling horny and full of mischief, but not all that submissive, at least not towards such a bunch of arrogant, ignorant wannabe doms. I was laughing as I closed the connection. Mr Big was going to be fit to burst, his cock so hard he'd have to finish himself off. He'd have to fantasise over me too, I was sure, but he'd be doing it with the certain knowledge he could never have me in the back of his head as he came.

There were members' profiles, and I checked his, just to see who I'd been tormenting. He hadn't put up a picture, but he sounded like Mr Average, forty-five, a warehouse foreman in Coventry, five feet eight inches and medium build. That was all, save for his listing as a dom.

I was still chuckling to myself as I went in to check on Gabby. She was as I had left her, curled up naked on the bed with her dummy in her mouth and the enema tube in her anus.

'Are you ready?' I asked.

She shook her head. I went back out to finish my wine, wondering what to do. Mr Big, I knew, would be sitting in his flat in Coventry, probably with spunk all over his hand. It was funny, and I was sure he'd be thinking furious thoughts about me, probably involving some horrible sexual revenge.

Gabby was going to be ready soon but, for all my behaviour, Mr Big had turned me on, and I was in a dirty mood but not a dominant one. Three nights I'd played nurse, letting my role slip only when it came to squatting on her face. Not that I minded, but now I was in the mood for something a little less passive on her part.

I pulled my skirt up, just far enough so that I could stroke my pussy through my knickers as I sipped the wine. My gusset was damp but, if I wanted to make it a great deal damper, the pressure in my bladder hadn't really built up enough to just let go. So I stroked and drank, feeling the pressure slowly build as I imagined myself on my hands and knees, mopping up my own pee with my knickers stretched taut and wet across my bum, showing because some vicious old harridan of a matron had made me pull my uniform skirt up . . .

All I needed was the vicious old harridan, but short of calling Anna there wasn't much I could do about it. I could get the fantasy though, or something close, better in other ways. I got up, feeling slightly dizzy, and went into the playroom. Gabby had rolled on to her front, and the tube was still protruding from between her little pink bum-cheeks. She turned to look at me and I saw that her eyes were glazed and half-shut. She was in the state of sleepy, uninhibited bliss it takes so long to reach, but in the end makes for the best, the dirtiest sex play. She had to be ready, and I turned the tap on the enema bag off, pulled the tube free and blew down it to force the last of the water up her bum. She gave a little whimper in response and hid her face in her pillow.

'You're ready then? Good. Relax and stick it up a bit.'

I slapped her bum and she obeyed, her cheeks parting to show the glistening ring of her bumhole with the white plastic nozzle sticking out of the centre. She sighed as I pulled it free. Her bumhole closed to make a wet, pink star.

'Up,' I ordered.

She rose from the bed and I took her hand. Her thumb went into her mouth as she trailed after me, to the bathroom, where she stood, watching me from her beautiful pale eyes.

'Turn around and bend over the bath, legs well apart.'

Her mouth came a little open as she pulled out her thumb, and she cast me a single, doubtful look as she went down. Bent, with her neat pink bottom pushed out and her long legs braced apart, I could see every detail of her bare, pink pussy, with the crease moist and ready. Her bumhole was distended too, bulging out from the pressure of the water inside. Her ring was twitching as she strained to keep her enema in, but she leaked a little, a runnel of water escaping from her hole to run down her cheek and drip from her pussy.

'Let it go, Gabby,' I breathed

She moaned, but there was no hesitation. Her bumhole spread, out and open, the contents spurting out, to splash on the radiator and all over the floor in a thick, pale stream. She was gasping, and mumbling to herself as it came, and clutching at the bath. It stopped, cut off abruptly. Her bumhole was closed, pulsing and wet with the bright pink centre splayed out like a little flower.

A little whimper escaped her throat as her hole opened again, erupting her mess on the floor behind her, and more, spurt after spurt to the sound of her gasps and sobs, each a little smaller than the last. I stroked myself as I watched, one hand pressed tight to the front of my uniform skirt, one boob cupped in the other, until at last her bumhole stopped pulsing.

'Are you done?'

A final trickle of fluid squeezed out of her bumhole, to drip from her pussy-lips. She nodded, panting, her soft brown hair bobbing to the motion. Again her anus opened, a last piece emerged and she stood up, her whole body trembling, her eyes bright and wide, her nipples straining to erection.

'Look what you've done, you dirty girl!' I snapped. 'Now I'll have to mop it up. Stand in the shower, now!'

She got in quickly, pulling the curtain to her body so that just her face showed. I took the bucket and a cloth and got down on my knees, pulling my skirt up to stop it getting wet, and began to mop up.

In my imagination the matron was standing over me, a huge woman with massive breasts and hips, much taller than me, bigger in every way, and horribly powerful. Her brawny arms would be folded across her chest, her red face set in real disapproval and real disgust, but also cruelty. I'd beg to be allowed to pee, but she'd deny me, telling me I had to have the floor spotless first. I'd know I couldn't hold it. I'd know it was going to come out in my knickers. I'd know it was what she wanted.

I worked slowly, letting my feelings build along with the pressure in my bladder. It was going to happen, soon, whether I liked it or not, in my knickers and down my legs, all over the floor, where I'd masturbate in it. In my fantasy the big matron would laugh at me as the wet stain spread over the seat of my knickers and yellow fluid ran through my gusset and down my thighs. When I was finished, she would tug up her uniform, pull aside her huge white knickers and casually urinate over my head.

That I could have, for real, not from a matron, but from Gabby. I looked up, meeting her eyes.

'Gabby, can you pee?'

She nodded.

'I'm going to do it, in a moment, in my knickers, and have a rub. When I start to come, pee on my head.'

'I will.'

I smiled and went back to my fantasy, mopping up the last of her mess before flushing the loo, then pulling up my skirt to show off the seat of my knickers. I could do it easily, but all I had to do was hang on and I was going to have a genuine accident, which would be so much stronger. I got down on my knees again to polish the tiles as my urgency continued to grow, until I was panting and curling my toes, shaking my head and clenching my bum-cheeks.

It just came, erupting into the gusset of my knickers as a sudden stab of pain broke my will to hold back. Then it was coming in earnest, gushing full blast to spurt through the taut cotton over my pussy and splash on the newly cleaned floor. I could feel it soaking into the seat of my knickers, and up over my pussy, hot and wet against my skin.

I reached back, snatching at my pussy, to feel the softness of flesh beneath the pee-soaked cotton and the dribble of fluid running through it. My mouth came wide; I caught hold of my knickers and jerked, tugging the wet material up into my crease to spray pee over my legs and dress. Again I jerked, pulling my sodden knickers tight between my bum-cheeks and against my clitty. I realised I could come, against my knickers, what Fat Jeff and Monty called a panty-wank, only girlie style.

Gabby stepped from the shower as I began to tug frantically at my knickers. My pee was dying, but still splashing about as I wiggled my bum and jerked at myself. It stopped, my pee-hole closed and at once I sensed a change in my pussy. I was going to come in moments, just with a few more sharp tugs to my straining knickers . . .

. . . and Gabby's stream erupted over my head, over my face, into my hair and down my back. I just screamed, already coming, my mind whirling with filthy thoughts as my sweetheart urinated over my head. It was her and, in my mind, the huge matron, and June, and Nikki, all peeing on me as I frigged myself to blinding ecstasy with my own soggy knickers. My muscles were twitching, my boobs jiggling in my bra, my bumhole and pussy in spasm, and all the while with Gabby's pee splashing in my hair and trickling from my fringe, on and on as I held it, never wanting it to end.

When it finally broke I sat down, right in it, breathing hard, the last of her pee pattering on the floor and into my hair. I'd come, but it wasn't over, and I forced myself not to relax. The matron would have taken me by my sodden hair and pulled my face into her pussy ... no, her cunt ... her huge, reeking cunt, to force me to lick her to orgasm. Not Gabby, but I wanted to give what she had given me, any way she pleased. I looked up through my dripping fringe, my eyes half-closed.

'Now you. What do you want? Anything, just say ...'

'Nurse me. Take me there as you please, but be slow.'

'I will. Let's shower.'

She disappeared behind the curtain and a moment later the hiss of water started. I was still shaking a little as I peeled off my wet clothes and stuck them into the laundry basket. She wanted me in charge, and I wanted it special, different, with me off to Dorset first thing in the morning. The idea came to me even as I climbed into the shower, and I washed quickly and wrapped a towel around my head as I climbed out. Gabby was already drying herself, and I took over, folding her in the big fluffy towel.

'You're going to get dressed,' I told her, 'in your office clothes; a white blouse, black lace panties, stay-ups, everything. And put your glasses on.'

Her response was a nod and a sigh as I smoothed the towel over one little breast, brushing her nipple. As I went lower she stuck her bottom out, spreading her cheeks deliberately to let me get between them. I dried her bumhole and cupped her pussy with a handful of towel, teasing her for a moment before letting go. She kept her bottom stuck out and I reached into the cupboard for talc, to shake a little on to my hand and pat it over her bottom. She gave a shiver of pleasure, and another as I talced the little pink star of her anus. Her special jelly followed, some

French stuff she ordered by mail, just a little applied to her bumhole with my finger, around her ring and a little way up.

Powdered and lubricated, she skipped out of the bathroom, and into the ordinary bedroom. I went to the playroom, wondering how I ought to dress with my nurse's outfit in the laundry. There was another uniform, not a proper one, but a ridiculous nylon thing Monty Hartle had given me as a birthday present. I could barely do it up across my boobs and the skirt was so short it left the tuck of my bum showing. I put it on anyway, along with a pair of big frillies, a fluffy suspender belt and stockings, all in white. By the end I looked more like a stripagram than a nurse, but it was going to have to do.

Gabby wasn't ready, so I nipped into the bathroom and waited. She came out a minute later, immaculate in her work suit, with her hair up in a neat bun, just a touch of make-up and her glasses on, giving her the air of cool detachment she valued for her work. I stepped out and she looked up, one corner of her mouth twitching briefly into a smile as she saw how I was dressed.

'Now there's no need to be embarrassed, Miss Salinger,' I said. 'This won't take a moment. If you could just pop your knickers down and come across my knee.'

I sat down and patted my lap. She gave me what I would have sworn was a genuinely flustered look as she tugged her smart grey wool skirt up and peeled down the lacy black panties I had ordered her to wear. I pulled the thermometer I had fetched from my pocket and watched her face set in consternation as I opened the case.

'In my bottom?' she questioned.

'Now there's no call for fuss, Miss Salinger. Come along.'

I patted my lap again, and this time she went down, lying across my legs as if for a spanking. Her bottom was slightly lifted, and I took hold of her skirt to inch it up, exposing her bare pink cheeks. The temptation to spank her was strong, but no more so than that to stick things up her bottom. Leaving the skirt pushed high, I spread her bum-cheeks, showing off her tight, greasy anus. She wiggled, her hole tightening.

'Now do stay still, Miss Salinger. This won't hurt a bit.'

It was the biggest anal thermometer we'd been able to buy, and was actually from a vet's and designed for horses. She knew, and I could just imagine her feelings as her anal ring spread to the gentle pressure of the bulb. Her hole gave, the soft pink flesh engulfing the bulb, and it was up, her ring closing behind it. I pushed it in a little way, to leave the shaft protruding from her open anus with the pink folds of her pussy on display below. I imagined her embarrassment, or any woman's, at being put in such a position in a hospital ward, or perhaps a busy A&E, the staff utterly indifferent to her humiliation.

'This will just take a minute, Miss Salinger,' I assured her, and slipped my hand on to the soft, puffy flesh of her pussy. 'I'm simply going to masturbate you, so there's no need to make a fuss.'

I began to tease her clitty, and the doorbell went.

'Why now?' she demanded in exasperation.

'Don't answer it.'

'I must. It could be important.'

'Oh nonsense, Jo Warren will have dumped her new boyfriend or something.'

'No, I must –'

'Let me go. I'll tell them you're asleep.'

'Yes, but if it is important –'

'It won't be.'

She had climbed off my lap, the thermometer still up her bum. I quickly got up and went to the intercom.

'Hello?'

'Hi, Pops, room for a big one?'

It was Fat Jeff. I hesitated, torn between telling him to fuck off and making Gabby suck his cock in her work suit with the thermometer up her bottom. There was really no choice.

'Oh it's you!' I answered him. 'Come on up.'

'Who is it?' Gabby demanded.

'Fat Jeff Bellbird.'

'Jeff Bellbird!'

'No nonsense, Miss Gabby. You're going to suck his cock.'

'Like this?'

'Like that.'

She nodded, now genuinely unsure of herself. I hid a smile as I turned to open the door, admitting Fat Jeff, as big and hairy as ever, with a hooded camouflage jacket open over a string vest and baggy green trousers. His eyes went straight to my cleavage, and lower, drinking in my smutty uniform.

'Oh sweet!' he exclaimed. 'Fucking gorgeous! Show us your bum.'

I twirled, showing him the seat of my frillies. He blew his breath out.

'Fucking gorgeous!' he repeated. 'You too, Gabs. Spanking you, was she?'

She hadn't pulled her skirt down, and it was quite obvious she was bare behind. Instead of answering him, she stuck her thumb in her mouth. He chuckled.

'Baby games, eh? Is your arsehole greased?'

She nodded shyly, never taking her thumb out.

'Show.'

She turned to push her bottom out, the thermometer still sticking out of her lightly greased anus. He

183

blew his breath out again and stumbled in, to lower his bulk on to the settee.

'Give us a show, yeah?'

'I'll do better than that,' I answered. 'Get your cock out.'

He didn't hesitate, but immediately began to rummage in his fly, to pull out the full bulk of his cock and balls, which he began to stroke. I joined him on the settee, feeling cool and in command. Gabby wasn't. She looked distinctly flustered, but she came down as I patted my lap, into the same position as before, only now with her head in Fat Jeff's lap. He took her by the hair and popped his penis into her mouth without preliminaries. She began to suck.

'Spankies time, Miss Gabby,' I announced. 'I don't want you coming until Jeff has, and your bum-warming will continue until he does. Jeff, you're to do it in her face.'

'Will do,' he answered. Gabby gave a muffled grunt around her mouth of cock.

I began to spank her, just gently, the way she likes it. It made the thermometer waggle in her bum as she sucked, a truly comic sight. I thought of the hospital again, and a respectable businesswoman made to suck some drunk's cock in a cubicle she'd been made to share, while her rectal temperature was taken. It was an absurd fantasy, even for the NHS, but fun, and I let it grow as I slapped her pretty cheeks and watched her mouth work on Fat Jeff's cock shaft as it swelled to erection.

She was pinking up nicely, and her pussy was getting slowly puffier, with her lips engorged and her hole wet and open. I paused to stick a finger in and suck it, then went back to spanking, a little more firmly now that she was fully aroused. Jeff had a firm grip on her hair, pulling it out of the neat bun she'd made so that he could control her sucking. His breathing was getting faster too, and I began to spank harder and faster.

I knew he was there when she started to gag, and then he had whipped it out and forced her head back, twisting her body. She gave a squeak of pain, gasped, and had her mouth filled with thick white spunk as his cock exploded. The next shot went in her hair and she tried to jerk her head down, with sperm already dribbling from around her lips. Then he was milking his cock slowly over her glasses and nose before popping it back into her mouth.

She began to suck again, and cocked her bottom up for rubbing. I thought of the businesswoman again, her face filthy with the drunk's spunk, her little knickers pulled down, the thermometer up her bare bum, finally losing control and begging to be brought to orgasm.

My hand went under Gabby's pussy and I was rubbing, teasing her clitty for a moment before slipping my thumb into her willing hole and giving her my full attention. Her bum was a glowing pink, but I began to spank again anyway, with my spare hand, talking as I slapped and frigged.

'Bad girl ... naughty girl ... who let her knickers down? Who let a man's cock in her mouth? Who's being spanked for it?'

Her pussy began to contract, squeezing on my thumb, and her mouthing on Jeff's slowly deflating penis became suddenly urgent. She was holding his balls, and had circled his cock between forefinger and thumb, to keep the blood in it as she sucked him and his spunk trickled slowly down her face. I rubbed harder, and spanked harder, trying to second guess what was in her head as her pussy once more tightened on my thumb.

'Feed on him, Gabby, suckle his spunk and swallow it down as I spank you. You're going in nappies, Gabby ... Gabrielle ... out of your smart clothes and into a nappy ... spanked for naughtiness and put in a nappy, Gabrielle.'

Her body went rigid as her muscles locked in orgasm. Her bumhole was pulsing on the stem of the thermometer, and right at her peak I eased it out, slowly, keeping the bulb in her hole so that she could feel it as she came.

'There now,' I said soothingly as I popped it out to leave her hole gaping, 'is that better? Now let's read your temperature, then straight into your nappy and bed.'

She gave one last shudder at my words and went limp, Jeff's cock finally flopping from her mouth.

'Nice one,' he said puffing. 'So how about you fetch me a beer, and I'll stick you both in nappies and do you together?'

Nine

I felt a little guilty leaving Gabby to deal with Fat Jeff's snoring bulk in the morning, but I had a train to catch. It wasn't direct either, but involved changing at Bournemouth and a long taxi ride. By the time I got to the cottage I was exhausted and used my Lance-Corporal's rank to order a hot bath. That made all the difference, especially having the two of them in just their white uniform knickers as they soaped me down and washed my hair. I had them dry me too, and powder my bum and pussy, Gabby style, before dressing again and parading them on the lawn in nothing but their knickers and boots. Remembering Mr Big, I took a cane out with me as I followed them.

Both were at attention, Nikki looking earnest, June trying to suppress a giggle. I went to Nikki first, tilting her chin up with the tip of the cane as I addressed her.

'Very good, Miss Knickers. You at least have some decorum.'

She didn't flinch, even when I ran the cane tip down across her chest, brushing a nipple. It was tempting to beat her, but unlike Stephen I wanted her to deserve it. June already did. I moved to her.

'Right, Miss Boots. The first thing I want to know is how come you told a certain Mr Big on UK Masters that I like to wet my knickers?'

'I didn't!' she squeaked.

'Oh no? Well, he seemed to know an awful lot about it.'

'It wasn't me!'

'That's not what he said.'

'Yes, but –'

'Touch your toes.'

'What are you going to do?'

'Cane you. Six of the best.'

'You can't! Master said you could spank, not cane.'

She was almost laughing, but there was just a touch of the hysterics about it.

'He did say that, didn't he? So what do you suppose he'll do to me when he sees your bum?'

'Cane you, hard.'

'Probably, so touch your toes.'

She hesitated, but she went down, all the way, to leave her knickers straining across her cheeky bottom. I stepped up beside her and yanked them firmly down, showing off her rude, colourful rear view, pussy, bumhole and all.

'Six,' I reminded her, stepping back and tapping the cane across her bum.

She gave me a genuinely resentful look, then closed her eyes. I brought the cane up, and down, full across her fat cheeks, to draw out a cry of pain, then a stream of abuse.

'You bitch, Poppy! You little bitch . . . oh, my bum . . . that is fire . . .'

'Nothing quite like the cane for discipline,' I said, 'and I think we'd better have an extra stroke for each time you call me a bitch, don't you?'

'No,' she answered sulkily.

'Yes,' I responded and cracked the cane down again, right under the chubby tuck of her bum.

'You fucking ... you ... you ... pig, cow, little ...'

'Uh, uh, manners, Miss Boots. Now stick it up again like a good girl.'

She'd moved, but she got back, now wild-eyed and shaking. I swished the cane near her bum, not touching, and laughed as her muscles jerked in fear. Her mouth came open, but she closed it without speaking.

'Could it be you're learning manners, Miss Boots?' I asked, and brought the cane down again, this time on target, with a smack of wood on plump girl flesh.

'Ow! Ow! Ow! Shit that hurts, Poppy, you fucking little ... pig.'

'Not very fast, evidently. Bum up, three to go.'

She blew out her breath and touched her toes one more time. Her stripes were coming up nicely, and I'd laid them well, three deep red welts evenly spaced and all on the meat of her bottom. I'd had the best teacher, but it was nice to know the knack hadn't left me. I tapped her bum again, between two welts.

'Hold very still, Boots, I'm going to give you a five bar gate.'

I whipped the cane down, landing it perhaps an eighth of an inch too high, and gave her bum a quick rub to bring up the colour as she abused me.

'Sh!' I urged. 'You know you deserve this, so stop whining.'

'I don't!' she wailed, with real feeling.

I shrugged and gave her the fifth, plumb between the two lower welts, a perfect stroke, as I discovered when she'd stopped dancing up and down and calling me names.

'Last one, darling.'

She looked back, her mouth a little open, her eyes full of emotion. I smiled back and tapped the cane to her bum at a carefully judged angle, lifted and struck. She howled in response and immediately jumped up, rubbing at her hurt bottom and bouncing up and down on her toes to make her tits jump. I stifled a giggle and waited until she had calmed down before making my inspection.

It was near perfect. The sixth welt lay diagonally across the other five, placed exactly at the far side of her cheek, but not quite reaching the highest line on my side. I ducked down to inspect her, tracing my finger across the last line.

'Hmm . . . fair, if I say so myself. Your bum's a bit fat really.'

'Thank you very much!'

'Don't mention it, and next time, don't tell on me.'

'I didn't!'

'Do you want another six? Maybe an ice-ball enema, like I got?'

'No! Not that, Poppy, red, red, red, and I mean that!'

'Ah! Diddums for Boots! Seriously, you told Mr Big, yeah?'

'No. I didn't tell anyone. It must have been Nikki, or Master.'

'It wasn't me, Mis– Corporal, I promise,' Nikki said quickly.

'Well it must have been someone,' I answered. 'Still, I feel a lot better for that, so enough punishment. Instead, there's an important bit of training you both need. Boots, run indoors and fetch two of those candles from the cupboard by the sink, also the lubricant Stephen bought for your pony-girl tails, and some matches.'

'What . . . what are you going to do, Corporal?' she asked.

'Teach you how to open your bumholes. Master's bound to want to bugger you, or stick your tail plug in at the very least. It's important you know a few things.'

She nodded, looking more than a little worried, but ran in, clutching her half-lowered knickers in one hand as she went. Nikki turned to me, and I saw that her expression was more uncertain still.

'So do you really think he will? Put it up our bottoms?'

'He's bound to. Men always want to, and it is nice, done properly.'

'I do want to, but I don't know if I can.'

'Oh you can. A girl can always take a man's cock up her bum, if she wants to. It just takes a little care and attention, and know-how.'

'And you're going to show us, with candles? You're not going to light them while they're up our bums, are you?'

'No, I don't think you're ready for that. I just need to make the wax a little smoother. Candles are good to start with, just the right shape.'

She nodded, so sweet, so nervous. I was smiling. I couldn't help smiling. June came back, now holding two candles, the lubricant and the matches. Her knickers were back up.

'What's the point of covering your bum, silly?' I laughed. 'How modest do you think you'll look with a candle up the hole?'

She stuck out her tongue, as insolent as ever, but her hands were shaking as she passed me the things.

'Best pop them off, both of you,' I advised. 'Down's best for spanking, but right off for anal.'

Both nodded. As I rounded off the ends of the candles with a match, both struggled their knickers off, leaving them stark naked except for their boots. Both were looking back over their shoulders.

'Bottoms up,' I instructed, 'down on your knees.'

They got down, slowly, to lift their bottoms. Nikki had her knees apart and her back in, spreading her cheeks to show off the tiny pink dimple of her bumhole. June was simply down, but as I met her eyes she moved, flaunting herself with her big cheeks well parted and her colourful hole showing. I got down behind them, trying to sound calm and authoritative against my urge to lick them both out from the rear.

'The first rule is always to use plenty of lubricant.'

I stuck my finger in the pot, to pull out a thick wad. They were watching, and looking distinctly worried. I divided the lube between my fingers, reached out, and touched, smearing the thick jelly on to their virgin bumholes. June gave a nervous giggle. Nikki stayed silent.

'The second rule,' I went on, 'is to take your time. Never rush, but allow your body to respond naturally. There should be no pain.'

I was working my fingers on their rings, rubbing the jelly over the little bumps and creases. June had already begun to sigh and was sticking her bottom up, thoroughly lewd and clearly ready for penetration. She fingered herself, I knew. Nikki didn't.

'Relax your holes,' I ordered, 'as if you were on the loo. Don't push, just relax.'

Nikki nodded, but it was June's bumhole which came open, a brilliant pink centre appearing in the dark flesh. I put my finger to it and felt her ring suck at the tip, then open. Gently, as if going up myself, I probed, easing her open until at last I could slide the full length of my finger up her bottom into the hot, mushy cavity of her rectum. She moaned and put her head down to the lawn. Nikki's bumhole was still clamped tight.

'Come on, Knickers. It won't hurt, I promise.'

She gave a little sob, and I felt her ring loosen, just a little. I pushed the very tip of my finger in and she had given in, her ring opening to the pressure with a wet, squashy sound. I just could not keep the smile off my face as I watched her hole squash in, penetrated for the very first time. She was tight, very tight, her tube close around my finger and her ring squeezing on my flesh. I began to bugger them, gently easing my fingers in and out to make their anal rings pull with the motion. June's breathing immediately became sharper. Nikki hung her head further down.

Soon both were open and juicy, their bumholes moist, slimy cavities, maybe not ready for a cock, but certainly for a candle. I remembered the barbecue, and Nikki's face as Stephen's cock had been fed into her mouth, straight from my well-buggered anus.

'Some doms,' I said, 'like to assert themselves by making a girl suck a finger that's been used to open her bum, other things too. It doesn't taste very nice, but then it's not supposed to. It's supposed to make the experience stronger.'

I pulled my fingers free. Nikki's bumhole closed soundlessly, June's with a soft fart. I shuffled forwards, extending my slimy fingers. Nikki had understood, and lifted her head to gape, as meek and obedient as ever. I stuck the finger I'd had up her bottom into her mouth and she immediately began to suck, as dutiful and submissive as anyone could hope for. June had turned, but did not look happy.

'Come on,' I urged, 'if you can't be good, be dirty.'

She gave me a little wry smile and abruptly her mouth had come open, to take my finger in and suck. I felt a familiar twinge of sadistic glee as I watched them, and kept my fingers in until I was satisfied what they were doing had fully sunk in.

'Good girls, that's enough,' I said, 'and another

lesson to learn there. If you take too much pleasure in something that's supposed to hurt or humiliate, your Master is likely to try something worse.'

June nodded as she released my finger. Nikki kept sucking for a moment, her tongue working firmly on my flesh, then let go. I sat back and took the candles. Both bumholes were ready, moist and greasy, the centres showing. I put a candle base to June's and pushed gently. She gasped, but it went in and I slid it up until just over half was buried in her rectum.

I could see just one of Nikki's eyes as she peeped back, and I wagged my finger at her as I picked the candle up. She looked away and I saw her bumhole tense, but I put the candle to her anyway, to twist it in the slimy dimple of her bumhole, and watch it slowly engulfed. A sob escaped her as her ring opened, but the candle was in and I didn't stop, pushing it deep as I went on talking.

'Other rules, never use anything that can break, especially glass. Not even bottles, no matter how thick. If you get a vacuum trap you'll have to walk around with it sticking out of your hole until you can fill it naturally. Never use anything you can't pull out either. Small things aren't so bad, but if you think what Stephen did to you on the beach was embarrassing, trying walking into A&E and explaining that you got a turnip wedged up your bum.'

June giggled, making the candle in her bumhole wobble. I gave her a gentle slap.

'I'm serious, Miss Boots, so listen. You can't feel pain in your rectum, only pressure. If you put a finger in, always take your rings off, and make very sure your partners do. Nikki, however submissive you may feel, however much you wish to be able to trust your Master, never forget that it's your body, and ultimately you are responsible.'

She gave the faintest of nods.

'Good,' I answered. 'Now relax and enjoy your first bum-fucking. Rub off if you like . . . no, rub off and that's an order.'

I took both candles, to push them deeper and pull slowly out, drawing low moans from both girls. What I needed was a strap-on, or anything else to really make a thorough job of buggering them. There had to be something.

'Touch, but don't you dare come,' I ordered. 'Go head to tail. Feel the candles in each other's hole. Fuck each other's bottom. Boots, turn around.'

June scrambled around, now eager, to take Nikki firmly around the waist and stick the candle well in. Nikki responded, gasping as her bottom was invaded once more, and quickly returning the favour. I went to open the shed, sure I'd seen something that would fit just nicely into a not-so-very virgin bumhole.

Sure enough, there was a set of gardening tools hanging on one wall. The handles were wooden, smooth and bulbous at the tip, also well varnished. They were perfect, and not only because the handles were almost exactly the thickness of a good-sized cock, but because the girls would look supremely ridiculous with the things sticking out of their bumholes.

They were as I'd left them, but more heated, now intertwined, each concentrating on the other's anus. I held up the trowel and the little fork I'd selected, showing off the handles. Both knew exactly where the tools were going, and June's face showed an immediate and delicious blend of consternation and pleasure. Nikki simply got back into position with her face to the ground and her bottom lifted.

She was such a cutie, so ready, so willing, so determined to give of her best. Stephen was lucky to have her, with her determination to be the perfect slave. I'd been the same, so I understood, and appreciated her more than he did, maybe more than any pure dom could. June was a brat, more my new style, less in need of punishment and more deserving of it. She was also deserving of six inches of trowel handle up her bottom.

'Ready, girls?' I teased. 'This will take a little more, but just keep those holes relaxed and they'll be up in no time and, believe me, they will feel good inside. You first, Boots, candle out.'

I'd taken hold of the candle as I spoke, and I eased it free. Her bumhole stayed open, well buggered and sloppy, as if she was used to it. I slipped a finger in, just to feel her heat, and stuck it my own mouth, my dirty feelings rising up over my efforts at dominance. She saw, and giggled, so I slapped her bum a few times as I sucked on my finger, just to let her know who was in charge. She stuck her tongue out and her bum up.

I picked the trowel up, showing her the bulbous handle once more before pushing it between her cheeks to her rude, wet bumhole. She gasped as I gave a gentle push, but it was going in, her bum ring pushing in, and out, stretching, pink and slippery as she took the handle. I had a couple of inches in, and her hole was gaping on the thickest part of it. Again I pushed, and watched the full, fat handle slip up into her bumhole until only a half-inch of wood pro- truded. She gave a little moan and came up on to all fours, as if being fucked in doggy position.

'Nice, isn't it?' I asked.

She gave a quick nod as her hand came back, to touch the handle where it was sticking out of her hole, then to rub, using her palm on her pussy as she explored her buggered anus.

'It's better with a cock,' I told her, and smacked her bum.

Her eyes came open as, still rubbing herself, she looked back at Nikki. I picked up the little fork.

'Watch, Knickers,' I ordered, pushing my finger into the jar of lubricant.

She too looked back, her big, impish eyes wide as she watched me smear the handle of the fork with jelly. Her whole body was shaking, but she stayed down and merely sighed when I extracted the candle from her anus.

'It's going in,' I told her, 'just like June's. Just relax.'

Her bumhole had closed, and looked impossibly tight, a little star of greasy pink flesh, impossibly small for what I intended. I moved closer, knowing I had to take my time, and poked the tip of the handle to her hole. She pushed out, as I'd told her to, and I saw her ring spread, her slippery flesh engulfing the rounded head until perhaps half an inch was in. Her flesh looked taut, as taut as June's did with the full bulk of the handle up her, and her hole still needed to stretch as far again. I pressed it in, very gently. She gave a whimper and I stopped, her anus now a glistening ring of straining pink flesh.

'Rub yourself,' I ordered.

She nodded and her hand came back to her sex. As soon as her finger was busy with her clitoris I pushed again, gently but firmly. Again she whimpered. Her hole pushed in, contracting, and I waited until she got control of herself and once more let it spread. An inch was in, almost to the thickest part. Again I pushed, and this time her ring spread to take the thickest part.

'Good girl,' I soothed, 'now you just rub that little pussy and you'll soon be done.'

197

Her answer was a sob. I pushed again, and in the handle went, up her bottom to the sound of little whimpers and grunts as her rectum was filled by the thick, hard handle. She was done, fully invaded, buggered, and soon to come over the feel of something big jammed up her bottom, for the first time ever. I had to come too, and quickly.

I sat back, watching as they masturbated eagerly with their little rings stretched wet and greasy around the thick tool handles. Both pussies were wet, their swollen lips quivering to the motion of their fingers, their pulses pulsing slowly, their bumholes sucking around their loads. I was wishing I was with them, three in a line, dressed in nothing but boots as something fat and hard was rammed up my bottom, preferably a man's cock.

My hands went to my jeans. I popped the button and pushed them down, knickers and all, baring my bum to the warm summer air. My fingers went down, front and back, to find my pussy and bumhole. I needed penetration, badly, and snatched a fat blob of grease from the tub of lube. It went up my bumhole, pushed deep in, hard enough to make me gasp. They were going to get there, and as I fingered my bumhole I was wishing they'd turn on me, get their revenge, bugger me with something impossibly large and make me suck it after it had been up my dirty hole.

June began to mumble obscenities and she was coming, her fingers busy on her sopping pussy as the trowel twitched and jerked in her bumhole. I took a candle, to stuff it firmly up my own hole, buggering myself as I frigged, faster and faster. June, finished, reached back to ease the trowel handle from her bottom, leaving her anus a gaping red hole. She saw what I was doing as she rolled on to her side. She grinned and I was babbling.

'Use me, June . . . darling . . . use me, up my bum . . . please . . . now.'

She swung round, crawling close. Nikki cried out in orgasm, her bottom tightening on the huge load in her tube, her fingers fluttering between her lips. June took my hair, to pull my head back, hard, and, as my mouth came wide, the trowel handle she had that moment pulled out of her bumhole was stuffed into my mouth.

I just came, my whole body jerking in orgasm, one hand snatching at my pussy, the other jamming the candle furiously in and out of my slimy bumhole, and sucking, in eager, filthy wantonness on the trowel handle. Jolt after jolt of ecstasy went through me, and all to the sound of June's laughter, helping to bring me higher, and higher still, to a plateau of twitching, blinding rapture.

June finally pulled the trowel out of my mouth and I began to come down. We collapsed, giggling, into each other's arms, and after a moment drew Nikki in. All three of us were laughing as I stripped, and we washed on the lawn, using the hosepipe, a big green bar of soap and a brush meant for scrubbing boots. It left us pink and tingling and, after a round of very large brandies, light-headed and more giggly still.

I was well pleased with myself. I'd done them both. Now Stephen could bugger them at leisure, and I would know that it was me who had given them their first proper anal experience. Even if he chose to bugger them both that evening, I'd been there first, and taught them just how good it could be.

There was a fair bit to be done before the cottage was presentable for Stephen, but as Corporal I didn't really see why I should bother. So I made a quick list and strolled down to the pub for a salad and a couple of glasses of white wine. I took my time, walking down to the edge of the beach with my second glass and sipping it as I watched small waves breaking on the shingle. Drowsy and a little tipsy, I let my mind wander to what I could do with the girls during the afternoon, perhaps a punishment, or simply having them perform for me.

I was fairly sure they wouldn't have done all the tasks, and when I went back I deliberately climbed the gate to make sure they didn't hear me, and peered in at the kitchen window, hoping to catch them being lazy or up to mischief. What I saw stopped me flat, horrified. There was another person with them at the table, a woman, fully dressed, drinking tea. For one awful moment I thought Kate Stanbrook had turned up unexpectedly, only to realise that she would hardly have been drinking tea with her husband's playthings. Then I realised who it really was – Anna Vale.

It took a good five seconds of staring blankly before I could even pull myself together enough to duck down out of sight. Anger, consternation and bewilderment flooded through me. She had finally caught up with me, and I was going to have to face her down, not an easy thing to do after years as her servant, obeying her orders, taking punishment.

I had to. She could only have come to see me, maybe to take me back. It had been over a year, but I had no illusions about how she saw me. I was her girlfriend, her maid, with an emphasis on the 'her'. In her mind she owned me, and her actions would have been little different if a piece of furniture had gone missing. All the time I'd been avoiding her I had hoped she would simply give up, or find herself someone new. Now it looked like the confrontation I'd been trying so hard to avoid had finally caught up with me. I could leave. I could go back to the pub until Stephen came. Whatever I did I would only be putting off the inevitable.

As I got up I could feel myself shaking, but I was determined. She had to be faced down, made to see that because I had once committed myself to her didn't mean I had relinquished my final right of self-determination, the right to change my mind. I went to the door and opened it quietly, only to freeze once more at the sound of her voice.

'. . . so typical of a man to have to assert his dominance by making you walk about with your drawers showing,' she was saying. 'Now an alpha dominant woman, such as myself, would have no need for such props.'

I remembered the ways she'd made me dress sometimes, and choked back a bitter laugh.

'I like my uniform,' June protested, 'and I like to show my bum. It feels good.'

Anna didn't answer, but I could just imagine the disapproving arching of her eyebrows. To her, a girl's bottom came bare for punishment or to cause humiliation, usually both. When she spoke again, it was to send a jolt right through me.

'Do come in from the corridor, Poppy. I know you're there.'

I went in, feeling very sheepish, and sat down at the table.

'Sorry.'

It was all I could think of to say. Suddenly I was near to tears, and feeling very small and very weak. If she'd simply taken me by my ear and dragged me off to the car, I'd have gone. If she'd ordered me to strip and touch my toes for the cane, I'd have done it. Only if she'd pushed me too far again would the submission she brought to me so naturally have been broken. What she did was pour me a cup of tea.

I don't know why, it seems ridiculous, but that tiny gesture made all the difference. It was hardly submission, but it gave me strength, at least enough to speak, and to ask, 'What are you doing here? How did you get here?'

'Do credit me with some intelligence, Poppy. Amber had a large parcel with a Dorset address, which was obviously what you were there to collect as your name was pinned to it.'

I shut up, feeling smaller and more stupid than ever. She went on, oblivious to the presence of the others.

'As to why, I wished to speak to you. I realise that you must feel rather foolish, running away like that, and that in the circumstances you would hardly expect me to welcome you back. Yes, I am aware of what you have said, but I am equally aware of what you think. I am prepared to forgive, Poppy.'

I just sat there, my mouth open, unable to find words. If I hadn't told her my feelings to her face I had certainly made them clear, yet she hadn't accepted them at all, sure that what she knew of my personality was everything, that I was incapable of going beyond my submission to her. To deny what she was saying was pointless. It would seem no more than childish pique, a tantrum, spiting my true need for the sake of my stupid pride.

'I am aware,' she went on, 'that there is some male about the place, down here, and that as he works he will presumably arrive this evening. While you submit to his clumsy efforts to fulfil your needs, think of me, and where I can take you. I am staying in a local bed and breakfast, Bay View. It is a little way up the hill across from the village. I will be waiting for you.'

She finished her tea and stood up, giving Nikki and June the faintest of nods as she pulled on her gloves. I still couldn't find words to express myself, and simply watched her leave, still staring at the door long after she had gone out. One thought dominated my mind, to show myself as devoted to Stephen and hope she saw.

He arrived late, with the sun already sinking behind the big hill to the west. He'd ordered lasagne for his dinner, which had been OK when we'd eaten it, maybe a little overdone. It hadn't benefited from being allowed to go cold and then reheated in the microwave. I was looking at the soggy, steaming mess and the burned bits sticking out at odd angles as June went to let him in. It went on the table anyway.

All I had on was my pinny, and he gave a pleased chuckle as he came into the kitchen. June followed behind, to come to attention beside me, while Nikki dealt with his case. He threw me his keys, which I managed to catch.

'Your uniforms are in the car, Poppet. Fetch.'

I made a hasty exit, hoping June would get the blame for the lasagne. In the boot of the car were the same three items they had, smart green jacket, brown punishment shirt and baby-doll. There was also a three-pack of white cotton knickers. I took them out, holding each up with a mixture of pride and submission. Now I could really be like them, his playthings, dolled up in a naughty little uniform designed to show me off as a man's sex toy.

What I really wanted was for Anna to see me, to watch me being paraded around by a man in my slutty little uniform, to watch me spanked, cock sucking, fucked up my bottom, and loving it. Not that it was easy to imagine her sneaking around in the undergrowth so that she could watch us through the hedge, but she was nearby, and she had to be curious.

I went in, wanting to change as soon as possible. There were smacks and howls coming from the kitchen, and I paused, torn between my desire to see June getting it and the prospect of my own fate. It was going to happen anyway, and I went in. Sure enough, she was being beaten, with a long wooden spoon, and had been bent over the table with her face an inch above the offending lasagne. Stephen looked up as I came in, paused, put the spoon down and quite casually pushed June's face into the lasagne. There was a heavy squelch followed by a bubbling sound.

'Eat,' he ordered, twisting his hand in her hair to force her to keep her head down. 'So, Poppet, do you like them?'

'Yes, Master. Thank you, Master,' I answered, to the squashy sound of June's face being rubbed in the food.

'Good,' he replied. 'I have a little discipline to impose here, but I want you dressed in ten minutes sharp, and don't forget your Lance-Corporal's stripes.'

'Yes, Master,' I promised, and scampered off to dress.

I made it, for once, washing in double quick time and pulling on the tight white knickers and my own boots. The stripes I glued on, holding them down as long as I dared before putting the jacket on; I was in uniform. It did feel good – naughty and deliciously exposed. The feel of air on my bum kept me reminded that my knickers were showing, yet with the snug jacket to make it very different from the deliberate exposure of a bikini. I was marked as a man's plaything, precisely how I wanted to be at that moment.

Back in the kitchen, June had been made to eat the entire lasagne and was licking the bowl clean. She was a mess, her face brown and filthy, with bits of mince and pasta stuck to her skin and in her hair, sauce running down her face and into her cleavage. He'd beaten her while she did it too, and her knickers were still down, with her bum a glowing red ball, blotchy with purple and still showing the neat pattern of cane marks I'd put there earlier. Stephen's cock was out and he was stroking it. Nikki stood meekly to attention in one corner, her panties rolled down to show the hairless pink crease of her pussy.

'Ah, Poppet,' he said as he saw me. 'I see you caned Boots?'

'Yes, Master,' I responded, with a sudden tight, cold sensation in my stomach.

'Fetch the cane,' he ordered. 'Knickers, you can pull up your pants now. Get dressed properly and go down to the village for a skate and chips.'

I went for the cane, my butterflies dancing crazily in my stomach. I'd known it was coming, but that didn't make it any easier. Back in the kitchen I hung my head as I offered Stephen the thin yellow stick he was about to beat me with.

'Over the table,' he ordered. 'This ought to get my appetite up.'

He laughed as I bent. Nikki was gone, but June was standing in the corner, her hands on her head and her smacked bum bare behind. I closed my eyes as the tail of my uniform jacket was twitched up.

'Another one who needs to lose weight,' Stephen remarked as he took a squeeze of one bum-cheek, and a bubble of humiliation rose in my throat to add to my fear.

Big, male hands took hold of my knickers and they were jerked roughly down, exposing my bum. He stood back and picked up the cane. I shut my eyes tight, clenching my hands and gritting my teeth, and gasped as the first cut caught me across my bum.

Again he struck, and again, each time laying a line of fire across my flesh and leaving me with one leg twitching and my breath coming in ragged, uneven pants.

'Hard case, are we?' he asked.

'No,' I managed. 'No, Master –'

He gave a sceptical grunt and struck again, harder and lower, right on my tuck. I gasped in pain, clutching at the table. Again he grunted, and suddenly I was being thrashed, the cane whipping down on me again and again, striking my bottom and thighs, curling around to catch my hip, cracking down to smack against my pussy pouch.

'Red!' I screamed. 'Stop . . . please . . . mercy. Ow! You caught my pussy . . . Master.'

'Then let that be a lesson,' he answered, dropping the cane.

I was shaking my head against the pain, but he gave me no time to get my feelings together. His hand closed in my hair; my body was dragged towards him and his cock was stuffed rudely in my mouth. He was already close to erection, and came fully hard as he jammed his cock in and out of my mouth to the tune of my grunts and muffled sobs.

'All week I've been thinking of this,' he grated, and came, right down my throat.

Immediately I was choking. Spunk exploded from my nose and around my lips, all over his balls and trousers. He kept it in, ignoring the frantic batting of my hands on the table top, emptying himself into me with a long, contented sigh. When he did stop I was left gasping, my face soiled with snot and spit and spunk, my throat and stomach twitching as I struggled not to be sick. He looked down and saw his trousers.

'Can't you sluts ever learn to just swallow?' he demanded.

He went to change, leaving me still puffing on the chair. Only when I heard the bathroom door shut did I dare to speak.

'He's in a rough mood tonight. Quick too.'

'He's been saving it up, all week, he told me.'

'Right . . . well I wish he'd taken a bit more time. I just wasn't ready!'

'Nor me. Oh my tummy!'

'You ate it, the whole lasagne?'

'Yes. He made me. I tell you, if he'd made me suck him I'd have been sick.'

'I nearly was. Why do men like to make girls choke on their cocks?'

'I suppose it feels nice. So I got lasagne and you got the spunk supper. What do you suppose he's going to do to Nikki?'

'Nothing, not now he's come.'

She gave a thoughtful nod, then spoke.

'Fancy a cuddle? He's got my bum all warm.'

'Yeah, but we'd better be quick.'

I got up. My pussy stung, and my bottom was throbbing, but I was there, high on submission and the rude, dirty way he'd used me. June was a mess, her jacket dirty all down the front, and her face a mask of brown muck. I was little better, with Stephen's spunk and my own mess all over my lower face, but I shrugged my new jacket off before taking her in my arms.

She was warm and soft, very much alive and passionate, kissing me immediately and cupping my breasts in her hands. What bad feelings I had just melted away as I took hold of her hot bottom. My thoughts turned to the way we had been treated, so casually abused, our bottoms beaten, our faces soiled. She'd been forced to eat a spoiled lasagne. I'd had a week's worth of spunk ejaculated down my throat.

Now the mess was mingling in our mouths as we kissed, and being smeared across our faces as we rubbed our noses and cheeks together in rising and ever lewder pleasure.

I wanted to lick her, from behind, with my face pressed between her hot, smacked bum-cheeks as I lapped at her pussy and bumhole. She gave no resistance as I went down, unbuttoning her jacket on the way to let her big breasts free. I suckled one briefly, and laid a trail of kisses down her belly, to her tummy button. She gave a little gasp as I sucked her piercing ring quickly between my lips, and another as I kissed the tiny triangle of pubic hair above her pussy.

She turned easily as my hands went to her hips and pushed. Her bottom came out, right into my face, and she giggled as my tongue probed between her fleshy cheeks. I could feel the heat of her beating against my face, and the roughened flesh where the spoon had caught her hard. For a moment I nuzzled, teasing myself, before wedging my tongue firmly up her bumhole, to lick at her, and swallow down her thick, earthy taste. She moaned and pushed her bum more firmly into my face. I burrowed deeper, right up her hole, feeling the rubbery little ring of her anus on my tongue.

I already wanted to come, and to do it with my tongue up her bottom. She could have peed down my chest, even filled my mouth, and I'd have just kept licking, feasting on her, bumhole and pussy too, until she came in my face. My hands went between my thighs, into the pouch of my half-lowered knickers and to my pussy. I wanted to feel her come, as I came myself, and shifted a little, pushing my mouth to her sex and wriggling my nose into the moist cavity of her bumhole. She began to moan immediately, and I could feel my pussy tensing when Stephen's voice cut in on us.

'You sluts can't leave each other alone for a moment, can you?'

He was standing in the doorway in a red silk dressing gown, his face set in an amused smile. I pulled back, trembling as I came down from the start of what had promised to be a glorious orgasm.

'No, Master. May we finish please, Master?'

'Yes,' he answered, 'in a moment. You haven't eaten yet, have you, Poppet?'

'I . . . I thought I was on a spunk supper, Master,' I answered.

'You were, but I've decided to be kind.'

He reached up to open one of the smaller cupboards above the main row. I saw some cans, big, with garish labels – orange text on a red background, some revolting-looking brown substance vaguely like meat, and a picture of a contented Labrador.

'I . . . I didn't know you had a dog, Master?' I managed – a really stupid question.

'I do.' He chuckled. 'In fact, I have four, one pedigree Irish Setter and three mongrel bitches, one of whom is about to have her supper.'

I swallowed hard, my stomach tightening still further. Had I not been on the edge of orgasm a moment before I'd have been babbling my stop-word, but I had been, and a truly horrible fascination was stealing over me as he took the tin down and placed it on the worktop.

'Are you going to be a good girl?' he demanded.

'Yes, Master,' I said, despite what every ounce of common sense and every instinct I had was screaming at me to say.

'Good,' he answered, 'that's what I like to hear. Boots, over the table a little more, bum up, legs well apart.'

She went over, lifting her bottom to make a plump, double mound of her cheeks with her pussy on plain show between. There was a faint pop as Stephen squeezed the handle of the can opener shut. An immediate smell of dog food filled the air. My stomach lurched once more.

'You're to eat it all,' Stephen instructed, twisting the opener, 'and to make her come. How's that, Boots? Aren't I a generous Master?'

'Yes, Master,' she answered.

She giggled, but the sound was nervous, and also full of relief. I wasn't surprised. She wasn't going to have to eat dog food. I was, and for all my revulsion I couldn't stop myself. I was going to do it. I wanted to do it, and I wanted to come with my mouth full of the revolting mess, my face smeared with it, my tits coated, my pussy soiled.

I shook my head, struggling to get a grip on myself, to find the will to refuse what he was about to make me do. No words would come, and all I could do was watch in horror as he peeled the lid back, took a spoon and dug it into the slimy, brown muck within the can. The spoon came up, bearing a large dollop of the dog food and the foul smell became abruptly stronger.

June's bottom was just a foot or so from my face, her pussy and anus sticky with my saliva. Stephen stepped close, holding the well-filled spoon, my last hopes that he was tormenting me fading, and then vanishing as he slapped the dog food between her cheeks, right on her anus. My stomach lurched as he squashed the mess down with the spoon, pressing it into her bumhole and up between her cheeks, over the mouth of her pussy too.

The smell was overpowering, and my urge to gag was nearly so. Still I could not find it in myself to

210

refuse, and merely watched as a second spoonful was slapped between June's big cheeks, this time on her pussy, wadding the tight hole with dog food to draw a moan of disgust from her. Stephen laughed and dug his spoon in a third time, to scoop out yet more and squash it to her sex, cramming her pussy-hole deep.

The fourth spoonful was pressed to her sex, caking her pussy-lips and clogging the little folds and grooves. The fifth went on top of the rest, and the sixth, the seventh higher, in the crease of her cheeks. Half the tin was gone and I was wishing fervently he'd owned a Chihuahua. An eighth was added, and a ninth, leaving June's bum crease piled high with reeking, lumpy dog food and her reddened skin speckled with bits of escaped jelly.

'Good girl, eat up!' Stephen laughed, and sat back.

I looked at him, and at the pile of dog food between June's bum-cheeks. He merely gestured towards it. I swallowed, forcing the bile in my throat down, and I was leaning forwards, my rational mind and my body in desperate rebellion against what I was about to do, but not my sense of submission. Then my tongue was out, poked in the dog food and I was tasting it, gagging on the foul, doggy taste and smell, but willing, more than willing . . .

Then I was eating it, my face right in the mess, guzzling it down and swallowing, my last vestige of restraint abandoned as I gave in completely to my need. Stephen laughed to see me, but I barely heard him, my whole being focused on the utterly degrading act he had made me perform, to eat dog food from between another girl's bum-cheeks, to put my face in it, to swallow it, to mouth and lick until she came, and I came too.

I slipped my hand down to my pussy, finding myself wetter than ever, my flesh puffy and sensitive, my clit a hot, urgent spot at the centre. June pushed her bum up, spreading her cheeks in my face to smear dog food over them and force more into my open mouth. I swallowed it, feeling the lumpy, slimy texture in my throat for an instant before it went down, and I had begun to masturbate.

'None of that!' Stephen ordered sharply. 'Can't you leave your cunt alone for a second?'

My hands came out of my knickers, sticky with juice. I had to come, but I had to obey too, or the reality of what I was doing would simply be too much. He'd ordered me to eat dog food and I was doing it, as his plaything, his slave, his bitch. My feelings stronger than ever, I went back to eating, taking a fresh bite and swallowing it, then burrowing my tongue in to find the wrinkly flesh of June's bumhole.

I heard the click of the door and a fresh, bitter stab of humiliation caught me as I thought of Nikki seeing me. Half the dog food was down my throat, the other half between her cheeks, up her hole and smeared in my face. Nikki gasped at what she saw, and with that sound I felt my tears start, rolling heavily from my eyes as I forced myself to swallow yet another foul mouthful.

'You can make her come now,' Stephen offered casually, and a great wash of utterly pathetic gratitude came over me.

Everything from her crease was in my stomach, or down my tits and belly, and I began to lick at flesh, cleaning her cheeks and the valley between, her bumhole, poking my tongue in to winkle out a bit of dog food which had lodged up her hole. She sighed and lifted her bum to encourage me, and I set to work on her sex.

Her pussy was full of it, wadded well in to form a disgusting slimy paste. I had to suck it out, and chew on it before I could swallow, but that left her sex merely smeared. I began to lap, more bits falling on to my tits as I became clumsy in my urgency. June sighed and I burrowed my nose up her bum as before, only now with her tight little hole squashy with dog food.

I heard Stephen's chuckle and caught the waft of fish and chips, which brought me one step closer to being sick all over June's bum, and then she was coming, right in my face, her pussy twitching, her bumhole pulsing on the tip of my nose, wriggling her bottom to smear what was left of the dog food over my face and into my hair, up my nose and into my eyes. I kept at it, until I heard her cry of ecstasy and felt her muscles lock, still licking, with dirty spit running down my chin, over her pussy mound and down on to my tits and into my knickers. Again she cried out, louder than before, calling me a filthy bitch and a slut and her darling, and then it was over and she had gone limp. Swallowing my final mouthful of muck and pussy juice, I sat back on my haunches.

There was no choice, I simply had to come. Catching up my slimy tits in my hands, I began to smear the dog food over them, rubbing it into my nipples and revelling in the disgusting texture. My pussy was going to be next, maybe with a handful of the dog food left in the can down my knickers to give me something to rub in, maybe . . .

'Uh, uh, no you don't,' Stephen said around a mouthful of skate. 'Now be a good girl, Poppet, and you'll get what you need. Your turn, Knickers.'

'Master,' I panted, 'please no . . . I couldn't . . . I'm going to be sick . . .'

'Not you, silly girl,' he said. 'You get to come now, for being such an obedient little slut. Knickers is the one who's had no dinner.'

She'd understood the first time, and was looking on in wide-mouthed horror.

'Well?' he demanded. 'Should I have to give my orders twice?'

'N – no, Master,' she stammered.

'Then get on with it,' he ordered. 'Up on the table, Poppet. You can prepare her, Boots, and make sure you get plenty up her cunt.'

I had to come, and it was only fair. If Nikki couldn't back out, then I wasn't going to refuse what I'd just given June. I got up slowly, and took June's place over the table, lifting my bottom into the same lewd posture. June came behind me and took down my knickers, just far enough, and reached for the can of dog food. Nikki stepped close, her nose wrinkling in disgust, her face set in utter misery. I spread my legs, stretching my dropped knickers taut between my thighs and June smeared the first dollop on to my pussy.

It went up, filling my hole as she pressed it in with the spoon and I was shaking my head in a mixture of dizzy bliss and self-disgust. I was having my hole filled with dog food and I was about to come over it. My stomach was full of it too, my evening meal, a can of dog food, mixed with June's pussy juice and Stephen's spunk, and I was about to come over it.

More was slapped between my cheeks, on to my bumhole and over my pussy, plastered on, thick and sticky and lumpy. Some went in my anus, and my pussy was bulging before she stopped, six good spoonfuls' worth now piled up between my spread cheeks and up my hole. It felt awful, filling me with that same helpless, breathless sense of being filthy dirty and utterly liberated that comes with a full nappy.

I stuck up my bottom, eager for Nikki's tongue as I focused on the feel of the wet, squashy mess

214

between my cheeks and the filthy thoughts spinning in my head. She was behind me, stripping, her top already gone, her hands at the button of her jeans. Stephen and June said nothing, both watching in disgusted fascination. Nikki's jeans came down and off, her knickers, socks and shoes with them. Naked, she got down on her knees and her face was hidden from view.

'Do it,' Stephen ordered, 'all the way, Knickers, every last mouthful, and make Poppet come.'

'Yes, Master,' I heard her answer, her voice weak, trembling.

He gave a satisfied chuckle and put a large chip into his mouth. She took me gently by my legs, her face touched my spread bottom and she was doing it, her face in the dog food as she ate her revolting supper. I'd done the same, revelling in it, swallowing it down, nuzzling my face between June's ripe, cheeky bottom, licking her anus and pussy, feeding from her dirty holes, Stephen's filthy little bitch . . .

I had to come, but I forced myself to hold off, to let it happen the way it was supposed to. Nikki made a queer gulping noise and I knew she'd swallowed her first mouthful. Again her face pressed between my cheeks, and this time her tongue touched flesh, between my bumhole and pussy. I felt her lips as she took in a second mouthful, and heard her gulp once more. She had less to eat, and with the third mouthful her lips found my anus, kissing my bumhole to suck the bits of dog food out.

That was too much. My head was full of dirty thoughts, full to bursting point, both submissive and dominant. There was the disgusting taste in my mouth and the feel of Nikki's lips on my anus. There was my filthy state, in nothing but dog-food-soiled knickers, and her, nude, her face smeared with the

same muck. There was myself as a grovelling, punished little bitch and her as the same, made to eat her
filthy dinner from my clogged pussy and slimy
bumhole.

I reached back, simply unable to wait, and began
to masturbate in the slimy mess of dog food and
Nikki's spit coating my pussy. Her mouth found my
pussy-hole . . . my cunt-hole, sucking, to draw out the
wad of packed-in dog food. My bum cheeks
tightened; my pussy began to twitch. Nikki made the
same queer gulping noise again, only louder. I
realised she was puking as I started to come, and as
my orgasm hit me, hot, slippery sick spattered over
my bottom and filled the pouch of my half-dropped
knickers around my snatching fingers.

Ten

I woke to a vague sense of loss, which I only managed to place when I realised that Nikki wasn't in bed beside me. She was on breakfast duty, so I rolled over, glad I wasn't expected to cope. I felt a little sore and a little weak, also mentally exhausted. It was no time to be made to eat spunk for breakfast.

Coffee was a better bet, and I finally managed to lever myself up on the pillows, hoping that Nikki would still be at the breakfast-making stage and not the cock-sucking stage. There was no sign of her, and June was still asleep, cuddled up to her pillow with her thumb stuck in her mouth.

Something was missing, and I realised what it was as I reached the kitchen. There was no smell of coffee, nor bacon, nor sausages nor any of the other things Stephen might have wanted, only the tang of the antiseptic we'd used to clean up the night before. He'd made us do it in our work fatigues, and stood over us with a switch until everything was spotless, but by the time we'd finished we'd been too exhausted for any more sex.

That meant Stephen had presumably woken up with an erection and come in to get Nikki. I began to make coffee, hoping to be able to drink it in peace, only for Stephen to call out before the kettle had even boiled.

'Knickers!'

I stuck my head around the door, to see him with his back to me, in his red silk robe, looking into our bedroom.

'Isn't she with you?' I asked even as it sank in that she very obviously wasn't.

'No,' he replied, his dominant tone gone on the instant.

'Well, she's not with us,' I told him. 'Maybe she went out for a walk.'

He didn't answer, but he was looking distinctly worried, and guilty. She'd been quiet after being sick down my knickers, but still obedient. She'd kissed me good night happily enough, but we hadn't had sex before sleep. I'd been too tired, also sore and pretty well satisfied. I'd offered a lick, but she'd only wanted a cuddle.

Now worried, I made for the front door. Sure enough, the mortice lock was off, and a piece of paper had been stuck into the letterbox. It bore a single word, 'sorry'.

That was the end of Saturday, so far as anything naughty went anyway. Stephen went into an immediate fit of guilt, biting his nails and walking around in small circles before he finally got his act together enough to go and look for her. I wasn't too worried, as I was pretty sure I knew where she'd gone, and it wasn't over the cliff, which was the first place he went to look.

June had guessed too, and agreed that we couldn't tell Stephen. She also agreed to spare me by going up to Bay View while Stephen went down to search the beach. Twenty minutes later she was back. Sure enough, Nikki was with Anna, and had no intention of coming back.

By the time Stephen returned he was at the end of his tether, but June had the sense to report that she'd been seen getting into a cab outside the pub that morning. Stephen still wasn't entirely satisfied, but finally calmed down when we pointed out that she had taken most of her things, all, in fact, except her three uniforms and a few bits and pieces that had been scattered around the cottage.

Hardly surprisingly, there was no more play that day. Stephen felt guilty because he was sure he'd pushed her too far. I tried to explain that it was more that he punished her when she didn't deserve it than what he had actually done, but it fell on deaf ears. I wasn't too happy either, because Nikki and I had got on well, and if she became Anna's partner that was the end of our relationship, or at least the best part of it. Only June showed any spirit, pointing out that the three of us could still have fun. Stephen obviously thought she was being callous and wouldn't go for it, to my relief.

He'd changed his mind in the morning, either that or his cock had taken over his brain again. We woke at nearly ten, and June was ordered to perform cock-sucking duty while I had breakfast. She complied, and so did I, insisting only that we were allowed coffee and bacon and eggs as well instead of the usual mouthful of spunk. He agreed, and there was a brief discussion of roles and stop-words as we drank our second and third cups of coffee on the patio. Finally he rallied himself.

'Right, enough nonsense. Strip off, both of you, and put your boots on. Today, you learn how to be pony-girls.'

It was a long time since I'd been a pony-girl – too long. I pushed my ill feelings over Nikki and Anna to the back of my mind and drained my coffee.

'Yes, Master. I'll fetch the harness.'

June was in just her boots by the time I got back, the rest of her clothes strewn any-old-how on the ground. I began to sort out the harness, separating bridles, body harness and wrist cuffs from the tangle of leather straps and laying the tails carefully out on the table. Without Nikki I could have a tail, which was good, so at least I'd gained something.

I stripped quickly and pulled on my boots, my body already tingling with the pleasure of naked irresponsibility that is one of the best things about being a pony-girl. Stephen obviously wasn't going to help, and had sat back, watching. June got confused in no time, and I had to help her, fitting the bridle to her head and tightening the straps, putting her wrist cuffs on and adjusting her body harness until it was snug around her waist and shoulders. As a final touch I tied her reins to the door handle and clipped her wrist cuffs to the back of her harness, leaving her helpless, with her boobs, bum and pussy all quite bare, the way a pony-girl should be.

Putting my own harness on was easy, all the little tricks coming straight back to me. June could only wait and watch, bound and helpless to get free, until I too was fully in gear, bearing our tails.

'Do you want to?' I offered, holding mine out to Stephen along with the pot of lube.

'Show me,' he answered. 'I'll do Boots.'

I nodded and twisted the tail around, to leave the butt plug sticking up. Just to know it was going up my bumhole, and in front of him, was enough to set me trembling. I lubed it up, making sure he saw that I put plenty on, then scooped some more out and reached back to slip my finger up my bumhole, pushing it deep and fingering myself for a bit to get it well up and open my ring. He watched, smiling.

With my bumhole juicy and open, I popped my finger quickly in my mouth and put the tail back between my cheeks. The tip of the plug slid up easily, and I couldn't help but sigh as my ring stretched wide to take the bulb, leaving me feeling ever so slightly stretched in my rectum. A twist of the harness strap and it was fixed in place, the plug well up my bum and the shaft rising between my cheeks to make the actual tail appear to sprout from the base of my spine.

I turned, showing them my profile and my rear view, each time wiggling my bum to make the tail swish over my cheeks. Stephen gave an appreciative nod and squeezed his crotch, took June's tail and stood up. Her response was to stick her bottom out, making her cheeks spread to show off the colourful little hole between. Stephen gave her a gentle pat, stuck his finger into the lube pot and slid it straight up her bum.

She gasped as her anus was invaded, but immediately began to purr and wiggle her bottom as he fingered her hole. Taking the tail, he dipped the butt plug into the lube, bringing it up well smeared. His finger came out of her bottom with a sticky noise and the plug went up, pushed deep with a single firm motion. She gasped again, but took it, her anus closing on the tail shaft before she stood and allowed him to fasten it off.

I stayed stock still as he clipped my wrists to my harness. It had been so long, but I could feel myself slipping into role, responsible only to the most basic commands, indifferent to my nudity or to the whole wide panoply of human morals. My bladder was already a little full from all the coffee I'd drunk, and I just let it go, my pee spraying out on to the concrete of the patio and running down my thighs to fill my boots. It felt squishy and warm, and in the back of my mind I knew I'd just ruined a perfectly good pair of black suede ankle boots. I didn't care. I was a pony-girl.

Stephen gave me a cut of the riding crop I'd brought out and I managed a pained snicker in response. A moment later he'd turned the hose on me, making me snort and stamp as I was hastily washed down with the jet of chilly water and left dripping in the sun with my nipples erect and steam rising gently from my skin.

He was laughing as he went, as cruel an owner as he was a Master. I considered running, but stayed, mindful of his crop as my welt was stinging quite badly. June also stayed, still and patient, just watching from the corner of her eye until he came back with the cart.

It was heavy, and clumsy, never designed as anything but an ornament. He still managed to attach our harness to the shafts after a couple of false starts, and climbed in behind us. His crop smacked on my flesh once more and we were off, trotting up the lawn, and back, in a broad oval as he slowly got us under proper control.

I was moving to the tugs on my reins and the flicks of his crop from the start, and June quickly got the hang of it. Soon he had us high-stepping and steering between two bamboo posts, cantering and making fast turns. He also had us running sweat and panting, with the sun hot on our aching bodies, our nipples stiff and our pussies wet.

At last he turned us back to the patio, where we were parked and unhitched from the cart. I stood as my reins were hitched off, the sweat trickling freely down my body, wiggling slightly to ease a sudden itch from the plug in my bottom. Stephen chuckled as he picked up the hose.

'Eager, are we? Maybe this will cool you down.'

He twisted the tap and the jet caught me full in the chest, splashing cold water over me, and June too. Before it had been a shock, now it was bliss. We revelled in it, letting the water play on our breasts and bellies, sticking our bottoms out to let him get down into our sticky creases, opening our mouths to gulp down as much of the cool, refreshing water as we could.

By the time he'd finished amusing himself he had his cock out, half-stiff in his hand. We were to be fucked, maybe buggered, our juicy bumholes surely tempting for his cock once our plugs were out, and certainly ready. Sure enough.

'Over the table, look sharp,' he ordered, once more picking up his crop. 'I think it's about time you learned how this feels up that cheeky bottom of yours, Boots.'

Neither of us moved, until a couple of well-aimed flicks of the crop had added new welts to our poor abused bottoms. With that we both bent, laying our torsos on the table, helpless to support ourselves with our bound hands, or to protect ourselves. I for one didn't want to. I wanted to be buggered soundly and spunked up, but it looked like it was going to be June who got the treatment.

He got behind her and I heard the sucking noise of her plug being withdrawn. She gave a little whimper and I pressed close, to kiss her, our lips meeting around our bits as for the first time in her life she felt a man's cock press to her bumhole. She gasped and I knew it was in, her anus invaded and her rectum being slowly but surely stuffed with penis as she began to grunt and pant into my mouth.

She took it noisily as ever, mumbling and crying out through her bit as she was buggered, but still trying to nuzzle me. I thought he'd spunk up her, eager to give the virgin the full treatment, but in what seemed like no time at all he was pulling out, to leave her bumhole to close with a long, soft fart.

It was my turn, and I closed my eyes as his fingers took hold of my tail plug. Slowly he pulled it out, to leave my bumhole gaping and slimy behind me, ready for cock. I got it, immediately, his bulbous helmet pushed to my anus and in, up into my rectum. Buggered, I began to gasp and grunt, no more restrained than June, with my bottom squashing to his pushes and my boobs slapping on the table top in time.

Again I thought he was going to spunk, and again he didn't, keeping it in me just long enough to leave me truly desperate for orgasm. I couldn't frig, not with my arms clipped up behind my back, or even rub myself on anything. All I could do was squirm on the table as he once more inserted his cock into June's bottom-hole. She took it with a series of little grunts, pop-eyed all the while, until it was wedged right up. Only as he began to move in her rectum did she close her eyes, and I saw her mouth go slack with pleasure, spit running out where her lower lip protruded beneath her bit.

I stayed still, my body focused on the two sloppy holes behind, and my need to have them filled. June was getting it, and it was impossible not to feel jealous as Stephen puffed and groaned his way to orgasm up her bum. I was hoping he would pull out, to finish up me, but when he suddenly began to push hard and June's noises grew suddenly pained I realised it was too late. A moment later I heard his cry of ecstasy and knew he had come in her rectum.

He pulled out, to flop into one of the garden chairs, not even troubling to force one of us to suck his cock clean. I wiggled my bottom, hoping he'd take mercy on me, but he closed his eyes. June looked round, right at me, her pretty face loose with reaction to her buggery, her eyes half-lidded. I kissed her, then stood, with difficulty, and nodded to the lawn.

She came, waddling slightly, and flopped down on the grass. I did the same and we rolled together, Stephen now watching with a sneer of casual amusement on his face. June swung one plump thigh over my head, and the sight of him was replaced with that of her naked bottom and pussy, a moment before it was all lowered into my face.

I was not comfortable, my body cocked sideways to spare my clipped-up arms, with a good deal of June's weight on my shoulders and head. My thighs came open anyway, around her head, locking her in place, and, as her tongue found my pussy, so mine found hers. We began to lick, in mutual need, lapping urgently at each other's pussy, and in my case also slurping up the spunk running from her well-buggered anus.

It was wonderfully dirty, bound and buggered, strapped up helpless and used as pony-girls then made to take his cock up our bottoms. My head was full of the taste and smell of pussy and spunk and sweat, leaving me dizzy with dirty pleasure as she worked on my clitoris, bringing me up and up towards orgasm.

My thighs tightened around her head and I was there, coming with her head clamped hard to my pussy. I stuck my tongue well in her dirty bumhole as the ecstasy washed away any last trace of inhibition, and I kept it there as my body shook and twitched in climax, swallowing my mouthful of spunk and juice an instant before a peak hit me, so high that I lost all control, to lie jerking spasmodically under her body.

I licked her again the instant I'd recovered, right on her clitty. Her thighs went wide, spreading her sex in my face and I redoubled my efforts, lapping and rubbing my nose into her pussy-hole and anus, faster and faster until she gave a final, ecstatic cry and once more buried her face in my sex. I held her tight with my legs until she had finished, still lapping at her all the while. When she at last rolled off we both collapsed on to the lawn, giggling in dirty satisfaction and at the sight of each other's sticky, soiled face.

'Sluts,' Stephen remarked. 'Into the shower, both of you.'

'Yes, Master,' June answered, pulling herself to her knees.

He came to unfasten us and we ran into the house together, to shower and to clean our tack. He stayed outside, as indifferent as ever post-orgasm, speaking only to demand a beer. I brought it out to him naked and wet, then went back to dry, powder and lubricate my slightly sore bottom-hole. We got into uniform, including clean boots, and, despite June's jacket being less than perfectly smart, put lunch together for Stephen.

June sat with him to eat, as per our new agreement, but I wasn't all that hungry and contented myself with a ham sandwich and a bottle of deliciously cold beer. The day was blazing hot, and I was soon beginning to feel a little drowsy after the morning's pony-girl play. Dozing on the lawn seemed a good idea, and I went in to fetch some suntan lotion, then strolled up across the garden.

We'd been showing off all morning, and in far ruder condition than simply being naked, never mind being buggered and going sixty-nine with June. It occurred to me to take a closer look at the hedge, just for the sake of security. It was beech, with the silvery little trunks intertwined and the dark green foliage making a pretty solid barrier. Only in a couple of places had rabbits or something made runs between the trunks, leaving little paths of golden sand. They were small, but ducking down I found I could peer through, to a little patch of grass among brambles, grass that looked suspiciously flat.

Curious, I pushed through, just managing to squeeze my body between the beech trunks before coming up on the far side panting and dishevelled. Sure enough, the grass in the glade had been flattened, and a narrow track between the bramble bushes had been cleared recently. We had a Peeping Tom.

I was not going to try and accost him, not on my own. He had probably seen me being very rude indeed, and might well not want to take no for an answer. Just knowing he'd been there had me more than a little scared, and I was about to burrow back through the hedge to fetch Stephen when there was a rustle among the brambles. I nearly wet my knickers, and was scrabbling at the hedge as a huge figure loomed up over the bushes, his grotesquely painted clown face leering at me in a dirty, idiot grin. Pee squirted into my panties ... an instant before I realised it was Fat Jeff. He was in camouflage of pale grey and faded tan, both jacket and trousers, and wearing a clown mask. I was shaking hard, and it took me a moment to find my voice.

'You bastard, Jeff! You scared me ... you made me wet myself!'

'Cute! Let's see.'

'Fuck off, Jeff!'

'Don't get mad, Pops. I didn't mean to scare you.'

'You didn't? What are you doing creeping around the bushes in that stupid mask then?'

'It was just a laugh.'

'Very funny.'

We went silent, both looking at the other. He shrugged, looking sheepish, and pulled the mask up.

'Sorry.'

'OK, just don't ever do that to me again. What are you doing here anyway?'

'I had to see, didn't I? I mean, old Soapy Stanbrook with three girl slaves? What a laugh!'

'Two girl slaves. Nikki ... Knickers has gone off with my ex, Anna, who is also down here uninvited. But how did you know?'

'Give me a break, Pops. You're talking to Mr Hacker here.'

'So you got his address off a computer at work?'

'Yeah, easy.'

'And the rest?'

'It wouldn't take Sherlock Holmes, Poppy. And I've been lurking in UK Masters and Slaves.'

'You have? Under what name?'

'Mr Big.'

'That was you? But in your profile it said –'

'And you believed it!? Get real, girl. Anyway, laugh, wasn't it? You are one fucking little prick tease, you know that?'

'I'd have done it, for real, only I didn't like your fantasy. And you had your fun with us later, didn't you?'

'Yeah, that was good.'

He nodded and put his hand to his crotch, rubbing an obviously swollen cock.

'You are an utter bastard, Jeff.'

'Yeah, and you love it. Nice uniform, by the way, and I love the panties. How about a blow-job, or a quick rub up your bum slit?'

'Jeff!'

'Or some clown action? You and the Indian-looking tart with the tits could –'

'Jeff, I don't know what you're on, but June and I are supposed to be down here as Stephen's slaves. You're not supposed to know!'

'Yeah, but he's going back this evening. I'm not. I've taken a week and I'm camping up on the hill. Tell you what, here's a game. There's a big bar of chocolate in my tent. You've got to get it, right, only if I catch you I get to fuck you –'

'No, Jeff . . .'

Then it struck me. If there was one thing I could absolutely guarantee, it was Anna's attitude to Jeff. He represented everything she despised most about men, from his dress sense to his habit of spunking in girls' faces. She had Nikki, but that didn't necessarily mean she had given up on me.

'. . . not now, anyway,' I finished. 'Maybe tomorrow.'

'Yeah, I meant tomorrow. Gabs coming down?'

'Yes, she is. OK, I'll tell June, who's Boots from UK Masters in case you hadn't figured that out . . .'

'Yeah, trust me on that one.'

'. . . and we'll play your game tomorrow if she can handle it. For now, just fuck off, will you? Go and wank in your tent or something.'

'I did, right after what I saw this morning. You are one dirty bitch, licking his spunk out of her arsehole . . .'

'OK, OK,' I cut in, feeling the blood rush to my face. 'Come down after Stephen's gone then. I'll introduce you to June.'

'Sure, but how about a bit now? What I'd really like is to rub off up that little white panty seat.'

'Don't be stupid, you'd get spunk all over my knickers.'

'So? You've wet 'em anyway.'

'So Stephen's going to want to know who I've been with. What am I supposed to tell him, that I met a Peeping Tom and let him rub up my bottom?'

'Yeah, that's true. Pop 'em down then, I'll do it up your slit. You love a good slit fuck, don't you?'

'Jeff!'

'Aw, go on, Pops, please. I'm fucking bursting for you here.'

He had pulled down the zip of his combat trousers as he spoke, to flop out his cock, the head already half out of the foreskin. I caught the cock smell and swallowed. He began to wank, rolling his foreskin back to show off the big, damp helmet within and the smell became abruptly stronger.

'Go on, Pops,' he urged. 'Look at the state you've got me in, and it's not like it was the first time, is it?'

I nodded. It wasn't. We had him quite well trained too, well enough to help us come even after he had.

'How're you getting on with that dirty German book? You got to the one where the fat railway guard pisses up the girl's arse?'

I nodded. We had, and had come over it together. It showed a scene in a railway siding, five pictures, with an immensely fat man in a green railway uniform and a young girl in a fur coat. The sequence showed him catching her, spanking her bare bottom, buggering her, relieving himself up her bottom, and laughing as she ran away with a mixture of spunk and urine squirting from her bumhole.

'My favourite, that,' Jeff said, catching up his balls to show off his now rigid erection. 'Come on, doll, stick that little round arse out.'

'No, Jeff . . . we can't do it here anyway. What if Stephen hears us?'

He nodded towards the hedge. I couldn't see over at all, but ducked down. Stephen wasn't there. Nor was June. It looked like I was going to get my bottom rubbed.

'Oh, OK! Honestly, Jeff!'

I stuck my hands into the hedge, to grip on to the two biggest beech branches I could find, low, with my legs set well apart and my bum stuck out so that the tail of my uniform jacket rose to show off my knickers.

'Like this?'

'Perfect,' he grunted. 'You have one gorgeous arse, Pops. I want to do you up your panties for a bit. I promise I won't mess them.'

'OK, fine, but get on with it, and you're to help me come, all right?'

He just laughed, but I knew he'd do it. Then he was behind me, his massive belly pressed to my back and his cock to the seat of my knickers, rubbing. I clung on tight, wishing he'd put a bit less weight on me yet revelling in the sensation of being so crudely used. I could feel the stickiness of my pee around my sex where I'd wet myself, and I was ready for cock.

'That is nice,' he sighed. 'I could spunk right now . . .'

'Don't. Pull down my knickers, fuck me.'

'In a minute. I like a dry cock on panty cotton.'

I held still, letting him rub as I waited for my fucking, a fantasy already building in my head. He'd scared me, and if he had been a stranger I'd have been screaming for Stephen at the top of my voice and he'd have got the toe of my boot in his balls. It hadn't been a stranger; it had been Jeff, but I'd still wet my knickers in sheer fright. Now I was to be fucked, by a fat man in a clown mask, a man who'd peeped at me, who'd caught me in my knickers and jacket, who'd talked me into letting him rub himself off in my bum crease.

'Put your mask on,' I urged him, 'and pop it in . . . please.'

He moved to pull the mask down over his face. I glanced back, to find the idiot clown grin staring me right in the face, the wide, painted eyes open in what

231

seemed to me a cruel lust, the fat red lips curved up in mirth. That was how he'd see me, with mirth and lust, turned on by my body, but amused too, at the outfit I'd been made to wear, at his power over me.

I pushed my bottom out more, to feel his balls as they pressed to the tuck of my bum. My cheeks spread, his cock pushing my knickers down between, tickling my anus and pussy-lips. I moaned in pleasure, no longer caring if he spunked up over my knickers or not, but needing my climax more than ever. Then, suddenly, he had jerked my knickers down and his hot, rock-hard cock was touching my bare flesh, rubbing hard, with his big balls resting in my lowered knickers.

'Fuck me, Jeff,' I panted. 'Go on, put it up, right up ...'

He moved, his cock head nudging between my cheeks, against my bumhole, on my sex, up it, hard in, all the way, out again and slipping in the wet mush of my flesh, not up my hole, but between my lips, right on to my clit. I cried out at the sudden, exquisite shock, and then he was rubbing between my sex-lips, his cock and balls caught in my knickers, using my wet pussy as a slide.

'Fucking gorgeous,' he grunted, and came, spunking in my knickers and over my pussy, on the ground under my face too.

I snatched back, bracing myself one-handed as I took his hot, slimy cock shaft and started to rub it on myself. He was still coming, pumping spunk up my wrist, and as I got the pressure to my clitty I knew I'd be joining him in seconds.

Only in my head it wasn't him at all. It was some stranger, some pervert, some Peeping Tom. I'd come out of the garden in my little green uniform jacket, my tight white knickers, my smart little boots. I'd seen the clown mask, screamed, frozen and been caught. I'd been made to pose. I'd had my knickers pulled down. I'd had my bum crease rutted up . . . been slit-fucked, fucked properly, and what had I done? Had I fought back? Had I screamed and cursed and begged for it not to happen? No, I'd grabbed his cock and rubbed myself to ecstasy like the dirty, lewd little tart I am.

I came, screaming out my passion once before biting hard on a mouthful of beech leaves to stop it happening again. Jeff was trying to pull back, and complaining about something, but I had him by the cock and took no notice, finishing myself off with his fat, slimy shaft on my clitty until I was fully satisfied. Only when I finally let go of him did I realise what he was saying.

'. . . you mind your fucking nails, girl. Jesus!'

'Sorry, Jeff,' I managed as he doubled up, clutching his cock.

He stood up, to remove his clown mask. He was red-faced and sweaty, also wincing slightly as he bent to inspect his cock.

'Fuck that hurts! You really dug your nails in, Poppy.'

'Sorry, I got a bit carried away. Anyway, there's no blood.'

He blew his fat cheeks out and nodded his head. I made to pull my knickers up, but had second thoughts as I felt the now cold wet in the crotch. Looking down, I found my gusset stained yellow and slimy with spunk.

'I was happy doing it up your cunt,' Jeff pointed out.

'Forget it,' I answered, slipping them off. 'I'd better go before Stephen comes out. If he catches me like this I'll tell him I was playing with myself.'

He nodded and reached out to pinch my cheek as I ducked down to the hole in the bushes. I went backwards, my bare bum stuck out towards the lawn, which would have been asking for trouble if anyone had been there to see. They weren't, and once I'd sneaked in and deposited my dirty knickers in the wash basket I discovered why. Both were on Stephen's bed, June in just her open jacket and boots, no knickers.

I let them be, quite happy to have some time to myself after the exertions of the day, and pretty drowsy myself. So I got into my bikini bottoms, retrieved my suntan lotion, took another beer from the fridge and a book of ghost stories from the cottage's limited selection and went out to sunbathe on the lawn.

Knowing Jeff was there made me feel a lot better about Anna. Monday now looked more promising than worrying. If Anna saw Jeff she would stay away, I was sure. Even if she didn't, the almost hypnotic draw she had to submissive girls would have no effect on him whatever. She might as well try to give orders to a brick.

I'd got to the point in the story where a gibbering ectoplasmic thing was chasing the heroine around a house, when I fell asleep. Inevitably I dreamed I was her, and the thing had leaped on to my back and was about to fuck me when I woke up to find myself pinned down on the lawn, only by something considerable beefier than any ectoplasm. It was June, sitting astride me, and before I could react a leather cage had been pulled on over my head. I made to protest but only got the gag piece thrust into my mouth, and a moment later she had fastened the buckle at the back of my neck. I managed a stifled protest as she climbed off me, but she just laughed.

'Don't get your knickers in a twist. Stephen's got to go in a few hours. Then it's just you and me all week.'

I staggered to my feet, instantly suspicious that she had planned some horrible revenge on me for bossing her around and beating her. Before I could get my hands to the buckle of my head harness she had grappled me. We began to struggle, June laughing, me still hazy with sleep. I'd have won, maybe, if Stephen hadn't appeared, holding more gear.

He made short work of me, June helping to subdue my struggles as my wrists were pulled tight into the small of my back and strapped up, a thick leather collar and lead fastened around my neck and my ankles put in heavy, leather cuffs. I was still struggling, and tripped over my cuffs the moment they'd been fastened together, to sprawl headlong on the lawn. June was doubled up with laughter, but found the control to reach down and tug my bikini pants off my bottom. Stephen joined her, pulling my pants further down before rolling me over. Gripping my ankles, he pushed, forcing me to raise my knees. My lead was taken, twisted once around my ankle cuffs and clipped off, to leave me bound and helpless with my bare bottom stuck out and my pussy showing, and available. He still had some gear, one of the pony-girl harnesses, which he opened and wrapped around my tummy before fastening it at the back and tying a length of thick, black rope to the rings at the rear. He chuckled as he stood up, but it was June who spoke.

'As you're bound to abuse your position as Corporal during the week, our Master has kindly agreed to allow me to take a little on tick. Are you nice and comfy?'

I shook my head.

'Ah, what a shame. Never mind, I'm sure you'll be OK. If you would, please, Master?'

Stephen stooped down, to lift me easily, cradled in his arms as he walked across to the edge of the lawn where several trees extended thick branches out over the garden. I was laid down, just in the shade. June had followed, and stood watching, her arms folded across her chest, her mouth set in a cruel little smile. She hadn't bothered to put her knickers on, or do up her jacket, and the plump mound of her pussy and one chubby tit showed, a look that now seemed more cruel than vulnerable.

She passed Stephen the end of my rope and he threw it up, high over a branch. One tug and I had been rolled over, two and only my forehead was in touch with the ground, three and I was in the air, swinging gently backwards and forwards. A fourth tug lifted me to the level of his crotch and he stopped, his muscles straining as he tied the rope off to the hedge. June gave me one last, sadistic grin and made for the house. Stephen checked his knot, gave the rope a single hard jerk and nodded in satisfaction.

'That will hold.'

I was belly down, and spinning slowly around. My bum brushed his sleeve as he made a quick check of the knots behind my back and I felt a new pang of vulnerability. He was going to fuck me, I was sure.

He stepped away, but only to the patio. Taking a chair he brought it close, sat down and calmly undid his fly. His cock came free and he began to stroke it as he admired my bound and helpless body. I wondered if Fat Jeff was watching, and if he too would have his cock in his hand.

June reappeared, and my sense of vulnerability and fear increased sharply as I saw that she was carrying the tawse, two fat rubber dildos and the pot of lubricant. Her grin was manic as she came up to me, and grew worse as she smeared lube on to the tip of the dildos. Both were black, knobbly and cock-shaped, only bigger than any reasonable-sized man's erection. A shiver went through me as I found myself seriously wondering if my bumhole could take it.

I shook my head, as she prodded one of the massive dildos at my pussy, twisting it to smear the lube over me. My hole came wide, stretching to the big rubbery plug, and it was in me, filling me like the fattest possible cock. She pushed it up, the knobs bumping on my sensitive flesh, leaving me bloated and my bumhole feeling impossibly small. Her finger found my anus, smearing my ring with grease, then slipping inside. She began to rummage around and after a moment stuck a second finger in, speaking as she buggered me, her voice mocking my own.

'A girl can always take a cock up her bum, if she wants to. Isn't that right, Poppet?'

Stephen gave a chuckle. His cock was hard, but he knew I could take that, and so did she. The dildo was bigger, yes, but there was something about her manner, and what she said that told me I had some horrible surprise in store. Her fingers came out; the dildo head was pushed to my bumhole, and I had forgotten about everything except trying to accommodate the monstrous thing in my rectum.

I pushed out, and felt my ring spread wide on the fat, slippery head, wide and wider still, until the first stab of pain came and I was wiggling my bum in a desperate effort to escape. She waited a moment, the dildo head just in my bumhole, then pushed again. Once more I pushed out in return, and once more I felt my bum ring spread, wide and wider still, stretched until my teeth were gritted against the pain and I knew I could take no more.

'Good girl!' June said sweetly. 'See, Master, she can take it.'

I was left panting, my bumhole agape, but plugged, with the head of the dildo wedged in. June slapped on

237

more lube and began to work it in, bit by bit, invading my bumhole and stretching my rectum, until both my holes felt bloated, seemingly right up to my throat.

With me safely stuffed, she stepped back to pick up the tawse. She was going to catch my pussy-lips, and I was shaking my head and writhing as she got into position to whip me, desperate to make it clear to her what she was about to do. Stephen just sat back to watch me whipped, stroking his cock. She was going to get my pussy; she couldn't miss, with my lips sticking out between my thighs.

The tawse came in with a whistle and smacked against my flesh, full across the fattest part of my bum. My muscles jerked and I was whimpering into my gag at the sudden, heavy pain, delivered before my body had had a chance to respond. Five minutes before I'd been fast asleep, and now I hung from a tree, bound and helpless to her whip.

Again she struck, lower, filling me with raw fear for my sex and setting me twitching and jerking in my bonds. I was spinning too, slowly, so the third caught my hip, cracking in so hard my hurt leg went into spasm, my anus too, tensing on the huge plug in my rectum. June burst out laughing at the sight.

It was the eighth, maybe the ninth stroke that caught my pussy-lips. It hurt crazily, and set me bucking and writhing in my straps, my pussy and bumhole in frantic, pained contraction, the muscles of my legs and belly too. June stood back, her hand to her mouth.

'Whoops, cunt shot! Sorry, Poppet.'

I turned to glare at her. The hot welt was already rising across my sex-lips, a burning line far, far worse than those she put across my already beaten bum-cheeks. It hurt, but it had got to me, and for the tears

238

that were threatening to start in my eyes I knew I was ripe for Stephen's cock.

He knew it too, and stood, lost to my view as he got behind me. The dildo was pulled from my pussy-hole, the full length of his cock slid up into my body and I was being fucked, his hands on the rope to make me swing back and forth on his erection. I was trembling, dizzy with pain and close to my limit, but not there, not quite. I could come, maybe, as I was. He would fuck me, leave me running spunk. She would beat me again, smack the vicious tawse to my sex, not hard, but hard enough ...

Stephen's cock erupted in my body as he drove it in, suddenly, hard, and his mobile rang. He cursed, still holding himself deep in me, only to pull out and dash for the cottage. June watched him go, then came close.

'Sorry, Poppy, I didn't mean to hurt you ... well, I did, of course, but ... oh never mind.'

Her hand came between my legs, to cup my hurt pussy. Her thumb went up me, her middle fingers to my clitty and I was being rubbed off, masturbated as my smacked bottom jumped and wobbled to the motions, as I swung slowly on the end of my rope, caught and bound, whipped and fucked, and finally brought to orgasm under my tormentress' fingers.

It was good, but it would have been a lot better if I hadn't been worrying about who had phoned Stephen.

Eleven

It was not Kate Stanbrook but only a work colleague, to my relief and, quite obviously, to his. He was plainly nervous when he came back and it broke the mood completely. Once I'd been let down we had supper together, and he left with only a kiss goodbye and not so much as a squeeze of our bums.

That left me to explain to June about Jeff. June being June, she thought the whole thing was hilarious, and I presented Jeff as working for Stephen rather than with him to keep up his pretence of easy wealth. I was still explaining when Jeff himself appeared, waddling ponderously across the lawn having found a larger hole in the hedge near where I'd been hung up for tawsing. He was a bit of a shock to June, but I cautioned him to be patient and we spent the rest of the evening in the pub, with Jeff buying the rounds.

I also made him go back to his tent, but only by sucking him off first. June watched, alternately giggling and giving little exclamations of disgust, then a major one when he took me by the hair and finished off in my face. I was just grateful he hadn't dobbed me or made me sick on his cock, and mopped up dutifully with my tongue. The night was spent in the big bed with June, cuddling and licking until we had both come to drunken climaxes.

In the morning I felt a touch rough, but not too bad, and I was very much looking forward to Gabrielle's arrival. I told June over breakfast, and she accepted the presence of a new girl with a shrug and a smile. I also explained that she was pure lesbian, a lie, but the best way of explaining why she wouldn't have anything to do with Stephen. Well pleased with myself, I went down to the beach for a morning paddle and to watch for her cab.

She arrived shortly before noon, greeting me outside the pub with a reserved peck and then something more passionate at the cottage. There was still no sign of Jeff, and I explained about him, and Nikki and Anna as we ate lunch. Ten minutes later he rolled in, nodding happily as his little eyes looked us over.

'So who likes chocolate?' he demanded, parking himself on a chair.

'I've told them,' I answered.

'Cool. You game, yeah?'

'Sure,' I answered.

'I will play,' Gabby agreed.

'Just about,' June put in, throwing him a seriously doubtful look.

'So long as you catch us,' Gabby added, 'you bring us into the cottage.'

'It doesn't have to be a fuck,' Jeff answered. 'Blow-jobs'll do. I've got my paintball gun, and masks. A hit and you're down, yeah?'

'A paintball gun?' June queried. 'On bare flesh? You didn't say anything about that, Poppy!'

'It's not so bad,' Jeff stated.

'No worse than a tawse stroke across the pussy-lips,' I added.

'I saw that, laugh, eh?' Jeff put in. 'There's a four-hundred-gram bar of chocolate if you make the tent, Boots.'

241

'Four hundred?' she queried.

'Four hundred,' he confirmed, 'and my spunk doesn't taste any worse than Soapy Stephen's. Are you going to eat that, Gabs?'

There was a pause as he forced the rest of Gabrielle's ciabata and pastrami sandwich into his mouth, then he spoke again.

'Tell you what. If I get you, you get done your favourite way. Pops gets her arse whipped; Gabs goes in a nappy . . . you've got some, yeah?'

'Yes,' Gabrielle admitted, colouring slightly in the face of June's sudden and astonished laughter.

'I'm fairly badly bruised,' I admitted. 'You can pee on me.'

'Oh gross!' June exclaimed.

'And we're going to have to wear clothes,' I pointed out, 'so it won't be bare skin anyway. For a start someone might come, and there are just too many brambles for bare legs.'

'You've got to show a bit of tit at least!' Fat Jeff protested. 'OK, OK, boots right, and bikini bottoms.'

'Bikinis,' I said, 'or tops.'

'Tops, bare underneath, and I've got to hit your bums?' he suggested.

I nodded and glanced to the others. Both looked a touch nervous but also nodded.

'How's about you, Boots?' Jeff went on, reaching back to pull a hunk of bread from the loaf. 'What are you into?'

'I'm not sure, you can tie me, maybe, or . . .' she began doubtfully, and trailed off, glancing towards the door as the gate clanged.

'Nikki?' I queried.

June made a face and went to the door. A moment later I caught Nikki's voice, then Anna's. Both appeared in the kitchen door, Nikki looking a little embarrassed in a print frock, Anna haughty and detached in a suit of lightweight wool and a pillbox hat.

'Hi, you must be Knickers,' Jeff said around a mouthful of ciabata. 'I'm Jeff. Hi.'

The last greeting was addressed to Anna, who was looking at him in open disgust. He had extended one huge and slightly sweaty hand. Nikki took it doubtfully; Anna ignored him. He went on, oblivious.

'We've got this really dirty game, right. I'm . . .'

He trailed off. Anna had raised her chin and was pointedly studying a postcard of Lyme Regis. He shrugged.

'Suit yourself, your loss.'

Anna's eyebrows rose in outrage, but she didn't reply, addressing me instead.

'Nicola and I are returning to London. We came over in the hope that you might see sense and join us.'

'No thanks,' I answered, finding my confidence so much stronger with Gabby there and, to be fair, Jeff.

She hesitated, glancing towards Jeff before she went on.

'Very well. I shall be here until four o'clock this afternoon. Nicola, once you have spoken to Poppy you are to collect your remaining things and come to Bay View.'

She turned on her heel and swept out with no more than a curt nod to Gabrielle and June, nothing to Jeff. Nikki sat down, looking more embarrassed than ever. Jeff spoke first.

'What an old witch! Who was that?'

'My ex,' I answered.

'My Mistress,' Nikki added. 'Sorry, June . . . Poppy.'

'I understand,' I told her.

'You sure got the Master worried,' June put in.

Nikki gave a wan smile, then turned to me.

'Can we talk, Poppy, outside?'

I nodded and rose, touching Gabby's shoulder as I went out, as much for my reassurance as hers. Nikki followed me out on to the sunlit lawn. I knew what she was going to say, more or less, and I also knew that with her I would have an answer.

'Would you come back?' she asked as she caught up with me. 'I . . . I would like it very much, and . . . and it is where you belong.'

'No,' I answered, taking her hand. 'It's where I used to belong. I've moved on.'

'Anna says –' she began.

'I know what Anna says,' I cut in, 'chapter and verse as she used to say. I would like to be with you too, Nikki, but I'm with Gabrielle, and in love with her. Nobody can have everything, and I'm afraid Anna can never have me. I gave her my trust, absolutely, and she broke it. Maybe with you, she'll have learned her lesson.'

She nodded, her mouth pursed.

'So you're staying with her?' I asked.

'Yes,' she answered. 'She's what I want, Poppy, what I need. Stephen . . . Stephen just wasn't.'

'I understand,' I told her. 'The thing with Stephen is that it's not his dominance he enjoys, but your submission. Anna's different, and who knows, maybe you'll work together. I wish you luck anyway.'

'Thanks.'

I hugged her to me, the feel of her slender body making me feel immediately protective and reminding me of what we'd done together. It hurt to think it was unlikely to ever happen again, but there was at least a little time.

'Are you going to play the game with us?' I asked.

'What's that?'

'Fat Jeff's hunting game. He chases us and gets to do what he wants if he catches us ... what we've agreed to anyway.'

'The guy in there? No!'

'Nikki, you're going to be with Anna now. That means no play except to her rules and, believe me, they're strict. This is your last chance ... No, never mind that. Play for me, Nikki, please.'

'I ... I can't ... I'd like to Poppy, but –'

'Has Anna forbidden it?'

'Well, no, but –'

'Then play! Never mind Jeff, he's just a dirty little boy at heart, no better and no worse than Stephen.'

'Yes, but –'

'OK, so he looks like a bear, big deal ... He's got a nicer cock than Stephen.'

'Poppy!'

She was giggling, a rare thing for her, and I knew I'd won. I snapped out an order.

'Miss Knickers, you will do as you are told and play!'

The briefest flicker of shock ran across her face and then she was wearing her wan little smile, and nodding. I gave her a squeeze and swivelled her around towards the house. June was just coming out of the door, talking heatedly to Jeff, who was behind her.

'How's your bum?' I asked Nikki. 'Bruised?'

'No,' she answered. 'You know me, I'm good.'

'Nikki's playing!' I called out to the others as they reached the lawn. 'Hand spanking, and no marks, Jeff, got that!'

He nodded, grinning.

I stood at the centre of the lawn, the landscape before me a broad and fuzzy-edged figure eight through my protective goggles. My breasts were bare beneath my punishment fatigue top, which was going to absorb the impact of paintballs, but was making my nipples sore. They were erect, and it wasn't just the rubbing. Below them I had only my bikini pants, and those pulled tight up between my cheeks to leave me bare and vulnerable. The tail of my shirt covered half my bum and, if I knew that was added protection, somehow it made me feel more exposed than ever. I'd borrowed a pair of June's knee boots, which added a final, lewd touch to the outfit.

The others were much the same, bum-cheeks on show, thighs bare, but otherwise covered. June and Nikki were in their punishment fatigue shirts, Gabby in just a cotton top that did even less to cover the pert cheeks of her bottom. She and Nikki both looked extremely nervous, June simply determined.

Somewhere in the brambles was Fat Jeff's tent and more chocolate than I would normally eat in a month. Somewhere else was Fat Jeff himself, armed with a paintball gun. If he got me, he was going to piss all over me. He had rope too.

'Time,' Gabby stated, glancing at her watch.

The fluttering in my stomach became abruptly stronger. Jeff had to be watching, probably just beyond the hedge where he'd rubbed off on me. I moved up the slope instead. Gabby followed. June moved the other way towards the gap near the whipping tree. Nikki stood irresolute, then darted after June.

After the brilliant sunshine on the lawn it was dim in the wood, cool too, and I found myself blinking and shivering as I tried to adjust. There was fear too, that Jeff might be lurking among the trees, or coming around to intercept us. He'd had us though, but not June or Nikki, and I was sure he'd want them, at least first. Sure enough, he was not in the wood, and we made the top without a problem.

Beyond were the brambles and the narrow, tangled paths between. I pointed to one and nodded, sure we should split up. Gabby nodded back and moved quickly away, running with her neat little bum bobbing behind her, the cheeks pink in the sunlight, then suddenly spattered yellow as paint exploded across them to send her hopping and yelping down the path, and clutching at her shot buttock the instant she'd got control of herself. Fat Jeff rose from among the bushes, his clown mask on, the grotesque face seeming to portray an obscene joy.

'Fucking ace or what?' he called. 'That had to be thirty metres, on a moving target! I am the man!'

Gabrielle didn't answer. Her face was pinched with pain and her eyes looked wet. She stayed put though, merely looking resentful as Fat Jeff came up to her, to take her under her bottom and lift her with casual ease, across his shoulder.

I'd ducked down, my heart hammering, but they were coming right towards me. I had to move, and ran. Jeff snapped off a shot, left-handed, and yellow paint spattered the foliage just inches from my leg, to send a pang of raw fear through me. Then I was away, beyond a thick clump of bramble and I knew I was free.

Still I ran, biting my lip and thinking of what Gabby was going to get. He'd put her in nappies, make her suck his cock, maybe fuck her. I was relieved, no question, but also very, very jealous. Still, there was always the chocolate, and I could be rude with Nikki and June.

I just had to find the tent.

The bramble paths were a maze, too tall to see over, and covering the whole rear slope of the hill, down to woods in the valley and fields inland. I paused, trying to think sensibly. He wouldn't have camped too near the cliff path, I was sure, or too near the village. He'd be in some secluded glade, where he could indulge his dirty habits after peeping at us without fear of interference. That meant up the hill, but not too close to the crest where people went, also probably near the fields.

I moved off, in silence, already sweating slightly in the hot sun. The hair shirt was hurting my nipples and I was wondering if I dared strip it off, when I heard a noise from behind me, a cry of shock, the pop of a paintball gun and a scream. Puzzled, I ducked low and moved back a little.

Jeff stood in the middle of the path, paintball gun raised to the grinning clown lips as if blowing smoke from the barrel. Nearer me, Nikki kneeled in the grass, sweaty and dishevelled, her little pink bum stuck high and spattered with yellow paint. I moved back, quickly, realising that he planned to catch us first, leave us in the garden and come back to molest us at leisure.

He still had to carry Nikki a good three hundred yards before he could chase me, and I was sure I could move faster, even in high-heeled boots. I ran off, up the hill, the sweat now trickling down between my breasts and over my tummy and prickling on my thighs and between my bum-cheeks.

Twenty minutes later I was a lot sweatier, with my shirt undone to save my aching nipples and my hair plastered to my forehead and neck. I was at the top of the hill, the brambles a great sweep of green and red and brown, all the way to the trees that hid the cottage. I hadn't found the tent, or seen June, but I knew Jeff was there, somewhere down slope.

There was no choice, and I started back, sure I'd passed the tent on the wrong side of a bramble clump, or one of the little stands of windblown trees. It had to be there, somewhere . . .

A pop and pain exploded across my right bum-cheek. I leaped up, squealing and clutching at myself, then gasping for breath as I turned in shock to find Fat Jeff's idiot clown face just feet away, grinning as lewdly as ever.

'Gotcha!' he announced, and thrust the gun back into his holster.

I shrugged and smiled, my anger at the sudden pain already fading to submission. He came up, but instead of lifting me, pulled a coil of rope from his belt. I made to speak, but he simply took my wrists, holding them together in one massive paw as he lashed them tight. Throwing the rope across his shoulder he set off, and I was forced to come stumbling behind.

He already had the others on the lawn, Gabby and Nikki, but not June. Both were tied, their arms lashed behind their backs, and gagged, with their bikini pants stuffed in their mouths and tied off so that bits of colourful material stuck out around their lips, green for Gabrielle, red for Nikki.

'Number three,' Jeff announced proudly as he tugged me through the gap in the hedge. 'Let's have those pants off, Pops.'

He let go of the rope, and jerked my bikini pants unceremoniously down and off over my boots.

'Open wide,' he ordered as I stepped free of them.

I did, and had my bikini bottoms stuffed in my mouth, filling my head with the taste of my own pussy and sweat. He pulled a length of cord from his belt, one of four, and tied off my pants in my mouth. A brief adjustment and my hands were lashed behind my back, leaving me like the others, bare from tummy to boot tops and helpless. He led me to them and helped me lower myself to the warm grass of the lawn.

'Fucking ace!' he drawled, looking down at us. 'One to go –'

He stopped and turned at a rustle from the hedge. June appeared, her face covered in chocolate, her fingers too, and even her boobs smeared. She was topless, her punishment shirt slung casually over her shoulder. As she approached she raised one brown, sticky hand.

'A big one for Miss Thing!' she called. 'Who got the choccy, and did not get her bum splatted!'

She stuck a finger in her mouth as she approached, sucking the chocolate off, and laughed to see the state we were in as she took it out.

'You ate it?' Jeff asked. 'The whole bar?'

'Sure,' she answered, 'that was the deal, yeah?'

'Yeah . . . suppose. How d'you find my tent?'

She just shrugged and stuck another chocolate-smeared finger in her mouth. She walked past him to the garden chairs, choosing one and settling herself into it with a fine view of the three of us on the lawn.

'Go on then, fuck 'em, all three.'

Jeff nodded and put his hands to his fly, pulling it down to flop out his cock. He was near me, and my heart jumped as I realised I was to be first.

'Two suck, one gets fucked, but if I'm going to piss on Poppy . . .'

He just let go, a thick jet of urine exploding full in my face. It went up my nose, and the next instant I was gagging and spluttering, with pee bubbling from my nostrils as his stream went into my hair, then to my front. He played it over my tits, making sure both got well plastered. One was bare, one covered, and he made sure to soak my shirt, leaving my shape clearly visible through the sodden cloth and my stiff nipple sticking up in a little wet bump. Then it was my pussy, my belly pissed on until I had streams running down to either side of my sex-lips, and between. Last was my back, his cock pulled up to make the piddle rain down on me, soaking my shirt and running down between my bum-cheeks.

He laughed as he urinated on me, and finished off with a last squirt in my face, to leave me with a single yellow drop hanging from the tip of my nose. My eyes were half-closed, and I didn't dare open them, but just squatted down on the lawn, dripping piddle, steam rising from my flesh. June had been laughing too, and called out as Jeff shook the last few drops of pee out into my hair.

'Nice one, Jeff! Now make her suck it!'

'Will do.' He chuckled, and bent to tug the knot on my panty gag free.

I spat the bikini bottoms out as they came free, only to have his cock pushed straight into my mouth. He tasted of piss, but my mouth was full of it anyway and I sucked, my eyes closing fully as the fat, fleshy cock began to swell in my mouth.

'Fuck me but that feels nice,' he groaned. 'How's it feel, Pops, pissed on and sucking cock? You love it, eh?'

There was no answer. He was right. My top was plastered to my boobs with his piss, my bikini pants sodden, my boots full of it, and I was sucking his cock in gratitude. He'd put me in a state of utter submission, feeling dirty and abused and soiled, and knowing that those very feelings would bring me to an orgasm beyond anything I could achieve without them. I was too busy with his cock anyway, sucking for the sake of my own deliberate degradation and wishing he would give me his full attention and come in my mouth, over my face, in my pussy, up my bottom.

'Hey, hey, don't get greedy,' he said suddenly and pulled back, his cock now erect and shiny with my saliva. 'That's got to go round between the three of you! Right, Gabby next.'

He reached out to loosen her gag and she spoke the instant she had spat it out.

'My nappy, Jeff.'

'Too right,' he answered. 'Suck on this while Pops goes to get it.'

He stuck his cock straight into her mouth and her cheeks sucked in as she started work. June came behind me, quickly releasing me, and I ran into the cottage, returning with one of the big adult nappies. Gabby was still on her knees, and still bound. Jeff pulled his cock out of her mouth as he saw me coming, and pushed her over on to her back.

I took her legs, quickly peeling off her boots to leave her naked below the waist. Lifting her by the ankles, I spread the nappy out under her bum, lowered her into it, spread her, pulled it up over her pussy and fastened the tabs at the sides.

'You've done that before,' June stated.

'Frequently,' I admitted as I helped Gabby get back into a kneeling position with the puffy pink and white rear of her nappy sticking out and just a little slice of bum-cheek escaping at each side.

Jeff was fully erect, his cock skin taut with pressure, his helmet a fat purple mushroom, truly obscene as only a man's cock can be. As Gabby took it in I shuffled up beside her, not feeling I'd really had my share. Jeff chuckled and lifted his balls to my mouth, the fat, sweaty sack so big I had to gape wide to accommodate him. Then we were feeding on his balls and cock, our cheeks together, the puffy material of her nappy pressed to the sticky skin of my thigh. I wanted more, spunk in my face, my tongue up her bumhole, whipping, fucking, buggery, anything and everything.

It was Jeff who stopped it, or we'd have made him come over our faces. He pulled back, leaving his cock and balls joined to our mouths with threads of saliva as we tried to take him back in. He caught us by the hair and pulled us off, laughing.

'Cool it, you two. I've still got to fuck Knickers, and spank her.'

I pulled back, reluctantly, and turned to Nikki. She was kneeling, as before, but June was with her, kissing her mouth, and with one hand down between her thighs to manipulate her sex.

'She ready?' Jeff asked.

Nikki nodded as June pulled back. She looked seriously nervous, but also dizzy with arousal, and as Jeff approached she abruptly flipped herself over on to her back, upside-down, with her slender legs spread and stretched out, her toes, shoulders and bound arms the only parts of her touching the grass. The pose left her pussy sticking up, ready for fucking, and I saw that she was smeared with chocolate, and not just her sex. Her bumhole was brown and sticky, and June had obviously stuck a chocolate-covered finger up it.

Jeff gave a pleased nod and began to strip, kicking off his boots, peeling down his trousers and a pair of huge grey underpants. Bare from the waist down save for his socks, he waddled over and began to spank her, slapping at her upturned bottom with his fat fingers and all the while pulling on his cock. She was soon going pink, and I could see her anal ring twitching to the smacks, a little pink hole opening in the chocolate with every one. Jeff didn't bother to hurt her though, but climbed on to her after maybe two dozen, throwing one colossal leg over her so that she was looking right up at his bottom and balls.

Her body looked tiny beneath his vast, pasty buttocks and tree-trunk thighs, and as he pushed his cock down it seemed impossible that it would fit up her tiny pussy. It did, of course, going up with a squashy sound as she accommodated him as every tiny woman has accommodated every huge man in history, with a nice, wet hole. He began to fuck her, a truly obscene sight, rising and falling with his big ball sac slapping on her pussy-lips and his buttocks wobbling to each thrust. I watched, cuddled up to Gabby, my feelings soaring as one dirty idea after another came into my mind, but it was June who voiced one of the filthiest.

'Why don't you bum shag her, Jeff? You'll be her first.'

'Fucking ace! Knickers, how about your first ever arse fuck?'

June reached out, to tug out Nikki's panty gag.

'OK . . .'

It was a whimper, barely audible, her whole body was shaking and she had closed her eyes. She'd said it though, and Jeff immediately pulled his cock from her pussy, leaving her hole gaping wide. His helmet was dripping juice, and he put it straight to her bumhole, rubbing the slippery white fluid in with the brown chocolate. She gave another whimper as her anus was lubed up, but as he lifted his cock she pushed, her ring pouting, the centre a tiny pink dimple in a ring of lumpy, slimy flesh.

'I spunk up this one,' Jeff growled, and pushed down.

Nikki gasped as her anus pushed in to the pressure of his cock. She was open though, June's finger had loosened her, and as he pulled up a little I saw that her ring was spread around his helmet. Again he pushed, and this time her hole popped, letting in the full, fat penis head. She cried out, ecstasy and maybe despair as for the first time in her life a man's penis invaded her bumhole, but it was too late to stop anyway, Fat Jeff driving down into her to force the meaty ring of his foreskin into her body.

He kept going too, pushing inch after inch past the straining pink ring of her anus and into her rectum. I watched, all the way, fascinated to watch her buggered for the first time, until at last the full length of his cock was wedged up her bum and his fat balls had settled over her empty pussy. Then he was bouncing on her bottom, his cock driving in and out of her slimy brown hole, and she was gasping and panting, crying out in pain but in ecstasy too as he thrust into her, harder and faster, a demented clown buggering a pretty young ballet girl.

I came close, meaning to lick her as her bum was fucked, even if it did mean Fat Jeff would be more or less sitting on my head. Gabby moved in too, from the other side, to support her I think, but at that instant Jeff grunted, stopped, snatched at his cock and whipped it free. Spunk erupted over Nikki's bum, in Gabby's face and down her chest, and then he had stuffed the full, filthy length into her mouth.

Her eyes popped wide as her mouth filled, but she was sucking, and swallowing down the mess of spunk and chocolate and juices as he milked himself into her mouth for three brisk pumps before pulling out. Nikki had stayed still, ready and willing, her little buttocks streaked with spunk, her gaping anus a pool of brown and white fluid, into which Jeff stuck his cock.

It went up, right up, in one motion, filling her anus with a loud squelch as spunk squirted out to either side and forwards, to run in a thick coating over her shaven pussy-lips. She let out a whimper as her rectum filled once more, all the way down, until his balls were pressed to her sloppy pussy. I ducked down, to grab him firmly by the balls and start to rub them on Nikki's sex. He gave a squeak of pain, but she moaned in ecstasy.

'Don't you dare move, Jeff,' I ordered. 'Keep it up her bum, and try to move your cock in her hole a little.'

'What're you doing?' he gasped. 'A cunt rub?'

'Yes, now be a good quiet boy.'

I pushed his balls more firmly to her, moving his slimy, sweaty sac to make the fat spheres within bump over her clitty. He grunted but began to move his cock in her bumhole, pushing sperm bubbles out around the well-buggered ring. She gave a low moan that cut off abruptly as I swung my leg over her face and lowered my bottom. Reaching down, I pulled my cheeks wide and settled my bum on her face, wiggling until I found the tip of her nose with my bumhole.

'Lick,' I ordered.

Her tongue immediately pushed up into my pussy-hole. I wiggled, encouraging her, and went back to frigging her off with Jeff's balls. She kept licking, with mounting urgency as I found a rhythm on her clitty, Jeff's balls bumping in the slime and sperm coating her sex. It was not comfy, with my body twisted back at an angle, and his huge backside right in my face, but it wasn't my comfort that mattered. It was going to be her last chance to come with a man, and with me, and I wanted it to be a good one.

Gabby joined in, pressing her face to Nikki's bum to lick at the junction of anus and cock, and June slipped her hands in, one to stroke Nikki's tits, one down the back of Gabby's nappy. Suddenly Nikki's tongue was up my bumhole, burrowing right in, and as I saw the muscles of her legs start to twitch I knew she was coming. I let her hold it, rubbing Jeff's balls to her in a steady rhythm and trying to ignore the exquisite things her tongue was doing up my bumhole, and let go my pee right at what I hoped was her peak, spattering her face and neck and tits.

An instant later it was over, for her, not for me. I was still peeing, and then sucking cock as Jeff pulled it from her bumhole to flop straight into my mouth. He pulled back, panting, but I'd got the taste, and was already pulling Gabby to me as he collapsed on the lawn. Nikki's legs scissored out as I emptied myself over her, and Gabby quickly mounted them, pulling me close, the blob of spunk hanging from her nose swinging forwards to transfer itself to my lip as our mouths met in an open kiss.

I was still peeing, and Nikki was wriggling under me, nuzzling in my bottom crease and licking at my hole. June was holding us too, her hands on our bums, squeezing and stroking as she pushed her face in between ours. We let her in, a three-way kiss, sharing the chocolate-flavoured spunk which was running down our chins and splashing on Nikki's already filthy body. Suddenly Gabby broke away, her back arched in ecstasy and her eyes tight shut.

'Yes, like that,' she gasped, and I saw that June's hand was pushed right down the nappy.

She was frigging Gabby, pussy and bumhole I was sure. I scrambled off Nikki, wanting to help my girlfriend come. Her legs were wide, across Nikki's body, and I burrowed my hand in under the edge of the nappy. Sure enough, June had her thumb up Gabby's bottom and her hand doing the rest. I cupped a cheek, kneading, and fastening my mouth to a neat little tit through her top. She moaned, and an instant later she was there, wriggling her bottom in our hands and mumbling in French.

I had to come too, but I was still holding Gabby when June cocked her leg over Nikki's head and sat squarely in her face. Nikki began to lick immediately, and I joined in, knowing that last would be best as I suckled on one plump tit. A moment to recover, and Gabby was with us, sucking on June's other boob as she cradled our heads. It took seconds, June going tense in our arms as she came in Nikki's face, and on the instant she had recovered all three had turned their attention to me.

Gabby mounted me as I went down, the seat of her nappy over my face. My thighs were taken, pulled up and open, and as Gabby began to stroke my tits both June and Nikki started on me, kissing and licking at the insides of my thighs, my pussy, my bum-cheeks and between them.

'Slowly,' Gabby told them. 'I'll say when.'

She was going to do me, properly, and on the instant my head was swimming with need and with the strongest, most shameful embarrassment. I couldn't have stopped her, not with the two of them nuzzling me between my legs and her weight on my body, her sweet little bottom firm and cheeky beneath the softness of the nappy, her long, slim fingers teasing my nipples . . .

I felt her thighs tense and a strong shiver went through me. One of them took my legs, rolling me up and I felt cool air on my bumhole, then the firm, wet tip of a tongue, Nikki's I was sure. Lips found my pussy once more, kissing, sucking on my clitty, just once, to leave me jerking and shaking beneath Gabby. Again her thighs and bottom tensed, and this time I felt her cheeks spread a little against my face beneath the nappy.

'Now,' she gasped, 'lick her . . . lick her hard.'

Instantly Nikki's tongue was burrowing up into my bumhole and June had begun to suck on my clit. I screamed, overcome by a sensation too powerful to handle, but even as they eased off I knew I was going to come. June sucked once more, gently, but this time she didn't stop, and as the orgasm began to rise in my head I felt the seat of Gabby's nappy start to bulge.

She did it, right in my face, her nappy pouch with it squashed out against my open mouth as it filled and I squirmed and jerked under the girls' tongues. I felt it bulge, heavy and fat against my face, and her pee as the front lolled out on my chin and neck, wet and heavy. She lifted at my first scream of ecstasy, making me watch as her load swelled out her nappy pouch, to hang, heavy and pendulous, right over my face as I screamed again, and with my third she sat down, squashing her full, fat load over my mouth and nose with only the nappy to protect me. My whole body locked rigid as it spread in my face, and then I was jerking and thrashing beneath her, writhing and bucking in unbearable ecstasy, Nikki's tongue well up my bumhole, June sucking on my clitty, and Gabby queened up on my face.

I blacked out for a moment, it was so strong, and even when my vision had begun to clear again I was left trembling on the ground, too weak to get up. They held me until I'd recovered, then helped me up, still shaking, but blushing too, well and truly satisfied but thoroughly embarrassed. They knew, and held me for reassurance as we went over to the hosepipe, to wash each other down amid fits of giggles and plenty of slaps to bottoms and legs, mainly mine.

We dressed as soon as we were clean and dry, and June even managed to bully Jeff into tidying himself up a bit. He was still the first ready, and it took Gabby, Nikki and I far longer, all of us in need of powder and cream and a good belt of brandy before we were ready. When we came out, June and Jeff were on the lawn, drinking beer and chatting. He had dressed, and she had put her shirt on, but still with the buttons undone. They looked up as we came out.

'Who's for another run then?' Jeff called.

I shook my head.

'You've got some stamina, I'll give you that,' June said.

Jeff shrugged.

'Plenty of food, plenty of spunk.'

'I have had enough, thank you,' Gabrielle stated.

'Me too,' Nikki added. 'I'm sore.'

'Aw come on,' he urged. 'I'll make it easy. The tent's up over the top of the hill, in a hollow with trees . . . red berries they've got.'

'How did you find it, June?' Gabby asked.

'I just ran away,' she answered. 'I figured I'd wait till he was despunked, then go searching. The trees looked a good place to hide, and there was the tent.'

'Lucky cow!' He laughed. 'Give us another go, eh? I'd love to fuck you, you're gorgeous!'

She shrugged. 'Maybe . . . yeah, why not. Come on, you lot.'

'I can't,' Nikki protested. 'I've got to go back to Anna.'

'Poppet, Gabby? Come on, it's no fun on my own.'

I'd sat down close to Gabrielle, my arm around her. June couldn't see my hand, and I gave three quick squeezes to Gabby's waist, our private signal.

'I will run then,' she said.

'Me too, if you are,' I added.

'Cool!' Jeff answered. 'I'll go down to the shop then and get some more chocolate.'

'A big bar,' June demanded.

'The biggest,' he promised. 'Start in half an hour, yeah?'

'You've got it. Bye, Nikki.'

He bent to give her a kiss, which she returned quite warmly, and shambled off, pausing only to untuck his shirt and hide his paintball gun. No sooner was he out of sight than Nikki stood up.

'I'd better go too.'

June held her arms out and Nikki came to her, then me, cuddling and kissing us both before giving Gabby a simple peck on the lips. I watched as she walked away, happy for her, hoping her relationship with Anna worked, but full of regret, a sense of loss both for her, and, to be truthful, because I knew it was the final break between Anna and I.

'She'll be back,' June stated, but there was no confidence in her voice. 'Come on, let's play. Aren't you two going to change?'

'What into?' I answered. 'Everything's in the wash.'

'Panties and boots?'

'No, I'll go like this. They're only old jeans, and those paintballs hurt like hell on the bare.'

She made a wry face, but stood and stretched, her breasts and bottom stuck out, her hands behind her head.

'He thinks he's clever,' she said, 'but he's not. I'm going now, and I'm going to follow him, get the choccy and come back down the cliff path while he's playing soldiers in the bramble patches.'

'Dressed like that?'

'So I look a bit kinky, big deal. It's not illegal. Coming?'

'No, we'll follow. Good luck, and this time, save us some chocolate!'

'Will do, bye.'

She ran off, squeezing through the hedge and into the wood. I settled back, laying my head in Gabby's lap. She began to stroke my hair. I was feeling quite game, but a little drowsy, and if she hadn't been Little

Miss Efficiency and kept glancing at her watch I think I'd have gone to sleep.

After a while I heard the cottage gate bang. I looked up, hoping that Nikki had changed her mind and come back, but sure it would just be that Fat Jeff had forgotten something. It was neither.

It was Stephen Stanbrook, and he was running as he came around the corner of the cottage.

'You've got to go, now!' he exclaimed. 'Gabrielle!?'

'I probably owe you an expl–' she began.

'Forget it! Just go, now! Where's June? What's the cottage like? Oh fuck!'

He ran for the cottage.

'Kate must be back,' I suggested.

'Presumably so,' Gabby answered. 'We had better take our things and leave.'

I nodded and we hurried into the cottage. Stephen was going frantic, desperately stuffing everything into a black plastic bin liner. We began to collect our stuff, and June's, pushing it into the bags any-old-how. Stephen only spoke to give instructions, until we had everything piled on the patio.

'Thank you,' he puffed. 'That's it, I think. Kate's down at the shop, but she'll be up any moment. Go now, through the wood and down by the cliff.'

He shot Gabby a last quizzical look as we began to pick up the bags, and was going to speak. The gate banged and he went abruptly pale. An instant later a woman's voice called out, commanding and slightly sharp.

'Stephen?'

There was nothing we could do, nowhere to hide and nowhere to run, at least not fast enough. Before we could have made it halfway across the lawn Kate appeared. She was a blonde woman, maybe forty, casually yet expensively dressed. Her look of mild irritation turned to surprise as she saw us. Stephen tried to say something, but no clear words came out. Gabrielle spoke instead, as calmly as if addressing a client.

'Mrs Stanbrook? I'm Gabrielle Salinger, this is my friend, Poppy.'

For a moment she still looked puzzled, and angry, but her face suddenly cleared.

'Gabrielle Salinger? The therapist?'

'Yes.'

'Ah, yes, of course. I've read some of your work, with great interest, but –'

'Stephen very kindly said we could stay the weekend at your charming cottage,' Gabrielle went on. 'I hope that was not an inconvenience?'

Kate hesitated, and shot a glance at Stephen, but when she spoke there was no hostility in her voice.

'No, no, not inconvenient at all. I'm just back from Korea, as it happens, a little earlier than expected.'

She was not happy, but there was no hint of suspicion. There was no reason for any, after all. There were two of us and straights don't usually go in for *ménage-à-trois*, while Stephen had been at home.

'Will you stay for a cup of tea?' she went on.

'We should really be –' Gabby began and stopped as Kate's mouth fell open.

I turned to see what she was staring at. It was Jeff, who was just pushing through the gap in the hedge. He was wearing his clown mask, but it had slipped up a bit, obscuring his vision and making him look more grotesque than ever with a fringe of beard sticking out under the clown's chin. That wasn't the worst of it.

June was over his shoulder, her big, rounded bum stuck out towards us, her wrists strapped up in leather cuffs, her booted ankles tied with rope. Her bikini pants were up, but the bright red thong was so thin it left the star of little purple-brown crevices around her anus showing. Both bottom-cheeks were not only smeared with chocolate fingerprints and yellow dye, but also showed bruises. There was no question that she'd been beaten, and hard.

'Got the little bitch,' Jeff called out, adjusting his mask. 'Who wants to watch me fuck her arsehole?'

NEXUS NEW BOOKS

To be published in February

PRINCESS
Aishling Morgan

Princess follows the (mis)fortunes of Aeisla, her compatriot Iriel, and their ad hoc band of nubile, amazonian warrior women as they are forced to flee their native Aegmund or face bizarre and public erotic punishment. Their passages worked copiously, they arrive by ship at the kingdom of Oretea. Political scheming, slavery and perverse punishments ensue in this, the fabulously inventive final part of Aishling Morgan's *Maiden* saga.

£6.99   ISBN 0 352 33871 7

THE SMARTING OF SELINA
Yolanda Celbridge

Blonde journalist Selina Rawe eagerly infiltrates Her Majesty's Prison at Auchterhuish, where corporal punishment is mandatory for wayward girls, along with more specialist treatments from a gorgeous resident nurse, while the lustful Hebridean mariners provide little – or perhaps too much – relief. Sapphic governess Miss Gurdell worships the bottom beautiful, and Selina is horrified to learn that hers is the tastiest of all. A novel of craven submission from the author of *The English Vice*.

£6.99   ISBN 0 352 33872 5

THE INSTITUTE
Maria del Rey

When Lucy is sentenced to be rehabilitated in a bizarre institute for the treatment of delinquent girls, she finds that the disciplinary methods used are not what she has been led to expect. They are, in fact, decidedly perverse. By the author of *Dark Desires*, *Dark Delights* and *Obsession* – 'The Queen of SM' *Caress*. A Nexus Classic.

£6.99   ISBN 0 352 33352 9

To be published in March

THE ANIMAL HOUSE
Cat Scarlett

The glamorous and self-possessed Violetta receives a chance invitation to stay at a dream French chateau. Following a casual, train-board encounter with a mysterious and self-assured man, it becomes apparent that her holiday opportunity is not as random as it seemed, and Violetta finds herself drawn into a community whose members take their pleasures disguised beneath animal masks. Behind the licentiousness of her holiday destination, however, she finds a dark tradition of Gallic libertinage and medieval torture she had not imagined, as the Sadean trappings of the chateau are revealed and used upon her in turn.

£6.99   ISBN 0 352 33877 6

HOT PURSUIT
Lisette Ashton

Lucy is Master Donald's second favourite. When she tries to ask him a favour, however, not only does he not hear her out but, in pique, he asks his favourite, Ginger, to discipline Lucy. When poor Lucy runs away, Donald and Ginger wonder if they've gone too far. But as they give chase, they realise that in their bizarre SM society it's really little Lucy who holds all the cards . . .

£6.99   ISBN 0 352 33878 4

EMMA'S SECRET WORLD
Hilary James

Becoming Ursula's slave was the most exciting thing that had ever happened to Emma. She is whisked away to the confines of an English country residence, where beautiful but cruel mistresses preside over a bevy of young and wayward girls. Their corrective regime demands ultimate sacrifice in return for absolute fulfilment, and Emma surrenders every dignity of adulthood to learn the discipline necessary for her training. A Nexus Classic.

£6.99   ISBN 0 352 33879 2

If you would like more information about Nexus titles, please visit our website at www.nexus-books.co.uk, or send a stamped addressed envelope to:

Nexus, Thames Wharf Studios,
Rainville Road, London W6 9HA